Stained:
an anthology of writing
about
menstruation

Curated & Edited by
Rachel Neve-Midbar & Jennifer Saunders

QUERENCIA PRESS

© Copyright 2023
Querencia Press

ISBN 978 1 959118 45 9

.

www.querenciapress.com

First Published in 2023

**Querencia Press, LLC
Chicago IL**

Printed & Bound in the United States of America

In the poem "she says that we should call my mother," Sheree La Puma writes: "no one but god knows why warm blood seeps / onto bare skin." To write about menstruation is to question and commune with all that is cyclical, to consider the body's ancient and admirable insistence on renewal. In this brilliant anthology, writers explore their own connections to the natural world and to society, blurring lines between body and Earth, mother and daughter, country and womb. This inspired and important collection of writing invites us to acknowledge the shared power, grief, and tenderness inherent in our experiences of menstruation. It gives voice to both our organic, physical selves and our spiritual, human experiences, blazing a path for further discourse and reflection.

—Joan Kwon Glass, author of *NIGHT SWIM* (Diode Editions, 2022)

Stained is a brilliant collection of diverse voices that illuminates a bodyscape both intimately personal and universally experienced by half the human race. These essays, stories, and poems resonate with the hopes, disappointments, shame, pride, humor, and metaphors our natural cycles encompass. Within these pages every reader will find their own story.

—Carol Cassella, author of *Oxygen* and other novels

Stained is centuries overdue—from under the cloak of shadow and taboo, this anthology sings a multifaceted womb-bearer chorus, a raw and liberating (wo)manifesto on menses. To praise the blood, to scream its pains, to moon-howl and swim in its rising tides, to warpaint each other in its earth-rust hues as we warrior for autonomy, to mourn the babies, to heal the bodies, to quench the burning, to carry the loss of possible futures, to deify the cellular mystery we hold—this writing names it all in the most glorious, visceral, and unflinching way. I am changed after reading this collection of voices from all over the world saying, in both harmony and dissonance, that this blood, this blood, this blood is the clotted dark fabric that connects us all.

—Kai Coggin, author of *Mining for Stardust, Incandescent,* and *Wingspan*

It would be impossible for me to overstate how important—and how very necessary—this anthology is. From blessing to betrayal, from celebrated to cursed to censored, from a long-awaited confirmation to a complete contradiction of identity, the works in this anthology show the full spectrum of the experience of menstruation in stunning, brave, and beautiful ways. This is the anthology I've needed all my life.

—Emma Bolden, author of *The Tiger and the Cage: A Memoir of a Body in Crisis*

Not unlike the sea, blood is often unpredictable and unruly in its arrival. Many of us with bodies that bleed found ourselves on the early cusp of adulthood prematurely; to bleed meant we were "unclean" before the eyes of God; our own fathers stopped hugging us once our periods started. *Stained* is a robust amalgamation of voices across, race, age, gender, faiths, and traditions. Governed by an interconnected system of 14 colors and adjacent images—Fig, Quicksand, Clot, Puce, Bruise, Scab, Strawberry Moon, and Siren, to name a few—*Stained* is an anthology that insists on the language of reimagination, reclamation, and above all freedom. The poems and stories here which make the sum of *Stained* are elegant, visceral, and exacting in their execution while also refusing a facile rendering of the body's elusive machinery. Here, the editors Rachel Neve-Midbar & Jennifer Saunders curate for us a rich body of work that was once considered "taboo" to speak aloud.

—I.S. Jones author of *Spells of My Name*

What happens when the language of menstruation is returned to us from the patriarchal imagination, unsteeped from the male gaze that equates periods with being both fuckable and unclean? *Stained: An Anthology of Writing about Menstruation* is an urgent response to this question, reminding me of what Cecilia Vicuña writes in in *Read Thread: The Story of the Red Thread*, "no one ever paints menstruation, or shitting, because they are idiots. can there be anything more beautiful than those red threads of blood?" Each poem and essay in this gorgeous anthology returns us to the viscous knowing of our bodies while resisting the tropes of misogyny that devalue and stigmatize our vitality. Under the shadow of a culture that grows more hostile to bodily autonomy every day, *Stained* is a battle cry, a vibrant clot, reminding us that our understanding and relationship to our cycle is not just a political act, it is necessary to our survival. It is the thread that leads us to our wildness, a reminder that we are animal and cosmic, that our lifeforce is both: "first blood is the heart's overflow, my earthy inheritance," and "A ceremonious sprig of bloodshot maroon, to tell us we will live beyond those who wish us gone." As Ross Gay writes in "Unclean. Make Me," won't you join me and "Fill your lungs/ with birth's florid shadow. This is the common dream of the living/ and dead: not only to meet/ the maker, but to taste its sweet. Even God/ should know this."

—Kendra DeColo, author of *I Am Not Trying To Hide My Hungers From The World*

Stained is a chronicle of the experience of menstruation: the joyous, the ravaging, the powerful, the embarrassing, the hope, the disappointment, the pain, the fecundity, the dissonance, the passion. If you've ever felt alone, you'll find someone in this generous anthology who'll tell you that you're not. All contemporary voices. All contending with or celebrating that primal blood!

—Ellen Bass, author of *Indigo*

Stained is a look at the taboo of menstruation, from those who have lived through the first blood to the onset of menopause. The chapters are divided by the many colors of blood: Strawberry, Crimson, Cayenne, Fig and Siren, the colors that bind us to one another and the earth, the blood from which we spring. Women everywhere will be grateful to read these poems.

—Dorianne Laux author *Only As the Day Is Long: New and Selected Poems*

CONTENTS

Introduction

This book is about breaking silence, about finding language. This book is about the womb-bearing body in all its permutations. The uterus that bleeds.

We want to talk about menstruation, to tell our stories. Half of the world's population is womb-bearing, yet the subject of monthly bleeding remains taboo. *Stained* celebrates a body that has long remained a site of contention and conflict. For centuries menstruating people have been forced to navigate social perceptions which stigmatize, marginalize, and undermine the female fertility cycle. The ability to write our menstruation stories, to speak out loud, is new, vibrant, and represents an emerging body of literature. The writers in *Stained* bring the abject, the blood of their bodies, to the page.

Stained rose out of the whispers, was born in a Facebook post where one woman asked in a closed group of over 4000 female and non-binary poets from around the world, "where to publish a poem about that secret subject: menstruation?" And the answers: journals where only women published, only women read. We saw the online trappings of whispers behind hands, subjects only suitable within the Red Tent. It was 2019. Hadn't we all just experienced a viral #MeToo, hadn't we all just read Kristen Roupenian's "Cat Person"? Would the shame imposed by patriarchy about this most essential part of our bodies never end?

So we sent out a call and hundreds of menstruators from all over the world, of every age and so many diverse cultural backgrounds answered. We put no limits on the call, any genre, any style. We wanted the stories to be allowed to come in any form they chose. We asked only one thing: we wanted new work. No reprints. We wanted to collect a vision of the menstruation story right now in this moment, with all that menstruators are facing today.

And the menstruators answered. They answered loud and proud, with incredible courage. The writers in *Stained* offer their menarche stories, sometimes magical, sometimes traumatic; their menopause stories filled with longings and goodbyes. But they are also writing all that comes in between, the stains, blood-soaked sex, the babies wanted or not and the bleeding after. Endometriosis, PMDD, birth control, body dysmorphia—and many, many stories of medical mistreatment. The leaking pad, the grossed-out boyfriend, the fear of being the first in class to get it, the fear of being the last in class to get it. Waiting for the blood to come. Waiting for the blood to end.

Writers deep into menopause sent us their menarche stories remembered as clearly as if that first stain of red had appeared in their panties just yesterday. Writers sent us their stories of pregnancy loss and poets sent us their stories of joyfully giving birth. Some writers focused on a single crystalline moment. Others looked back over the lifespan of their menstruation and recounted how the ebbing and flowing of menstrual blood had shaped their lives. Grandmothers wrote to their granddaughters. A granddaughter reached into family history and wrote about her grandmother. We received a story of an apocalyptic future in which the needs of the environment clashed with the need for protection products. We received stories and poems of bleeding while traveling, bleeding while playing sports, bleeding while having sex, bleeding while dressed as Roberto Clemente for a fifth-grade history project, bleeding while practicing yoga. The writers collected here bled in doctors' offices and emergency rooms and operating theaters and punk rock shows. They bled from bodies that don't match their gender identity and that don't feel like theirs. They bled. They bled and they wrote their most personal stories. Some of which defined the blood of their bodies as an expression of their selfhood, an aspect of their own magic.

Upon reading the hundreds of submissions we received, we realized that the mark of the stain not only defines a menstrual incident, but also marks the body's shame. Each body experiences a menstrual event in its own way. Depending on factors like education, support, and family dynamics, what might be straightforward, exciting, and natural for one might be experienced as traumatic and unwelcome by another. No menstrual experience, no stain, is equal.

We began to divide the work into sections, each named after a color: the colors we all see and have seen in our protection products, in our bathwater, on our clothes, our sheets, on the tissue we have used to clean ourselves, on our thighs, on our hands. The colors we see every month aren't ambiguous euphemisms. For the first time we attempted to name these colors, their shades and essences. How many ways can one say "red?" And what might be the color of the absence of blood? Anyone who has menstruated knows that "red" doesn't begin to cover the tints and hues of menstrual blood.

We thought it would be easy, finding names for 10 different shades of red. We turned to the cosmetics industry, but we quickly realized that none of those names matched the emotional valence of the work we were reading. We needed to come up with our own names. We created a palette of 25 shades, the full rainbow we see each month. Then we had to name them. We spent hours talking about what a certain orange color meant to us and, in naming the various shades, we developed our own language. Soon we were able to read a story together and say, almost simultaneously, *oh, that's puce.* We divided the anthology into fourteen sections, each named after a color, an emotional valence, from "Fig" where the experience might be straightforward to "Bruise" where the experience might have been one of pain or suffering, to "Siren," where the stain might be empowering. The simple mute objects of our very bodies finally allowed to speak. The stain.

The writers in *Stained* are not frightened or disgusted to look deeply into their bodies, nor to examine what comes out of it. In her piece "When It Rains It Clots," Emily Reece Fontenot writes of her fascination with the blood clots she passes each month. "I would love to study them. Take them apart and figure them out. Catch them as they fall and inspect them under a magnifying glass and a bright light." Anndee Hochman writes of breathing in the "earth and salt and rust" smell of her menstrual blood.

Writers from vastly different backgrounds speak the same whispered language, passing messages back and forth, touching on the same reverberating themes. From Ireland, Claire Loader writes:

> [y]ou joke and say we should never be trusted—
> that anything that bleeds
>
> for that long and doesn't die
> could never be right.

Meanwhile in the Pacific Northwest of the USA, Kelli Russell Agodon asserts "I will bleed and live and you will bleed and die." Two writers from across the world title their poems "●."

One of the most abject of our menstruation stories is bloody sex. LA-based poet, Alexis Rhone-Francher adventurously tackles this subject in her poem, "Bloodbath." Her short solid-syllabled rhymes create a strong back-beat as the poet allows the rising desire that sometimes occurs during menstruation to become a literal 'bloodbath' of stains:

blood on his penis
blood on my skin
blood on my pussy
when he sticks it in

Another sex-during-menstruation poem reveals the exact opposite experience of Rhone-Francher's. Fifteen-year-old poet Ada Donnelly's poem "I Met a Guy at My Rich Friend's House Party" is a poem about two kids. The boy, with all the finesse of a fifteen-year-old, is trying to "woo" a girl by masturbating in front of her and suggesting that they watch some porn. When the poet tells him she has her period, he first accuses her of lying, then finally desists in his amorous attempts. Donnelly finishes her poem "Oh, how nice it would have been if my then boyfriend cared more about my safety / than he did some blood and tissue."

Menstrual stains are also a focal point of fertility: bleeding during IVF, <u>not</u> bleeding two weeks after a wild night with a stranger, bleeding after miscarriage, bleeding after abortion; the six weeks of blood after childbirth as in Israeli poet Geula Geurts' poem, "Lochia."

"We need a new name for the menopause, like 'Queen Bliss' or something. ('Queenepause' would be great if it didn't sound like a disease.)" writes Aduro Ojo, a British-Nigerian writer. Extreme bleeding can accompany uterine illness as poet Kristin Prevallet writes about in her poem, "What the Fibroids Said,"

Sitting snuggly in my belly, I have seven fibroids,
and my body collapses around their weight.

The blood is pouring buckets
from what is most open
in me: my lost babies, my
loneliness, and my beauty aging
into wisdom... but not without a fight.

"There is a silent chaos that follows me / shadowing my movements and biding its time," writes Filipino-American writer Leila Tualla about premenstrual dysphoric disorder.

However, there are those writers who push beyond even this courage—whose bodies are not matched to their true gendered selves. These are writers whose bodies might menstruate or not, but for whom monthly blood can become the trigger of excruciating dysphoria when the body's gender doesn't match the person's identity. In their prose poem, "Dysphoria," Marty Head writes:

> so let's talk about dysphoria, and what it's like
> to be a non-woman isolated in a woman's body,
> and how every time i feel that slick red smear
> between my thighs i'm reminded of what my
> body can do, and how very much i do not want
> that burden, and how, and how —

And yet, still we exhort ourselves to make friends with our bodies and love the least favorite parts of ourselves, even if those parts cause us illness and pain. Chris Talbot-Heindl in "Chris & Crampus: Besties Since Evacuation Day 2015" takes this advice to a profound and beautiful extreme. After their hysterectomy, they asked their doctor if they could keep the removed uterus. Astonishingly, he complied. Through this creative and astounding solution Talbot-Heindl captures the struggle they experienced of gender dysphoria throughout their menstrual life. Once the uterus no longer causes Chris physical and emotional anguish, it becomes a beloved, something that brings Chris great comfort. This story is empowering.

In these pages pain what seems almost inexpressible, through language, through courage finally finds expression. The writers in *Stained* have removed the taboos and created the magic through specificity, through finding the language to express reality, and thus break through the past to tell a whole new truth. These are writers unafraid of the body: the body imperfect, the body unbeautiful. The body external and the body from deep within. Over 100 contributors offer work that reaches deeply into their personal experience, allowing other menstruators to find the solidarity and support for their experiences too.

Rachel Neve-Midbar and Jennifer Saunders

gadflies grant menses
    —Amy Bobeda

gadflies granted menses————
there were no words before *estrus.*

menstrua once meant solūtiō
the birth of language dissolves
red pebbles in water.

women, sticky, leave the forest
red, a hand, painted round stone
lines annotate our imperfections.

la lengua es symbol's memory
—————————————————pink permeates————

now, in the shower a study of blood
dreamed by a single dreamer, *we*
labor *red* into language.

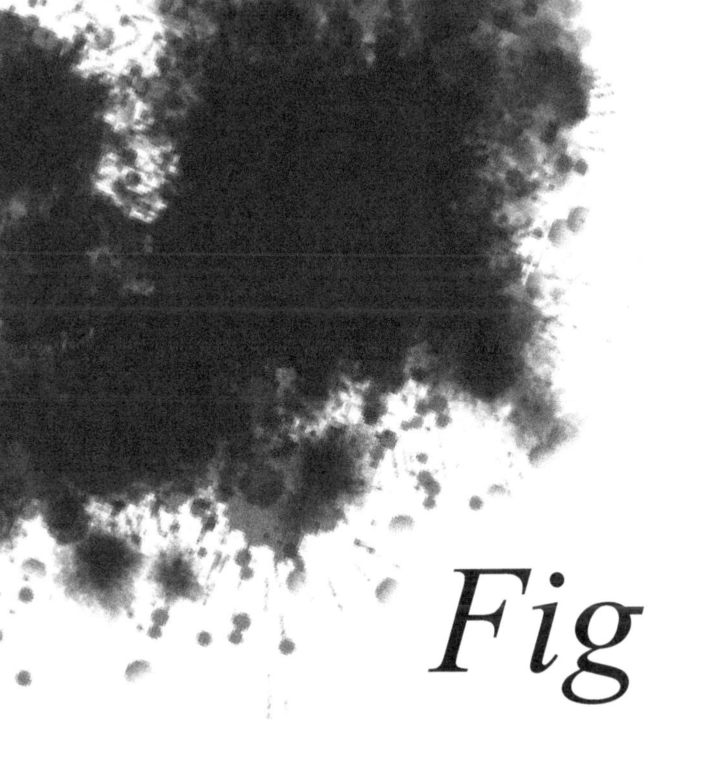

Fig

she says that we should call my mother
        —Sheree La Puma

no one but god knows why warm blood seeps
onto bare skin. not the man on the corner with
his sign *<jesus>*
not mom/not dad/not the nurse
dabbing at my feet.
hot/blade/cool/sponge
i come to be healed.
you strip bone from
twig, sew up
the girl in me.

little hour before the ache, my womb is a sieve
<self-purifying>
i cling to what's left of childhood.
downed like the trunk of a new
persimmon tree, silently/waiting
for *confession. oh, holy one,
life swells/wide & hungry. like
salmon spawning a river,
a generation passes
through me.

***

she says that we should call my mother,
that first blood is the heart's overflow,
my earthy inheritance.
she says that i am an evolving
<landscape>
destined to be a home
& it's up to me to invent
my own rituals.

The Good Doctor
        —*Caitlin Grace McDonnell*

Somewhere I'd seen abortion linked
to infection, so my insides
were a village hanging
the idiot, a room
full of flames.
The women's clinic was the only
place in San Francisco I belonged.
The soft table where I could unload
my rucksack of questions
          personal history,
dried hay & stones. *Okay,* the doctor
          said, looking over my chart.
I'd been going every few weeks, like church.
She put down her clipboard. *Sometimes...*
(That's when I saw her face for the first time)
Even though we know intellectually
 we've done nothing wrong, our feelings
  haven't caught up. A lot of women
experience feelings of guilt
or think they'll be punished.
Can I show you something?
          She held up a mirror,
a speculum, took time
making sure I was ready,
my legs up and hitched,
she put the tools in my hands.
          Everything looks really healthy
in there, she said, and I tilted
the mirror, wet and pink.
          That's just what it's supposed to look like.
My cheeks were wet with relief
and waves of truth.
Was this what being mothered felt like?

Blood: A Periodic Chronicle
    —*Anndee Hochman*

The box arrives unmarked, like bootleg gin or illegal fireworks.
You've been waiting, checking the mail, ever since your mother said
okay, but you're a little young, then wrote a check for $2.50 to the
Personal Products Company in Milltown, New Jersey. Now you run
upstairs and stash your shameful prize in the blue-tiled bathroom, the
cabinet under the sink, where your father never looks.

Soon you've memorized the contents: half a dozen Modess
pads, long and cushiony, like mattresses for sleepy Barbie dolls. A Y-
shaped, stretchy belt that you are too nervous to try on. A booklet
called "Growing Up and Liking It." You lock the bathroom door, sit on
the toilet and read.

> *What happens when I grow up? It's the time*
> *when you're old enough and grown up enough to*
> *think for yourself, choose your own clothes, add*
> *a dash of lipstick or powder, a glint of nail*
> *polish. It's the time when you begin to notice*
> *boys, and, what's even better, they begin to*
> *notice you!*

The girls pictured on the booklet's cover, in their bouncy
pigtails and empire-waist jumpers, don't seem to be wearing a dash of
lipstick or a glint of nail polish. Did they even choose those clothes?
You are wearing purple hip-hugger jeans that you begged your mother
to buy, from a store where the pants are kept in metal trash cans bolted
to the walls.

Inside the booklet are more photos—a white teenager (see:
they're growing up!) with bouffant hair, a Black one with a pressed
bob—and line drawings that remind you of the plant diagrams in your
science book.

One shows a hairless, legless female body—no breasts, no
armpits—with that triangle of uterus, each fallopian arm curling
around to palm a lumpy purse of eggs. You imagine blood dripping
from the half-hourglass of womb like red, wet sand.

Vulva, labia, and clitoris don't even earn a footnote. You will not know these words, or touch those parts of yourself, for years.

You read the booklet obsessively, as if you can summon your period through force of will. Actually, your mother was right: *you are a little young.* Meantime, you will acquire braces and John Lennon-style gold-framed glasses. Your mother will buy you a bra from Dolgonos Shape Shop on Haverford Avenue. Your hair will become an untamable frizz, and Neil Sukonik will whisper to you, one afternoon when Ms. Smith has dimmed the lights for a filmstrip in biology, "Did you know my dick's an outgrowth?"

> *Because everything is so new to you, you feel*
> *confused, puzzled and unsure of yourself, at*
> *times. Suddenly, you become moody and short-*
> *tempered. You cry easily. One instant you're*
> *happy, the next, you're blue. No one seems to*
> *understand you.*

On a car trip to Montreal, the summer you are 12, you check at every rest stop toilet stall; no, the dampness in your crotch is only sweat. Your best friend has started—you know because you snooped in her bathroom closet and spied the flowered box. Though you two have whispered about Judy Blume's book, *Are You There, God, It's Me, Margaret,* you do not talk about your own periods, or about the bras you both now wear, their straps visible under sleeveless summer shirts.

At the end of sixth grade, boys write crude rhymes in your autograph album about which girls they believe "stuff" and who is "flat." Someone in your class has told you it takes four hours to have sex. On an afternoon "date" with Michael Mogil—grilled cheese sandwiches and board games in his apartment—he asks if he can kiss you, and you say no, because you find the idea repellent and a little frightening. He asks again. You say no. Then you take off the ID bracelet he has given you, the one you've been wearing safety-pinned beneath your sleeve, drop it unceremoniously on the bed and tell Michael that you want his mother to take you home immediately.

*When you are about twelve (sometimes
younger, sometimes older), you will begin to
menstruate (men' stroo at). Menstruation is one
of the most important things that happen as you
grow up.*

When you finally get your period, one summer afternoon in your 14th year, it is anticlimactic, just a swish of sienna in the crotch of your Tuesday panties. You tell your mother, who probably tells your father. You use one of the Barbie-cots from the Modess box, but you can't figure out the belt, so the pad slides around between your legs, making you walk like a toddler in a soggy diaper.

You want to swim with your best friend, but you're too scared to use a tampon, so you grab a fresh pad and hope your tie-dye Speedo is tight enough to hold it in place. After two laps of breast-stroke, it feels as though you have a wet, rolled washcloth between your legs, and when you go to the bathroom, which reeks of Lysol, Coppertone and pee, you see a spot of red staining the pattern of your blue-and-white swimsuit, as if something bled into the surf. You wrap a towel around your waist and tell your friend you're too tired to swim.

*True or False: The menstrual flow makes you
feel weak. It's o.k. to have a permanent while
you're menstruating. People can tell when you're
menstruating. Staying in bed during the first few
days of your period is a good idea.*

Ms. Pinto, the health teacher in your high school, uses chalk to draw the female reproductive system on the front of her plaid kilt. Ms. Pinto also coaches girls' field hockey, and everyone thinks she is a lesbian, though no one actually says this out loud. On the first day of class, she tells a story about a former student who didn't know she was supposed to remove the cardboard applicator after putting in a tampon. The girls laugh nervously. The boys look shell-shocked. Ms. Pinto gets reprimanded by administrators for chalking a uterus on her kilt when the parents come for Back-to-School Night. You adore Ms. Pinto, though you're not sure what a lesbian is or does. You never raise your hand to ask.

*Chances are that you have heard about the
internal method of sanitary protection called
tampons...Applicator tampons are made with an
applicator tube and plunger...The other type of
tampon is inserted easily, naturally, without an
applicator.*

Your mother doesn't believe in tampons. She is wary of putting any kind of "foreign object" inside the body, an attitude consistent with her avoidance of X-rays, ultraviolet hand-stamps, Red Dye #2, and the fluoroscope at the shoe store. But you are 15, and you insist that she buy you a box of junior Tampax. You want to swim and play tennis without a diaper between your sweaty thighs.

In the blue-tiled bathroom, you strip the paper from a tampon, which looks like a blunt-tipped cotton cigar. How will you know where to put it? The peeled, cross-sectioned figure in the instructions is no help. One foot on the toilet? Squatting over the bowl? You poke blindly, painfully, until the tampon tip is stained red and the cardboard sticky. You toss the whole thing in the trash and slide a pad into your underwear.

But that summer, on a trip to Orlando with your aunt, uncle, and cousins, you try again, and half-succeed—that is, the tampon is somewhere inside you, but apparently not correctly, because you can feel it pinch and burn with every step. "Why are you walking like that?" your aunt wants to know, and finally you confess.

"Follow me." In a bathroom in the Magic Kingdom, where "It's a Small World, After All" tinkles through the intercom, your aunt sits on a toilet with a tampon in her hand. "Like this," she says, and it vanishes from her fingers. "But it has to go all the way in, otherwise it hurts. Now, you try."

Will it disappear inside you? The instructions showed a door at the end of that corridor, but still, you worry that the string will vanish and you'll need help—from tweezers? a chopstick? a doctor?—to fish the thing out.

But you manage, with your aunt coaching from the next stall, to push a Tampax far enough inside that you can walk without wincing. You wash your hands and skip all the way to Tomorrowland.

It is January of your senior year in college, and you've spent winter break having friendly, nightly sex with Barry in the guest room of his parents' house in Detroit. Your future scrolls out like fresh parchment, thrillingly and terrifyingly empty. You are pretty sure Barry will be no more than a footnote.

Then your period is late. You check and recheck the calendar, review your sex for any reckless moments. Barry likes sheepskin condoms that carry a fecund, barnyard smell, but he never objects to using one. You've been careful.

Still, you remember Ms. Pinto's biology lessons. Sperm are single-minded creatures; maybe one spunky overachiever has succeeded, and a clump of you and Barry is already drifting down the Fallopian slide, setting up house in your uterus.

You memorize the number of University Health Services. You imagine the metal instruments that will scrape you, like tugging barnacles from a seabed. You wait. You pray. You pray for an empty womb, you pray for the little bundle of cells to self-destruct, you pray for the tide of blood that will give you back your life.

You are in the bathroom of Sterling Library, taking a break from *The Woman Warrior,* when the first pink spot appears. You rummage for a tampon and waltz back to your study carrel. You never tell Barry. A month later, you break up with him, by phone. But for some reason, you keep a few of the sheepskin condoms. You think of their animal smell, and the luck of the draw, and the baby you and Barry will never make.

In your twenties, your periods abruptly stop. During that time, you begin to kiss women, fly across the country for a weekend to tell your parents that you are a lesbian, develop anxiety attacks, fall in love with the woman who will become your life partner and drop nearly 20 pounds.

You believe your body knows that this would be a really terrible time to grow a baby. Still, you worry. You explain to Dr. Liu that you cannot possibly be pregnant, that you have only slept with women for the past three years. He inserts the speculum, not gently, and you grimace. From the area of your feet, his voice muffled by the paper drape, he asks, "So, I take it you've never had normal intercourse?"

A homeopathic doctor prescribes some medicine that looks like BB shot and tastes like truck stop coffee. You gulp the pills obediently, but they do not make your period begin. Another doctor advises taking progesterone every three months so you can shed your uterine lining, like a seasonal clean-out of the garage.

Finally, on the night you are to give a reading from your first book—a book in which you tell your coming-out story and write about all the ways there are to make a family—you feel a couple of light cramps, like an old friend glad-handing your womb in a "Hey-it's-been-a-while" gesture. You bleed for the first time in five years.

Here's what the book does not tell you: That periods are a mess. That blood—sticky, clotted, bright, in every shade of rust and red—will smear the toilet seat and spot the tile floor, that it will streak the insides of your thighs and linger, a scarlet pentimento, no matter how hard you scrub your panties in cold water.

The Personal Products Company does not explain that your blood will rise and ebb like tides licking the shore, like the magnetic slurp of the moon. That you will menstruate in sync with female housemates and skip cycles when you travel, get the flu, or suffer panic attacks.

It does not say that when you are a mere flutter in your mother's womb, your pinprick ovaries are already packed with 6 million egg follicles—about the entire population of Missouri—and then there is a massive oocide, so that by birth a mere 1-2 million are left. By puberty you'll have just 400,000 eggs, and every month after that, 1,000 more follicles will dissolve into not-people. The booklet does not whisper about accidents or awe or the wild unlikelihood of any human actually being conceived.

> *Do women always menstruate? Menstruation*
> *does not occur during the time a baby is growing*
> *inside a mother's body. And women stop*
> *menstruating when they are between 40 and 50*
> *years of age.*

At 56, after 13 months of no circles on the calendar, you give away the remaining pads and tampons to your housemates, who are in their 30s. Then you schedule sinus surgery to recover your lost sense of smell. Your ENT, whom you adore for her utter lack of bullshit, says that the first few days post-op will feel like "you're having a period out of your nose." You prepare by folding gauze squares into little pads, sanitary napkins sized for American Girl dolls, that you can tape to your upper lip to catch the flow.

And then you start to bleed. From your nose, yes, and also—surprise!—from your vagina, through your vulva, words you can now say without stammer or blush. An actual period, crimson rill with little blackish knots, blood you can smell because—hallelujah!—the sinus surgery actually worked.

The booklet never imagined that your uterus would make up the bed for a baby 12 times a year for 43 years, give or take a few, and every time, it would strip those bloody sheets and toss them down the chute. You would marry a woman. Your body would not grow a baby. You would become the mother of a daughter, even so.

You sit on the toilet, tiny pad under your nose and larger one in your hand. You bow your head to drink it in—one final sniff of earth and salt and rust.

Buckwheat Honey
>—*Mariah Ayscue*

When I'm on my period
I crave buckwheat honey.

And my period has gotten
more painful over time.

With cramps of
imposter syndrome
around my manhood
And stomach sickness
to remind me of
my gender dysphoria

I attempt to
remind myself
that I am
a human being.

I am deserving of
softness,
gentleness,
grace,
forgiveness
and redemption songs.

But, when I am
on my period
It's hard.

I didn't have
buckwheat honey
this time around.

But, after showering in
leaf, leather, and steam
my friend
who is also trans
was like
We're going on
an adventure
to the forest
of buckwheat honey!!!

And so we went hiking
at South Mountain reservation
And followed the stream
to a waterfall.

And this radiant Joy
overwhelmed me.

And kicked off my shoes
I took off my socks
And ran barefoot into the waterfall.

And I was like
if being a boy is like
being a Mountain
Then being a man is like
creating waterfalls.

And trans care is like
craving buckwheat honey
and getting showered
in an abundance of sweetness.

And when we were
frolicking into this waterfall,
I knew I was free
And that sweetness
surrounds me
always.

The Flowering
> *—Lauren Rheaume*

I got my period when I was nine years old, the month before my 10th birthday. I brought my mother upstairs to my room, where I pointed to my stained underwear, since I had no language for my condition. I didn't know what a period *was*—I didn't know what was happening to me.

"Oh," my mother said, nodding. I felt reassured at her acknowledgment—she had an explanation. I probably wasn't dying. My mind slowly started to shift from alarm to curiosity. I don't remember the conversation afterward, how my mother explained what periods were. But I knew that because of it I had a new responsibility, a new awareness about myself.

Since I was five, I'd attended a small Catholic school in my town. I'd always been an early bloomer—in 4th and 5th and 6th grade I was one of the tallest of my classmates, and I curved my back into an arc often, slouching to hide my growing chest. I'd picked up that these were things to be embarrassed about, and certainly not something to flaunt. I started the work many girls learn young: the work of making myself smaller. I'd hope to God no one discovered the pads I kept in my desk because I thought my period was a secret I was supposed to keep. I didn't know how to talk about it with anyone, even the other girls in my class, my friends. They didn't talk about it with me either, but it was a while before I realized this was because I was the only one.

In freshman year of high school, when I was fourteen, I came home from a particularly frustrating volleyball practice and asked my mother for a tampon for the first time. No self-respecting girl wore a pad underneath those spandex shorts, I told myself. Too obvious. Tampons were another way to hide the truth. Mom brought one to me. I put it in and felt lighter already—it was much easier than I thought. It felt like my victory from the year before, when I finally touched my eye and put contacts in myself. I was becoming more refined every day. And what is *refinement* anyway? Hiding the embarrassing? Hiding flaws? Hiding the ugly reality?

The problem came later when it was time to take the tampon out. I'd read the entire little folded paper in the box, and I was already panicking over the likelihood of toxic shock syndrome—I vowed to never leave a tampon in too long, just like I vowed to never sleep with my contacts in.

As I pulled on the tiny string attached to the tampon inside me, I could feel my jaw tighten with the effort. I imagined that it would just slide out, but *no*, as I yanked on the string harder and harder, I started to think that something might be wrong. I was strong, but what if it hurt something inside if I pulled too hard? Again, I called my mother upstairs, and I explained the situation. After some back and forth, it was decided that I would lie on my back on the bathroom floor, my mother above me like a midwife, standing with her knees bent, pulling on this tampon with all her might. But it didn't work. After a little while she was huffing, and I was cursing.

"I think it's flowered inside," she said, between pulls.

"Flowered? *Flowered?!*" I said, groaning, my eyes on the ceiling and only the ceiling.

"It flares out at the end inside when it absorbs moisture." It wasn't until later that I was able to picture this: the string a stem and the tampon narrow at the base, widening as it went up inside me. So often we use flowers to describe women—blossoming—all that, but right then I found the image disgusting, the experience traumatic, and I thought *fuck everyone and their fucking flowers*.

I said, "Mom, I'm going to swear."

"Fine!" she said, out of breath, pulling with all of her body weight.

"Fuck! Fucking shit!" I yelled. How horrifying, to have to ask your mother to do something like this, to need help with something like this. As if having a period wasn't embarrassing enough.

She yanked one final time and it came out. We threw it away, never to speak of it again.

Gravida 0, Para 0
—*Kim Roberts*

Only the females of three species—
killer whales, short-finned pilot whales,
and humans—outlive their fertility.
So menopause is a biological rarity.
They also call it "climacteric,"
as if it were weather, a storm passing
through your ovaries. I read recently
that the death rate from pregnancy
and childbirth in the U.S. is rising;
no one knows why. It's more than doubled
in the last 25 years. Michael Cant,
who studies killer whales,
says, "You have to not only look at the gains,
but the costs the species would suffer
if they continue to breed." Once I told
my doctor if only I was not estranged
from my mother, I'd know what to expect
from menopause. "That's ridiculous,"
the doctor said. "Your mother had children.
You've never even been pregnant.
Her experience would have no bearing
on yours. Feel badly about the estrangement
if you like, but not because of this."
All women are different, but the basic menu
 (what the Japanese call *konenki*)
remains the same: hot flashes, bone loss,
fluctuating estrogen levels, poor memory,
sleeplessness, vaginal dryness,
higher risk for heart disease. The mystery
is why I feel better than I have in years.

It Stops For Awhile
    —Sarah Lilius

My uterus playground fills
with fluid instead of dirt.

They punch and kick important walls
no one remembers.

Ten months of rest
for each child.

Boys slide out at slow speeds
then it's back to work.

Giant hospital netting
catches the mess.

The grand finale gushes
like an event unscheduled.

Confused hormones,
lining builds and unbuilds.

I made life.
In my arms, they grow.

This is everything,
treat me like you know it.

When It Rains, It Clots
—Emily Reece Fontenot

I like to sit on the toilet after a long day of bleeding, legs spread wide, and let the clots pass as they will. I guarantee they each weigh at least three ounces themselves. Sometimes I can match the cramps that doubled me over with the clot that passes later. Like that's what all the fuss was about.

Tampon boxes are labeled with capacity guides—capacity weighed in ounces. They don't count the clots. Only the blood from the free flows counts, which sucks because the majority of the blood I lose once a month comes as clots.

I would love to study them. Take them apart and figure them out. Catch them as they fall and inspect them under a magnifying glass and a bright light. I imagine stretching them out and like cool Photoshop videos dragging them over and painting a room with it. I wonder what they look like when they're inside of me. I wonder what a baby can do with it that I can't.

In movies where demons are birthed, they look a lot like these clots. They slink and slither out of the woman, a thick and gooey dark red, almost black glob. Just like a clot. And then the beast tears its way out of the sack and goes off to do its wretched deeds. I wonder if that was a man's decision. That he envisioned the most terrifying thing that could come out of a woman and decided on a completely normal thing. He likely never thought it possible. Thought menstruation blood was just like the blood that leaks out of your skin from cutting yourself.

Or maybe it was a woman. Someone who also wanted to investigate the slimy thing. Tear it apart and see if it was solid matter, see what it looks like on the inside, see what it holds. I don't imagine my clots hold baby demons. Still, I hope it was a woman.

Blood For Eggs
       —Raye Hendrix

When it comes time to slaughter
the hogs it's the men

who do the slicing but
the women who make use

of the remains—know how
to clean and cook the skin

and muscle—substitute
the blood for eggs.

The men won't eat the dark
concoctions but their Irish

wives who settled this valley
and their daughters

have no issue—which
they say is because women,

like Christ, are used
to sacrifice and stains.

When I ask my mother
how she learned to live

with all that iron she tells me
again of the womb

and crucifixion—the duty
and the nails. She says

the only women who
should be afraid of bleeding

are the ones not washed
in the blood of the Lamb.

Senior Confessional
> —*MaryAnn L. Miller*

I prefer this drier
subsistence
to that juiced-up
building and bursting
that birthing of gratuitous
mucus and blood
that scheduled shriving
deep muscle penance
years breaking eggs
one at a time.

Period Ode
> —*Cynthia White*

Some say the hassle, others say pain,
still others say most monstrous
are the down & dirty rages,
the fleets of tears.
I say what afflicts me
is your absence. Darling phantom,
for years you were the rare thing
I could count on.
In the beginning, a napkin
caught your curds & whey,
fresh & glistening & warm
to the touch. Later, a tampon
so I might swim. Move
in tight jeans without shame.
On the rag, we all said. Little red,
your disguises are legion—
Lingonberry season. The English have landed.
The curse, the blob, Aunt Flo. Falling off the roof,
my mother's quaint phrase.
Would I rather be young?
I can't say. Only
that when I mourn your loss,
I mourn wicked power. Outrageous
dark magic. As if the source began
& ended with our tidal trysts,
as if the world doesn't carry on
heedless, blooming & fruiting & giving bloody birth.

Quicksand

Rose

> *—Amy Hsieh*

I bleed liquid rose
into water—red,
slowly opening smoke.
Plumes of an old future.

Petals shed in my panties.

Having and losing
count of moons, small pearls
slipped
between fingers.
Night skies in the window
still framed for fairy tales.

My breasts grow cold,
an unpicked orchard.

Just how many names for Rose?

I zip up,
trying to grasp
a thinning bouquet
in my body.

The Grey Rose
>   —*Kelly Gray*

These days, virginity is said to be a construct. When I was 13, it was not a construct, it was a place between my legs, just past where my fingers could reach, where I felt a pause. At the time, I had a friend who took me places I had never been before. She was three years older and had a boyfriend who was twenty-five. She told me about their sex and I noticed she seemed to without pause. She played music on subwoofers he'd installed in her car and drove around the twists of our backroads as if in a trance, unable to hear the screeching of tires over the sound of bass. Her mother had a small cabin tucked into the shadows of the ridge and they threw parties that spread into the night, dark parties and adults that made me slightly queasy when I wasn't drinking. This is where Tattoo John pulled out his gun and worked in a small grey rose below my collar bone among the bearded men cheering him on. His hands were dirty and looked like white bark. Droplets of blood sprung from the petals. I pressed a napkin to the tattoo and gave it to my friend before she disappeared into a wall of bamboo with a man, ignoring our calls to come back for her matching rose.

Weeks later she drove me to her boyfriend's townhouse and left me downstairs with his two housemates. We sat on a long L shaped faux leather couch with a huge screen TV in front of us blaring sports announcements. The men pushed a bottle of Peach Schnapps across the coffee table towards me. I drank, politely, watching the television with my hands in my lap. When my friend came downstairs, she was loud and smiling as she grabbed my hands, pulling me upstairs. "It's time for you. He said he would do it for you," she said gleefully before she pushed me in the room and closed the door behind me. His room was stark. A dresser, a bed, stacks of speakers and subwoofers. He asked me to lay down on the bed and as he pulled off my pants, I remember thinking, this is it, I'm not going to be a virgin anymore. I couldn't look at his face, his weight felt like it would crush me. There was a sharp pain that caused me to gasp, and when I bled, he laughed. He said he hadn't thought it was true, which confused me. He rolled the condom and himself off the bed at the same time. He asked me to get up, and I had to look away because my throat was beginning to convulse. On the bed the shape of my body was caught up in the sheets, marked in the center with a red wet blossom. I felt a hollow rigidity take to my core which I used to calm my knees from shaking as I walked down the carpeted stairs. My friend drove me home, the bass vibrating through my back and arms. She did not turn down the volume when I opened the car door in my driveway. Before I walked through the gate to my home, I knelt to vomit between the roses and jasmine, feeling blossoms on the side of my face. When I took a bath that night, there was no blood. Only a soft place inside me that led to a thousand future pauses.

premenstrual dysphoric disorder
     —Leila Tualla

There is a silent chaos that follows me,
shadowing my movements and biding its time.
It manifests quietly, slowly gathering its power.
I can feel myself leaving for a moment before this version of me
slips through the cracks and comes alive.
I succumb to her power, leaving nothing
but tears and fire in our wake.

She is passion; blindly going on instinct and fueled by turmoil.
She is my shame, my guilt, my walking nightmare;
A monthly companionable adversary and a savior I can call by name.

Our foundation is built on her intensity,
and as the moon shifts back into the shadows,
I surrender to this phase.
She slips away, leaving me exhausted and wounded.

A few more days of rest,
a few more moments of clarity,
a few more rounds of daylight,
before
a scream is uncurled, refusing to be held back
and sorrow pierces through my fragile defenses
that she emerges out of the shadows and takes her place once more.

My Uterus Says No
        —Rosemary Royston

to the thin tube whose goal
is to extract a slice of endometrial tissue.
This is not a surprise, my uterus

has said *no* before. *Remember that other*
failed biopsy attempt? I say.
But the ob/gyn pays no mind. She

props open my cervix to gain entry
into an uncooperative uterus. *No.* My uterus,
unconcerned about minimal spotting,

is not interested in offering a sample.
The doctor and I are determined.
Tell me a story! I blurt, and up from the stirrups

floats: *My husband was bitten*
by a rabid raccoon while fishing yesterday.
No way! I say, briefly distracted

before my scream of pain erupts.
The doctor shakes her head,
I can't torture you like this. She pulls

out the tube and speculum while I wipe
tears, wondering how many shots
are required for a rabies bite, and what

one does when her uterus
defies entry, the lining continually
thickening, unyielding.

Red Letter Days
  —Jan Chronister

In February
I make sense of the year—
plan trips
schedule visits
count weeks by four,
skip through months
like hopscotch,
throw a stone,
avoid where it lands.

I mark the first day of periods
so I won't give a lecture
attend opening night
travel too far from home,
make sure summer weddings
writing classes
are far away from
migraines and cramps.

I dream ahead to Christmas
with my daughter in Seattle,
realize with dread
I just circled a red letter day.

Missing
            —Eleanore Dykes

You are running late.

I was expecting you to be here already
need you to arrive as soon as you can
or send me a sign you're on your way
because I am worried about you
concerned you might have gotten lost
or stopped by something unforeseen
an unplanned event preventing your safe arrival.

It is a cruel irony
but your regular visits bring me relief
even though I am cramping
and clotting
and irritable
and tender
and sore
and I've come to rely
on your punctual company.

Then at last you show up
fashionably late and a little dramatic
in all your bloody glory
and I breathe a sigh of relief
I didn't realize I had been holding in.

Monthly Courses
—Sarah Rose Thomas

My breasts feel heavy like my milk's come in
But the baby's almost three
And we're all done with that

Blood was shame when
I started bleeding
the first day of 7th grade
Even though the guidance counselor warned us
Gave us free pantiliners
One tablespoon of blood, ladies,
Over the course of five days,
That's not too bad, now is it?

I used to look at my stepmom's
Super absorbent tampons
Who the hell bleeds that much?
They don't tell you that when your cycles start again
Everything is worse

After four sons
I can stand under a hot shower
While it feels like a clawed thing
Is hanging from my womb
The weight an ache I never carried
Before motherhood opened it up

This is the story of a woman's cycles
One way to measure the history of a body
Monthly I'll return to this reminder
The fruitless ovulation
The *How can there be so much blood?*

The flush of pain and pulse of emptying out
Letting go of the time when I was prenatal
Bleeding away the years I'll be postpartum
Waiting until I make the next transition
And this monthly ritual is slowly burned out of me
With heat of my body's own making

On Cue
>   —*Margo Berdeshevsky*

Was thin. Was an actress. Was it the year after Roe v. Wade, yes,   two
actors married a year, & ready to be Caesar & Cleopatra, not ready to be
mommy & daddy, no   skills for agonies of babies & discipline & griefs.
That much they knew.   She was scraped   & they went on to court

Oscars, for suffering on   cue. Was a year later the gynecologist
pronounced her pregnant. Again. Lay thin & imperfect on the hospital
stretcher awaiting cleansing that would return her body to her. He came
to her side to say "all ready now, dear," &   at that instant she bled, a
gush that flowed all

over her starched white sheet, river of relief   she was not pregnant
he'd made a terrible mistake. In dim rooms where she lay   other women
to her left   to her right, so many silent   one humming, one crying
she knew why   or she didn't   but she was an actress—there were
other roles to play. Went on to cry   on cue.

~

Home in an embrace & passion of sex again   she stopped. Remembered
being nine in a foreign hotel her mama jaundiced & flailing, a dying
swan, a hepatitis devouring her liver, mama begging a nine year old girl
keep her company in case she died.   "Learn the combination of our
luggage, baby.   Don't cry.   Never mind. Never mind. Read to me,
baby," piss-yellow mama begging her, "Distract me, baby, read!"

Only book in that room is what mama's been reading all summer long, a
doctor-story-fat-blue-covered-book named *Not As A Stranger*.   "Read
until I sleep, I can't concentrate when I read it baby, words are too small
& my head's all trillium or lilacs ... will you just read for chrissakes,
pleasssse? Help me, read, babe,"   & she did. Scene the girl reads out
loud in her good-little-daughter voice, blond braids an unkempt crown

on top of her head, wannabe actress, wannabe hunter, wannabe-saint voice is: an abortion with a wire coat hanger. "What *is* that mama?" No answer. The mother drifts, dozes, doesn't know.

The girl remains coldly sleepless seeing wires. Seeing blood clots. Seeing a sharp & low newborn moon hung in the hotel window, covered in its own blood. Hearing a high voice she doesn't understand. Awake. Mama is awake. "Baby! This is the combination of our suitcases: *O - O - 1 - O - O - 5.* You're a saint, baby. I want you to memorize that, *please.*"   She tries.   Loses a zero.   Her hands are fists.

 "Try, damn you. Say it again." She says it wrong.   "Again!   You use it in case—if I die." But the mother drifts. Is sleeping again. "Babyyyyy," She hears her mama's whine. "Don't forget. please, my darling." And for awhile she sleeps.

~

The actress cannot sleep. Or make love to her husband. Not that night, not for a long time. But she can always do—what her directors love about her, she can act. Can make it real. What makes her husband nervous and angry. What makes him whisper one night in the dark, if she does not have a baby she will never be a real woman.   But she is an actress. And, she can cry on cue.

What the Internet Told Me About Menopause
—Kelli Russell Agodon

They say not to worry as I turn forty
and start having doomsday thoughts,
imagining my own death.

They say hormones and dry skin.

They say anytime between thirty-five
and fifty-five. They say hot flashes, cold
flashes, flushes. I say, *Royal?*

They say loss of libido and hair loss
(with the benefit of random facial hair).

I say, *A good look*
for a squirrel.
I say, *A good look*
for a forty/fifty-something woman
not having sex.
I say, *I'm going to keep having sex.*

They say sleep disorder, night sweats,
mental confusion, disorientation,
dizziness. I ask, *Where am I?*
What was I going to write?

No one said I'd return to listening
to Aretha Franklin, no one said I might
cut my hair short.

They say anxiety, irritability, depression.
I say, *What else is new?*
I say, *Bring it on!*

They say burning tongue, electric shock
under the skin.
I say, *Seriously? Who is writing this stuff?*

They say osteoporosis after several years.
I say, *Wanna sign my cast?*
I say, *Got milk?*

No one says, MILF.
No one says, Body by Yoga.

They say if my pants don't fit,
it could be my thyroid.
I say, *Or evenings*
with glass of wine and a pocketful of chocolates.

No one says I might not notice
when others stop
noticing, when I move from *miss*
to *ma'am*. I say, *Sometimes*
I notice.

Red Clay

I the Already
      —Jennifer Schomburg Kanke

See me in that moment when other girls all turned to me
and I had a chance to become their queen.
I, the already bleeding. I, the already budding.
I, the already ten-year-old woman.
Do I wish I could relive it? Such beautiful
possibility, when I could have said something cool,
but instead shrugged, *I don't know,*
you just get a pad and go on with your life,
so that when the next girl started four months later,
some Heather or Amy, she took my rightful place.
She understood so much better than I
how our bodies would begin to define us,
though maybe I knew that too, knew it
and just walked away bleeding.

From One Girl to Another
    —Vicki Iorio

*And from that day on everything seems different. At first you feel new
and strange.....the way a butterfly must feel when it suddenly discovers it
has wings*

Nine year old summer. I fall out of a tree. After disposal of buds and
twigs, the cleansing of wounds, a deeper blood remains.

*Girls have some crazy names for it: my friend, the monthlies, Aunt Flo,
grandma coming to visit, falling off the roof, getting the pie*

My mother tosses me a box of Kotex. Tells me to stay in my room.

*Have an excuse when the boys ask you to go swimming...you can don
your play suit and get a tan while the others swim. Don't tease the boys
they might throw you into the briny*

I am a fish but mom won't let me near the water. When my best friend
Robert, my pool pal, his lunch wrapped in a beach towel, comes to get
me, Ma slams the door in Robert's face.

*And you need never feel the least embarrassed to ask for a Kotex in a
store----- even if it's a tall, young red-haired lad on the other side of the
counter. He'll give you a box of Kotex without batting an eye.*

Yeah right

*Tampons and the 'internal' method. Frankly most authorities say most
young girls shouldn't use tampons without first consulting their
doctors.......a brush with the hymen*

Ma pounds on the locked bathroom door. "Are you using a Tampax?"
Threatens to call my father or the fire department.

*Keep your hair clean and tidy. Wear fresh clothes......sprinkle Quest
powder on the pad to stop the odor, this will give you poise and make you
more attractive*

By age 13, I go with the flow, don polka dot frocks, go under the
boardwalk with boys.

*If you depend on your memory you're sure to get mixed up..... If you stop
for an overlong time then check with your mother and go to the doctor
for a good frank chat. He can probably fix you up in time*

Or call you a stupid girl.

Female Protection
>   —*S.L. Wisenberg*

Istanbul, 1987

We were strangers and our eyes met as we both left the tourism
office. He smiled and I smiled, and it was very early in the morning,
and I'd just arrived and didn't have plans. He was Austrian, spoke
English, was tall with acne still on his baby face. His name was Stephen.
He asked if the American dollar was strong—physically—if it would
hold up to washings if he sewed it into his clothing. We walked
through bazaars and tea gardens and ate in cheap restaurants I couldn't
find again after he left. We talked about the Big Things you talk about
with strangers because you don't have enough intimacy to talk about
the petty stuff. The morality of violence, World War II, the Baader-
Meinhoff gang. I was his first Jew in the flesh. He'd seen a rabbi once—
on TV, part of a series. He left a day before I did and after that I
realized he had been my protection. Because I wasn't wearing a
headscarf and skirt the men knew I was Western and therefore
hounded me.

Vienna, 1992

I stayed with Stephen and his sister. He took me to the
Nashmarkt for sheep-cheese sandwiches; to his medical school, a
building that smelled of formaldehyde and had worn stone steps. He
wanted to show me daily things and tourist things and I wanted to do
research. Jewish research. But to come to Vienna and not want to see
St. Stephen's Cathedral or view the Klimts and Persian miniatures in
the Belvedere Palace—instead to concentrate on tribal history—that
seemed narrow, parochial, stuck in the past.

I had my period. I didn't know where to throw my tampons
and pads. There was no trash can in the bathroom. I was afraid the
tampons would plug up the toilet. I was too embarrassed to ask
Stephen what to do with them. His sister wasn't around. I stuffed my
used feminine hygiene products into the bottom of the kitchen trash. I
put some in my knapsack and tossed them in garbage bins on the
street. That whole week I felt very bloody, very Jewish. Once we passed
by the Jewish welcome service on Kaertnerstrassse and I wanted to stop

in but not while Stephan was with me. My Jewish shame seemed the same as my menstrual shame, the clot that I scrubbed from the floor of the square bathtub. What to do with the unmentionables. Why bring up the Jews, those unmentionables? There was an outdoor exhibit downtown on the reconstruction of the city after the War. There were giant panels of blown-up black-and-white photos of rubble and after. Stephen told me he was tired of the war being thrown into his face. In school he'd always had to write essays about it. The past was past. And here I was, come from the New World, wallowing in it. He didn't say that. I thought that.

It had been interesting to talk about Jews when we first met, in Istanbul, I imagined him thinking. But once was enough. On to the next topic.

I didn't leap then from the personal to the body politic. Unlike Germany, the defeated power, Austria, as an "occupied" country, has not had to examine its anti-Semitism and eager participation in the Final Solution. After all, it was an occupied country. Not their responsibility, no need to mea culpa like Germany. And even German historians had started: *Enough is enough, how long must we be guilty?*

The Cold War had just ended, but Vienna was supposedly still full of spies. The heart of Europe. I was a spy in old empire, a Jew masquerading as an innocent American tourist, pretending concern for Sacher tortes and baroque palaces and Their history, visiting, say, the museum of resistance and looking impassively at the artifacts: chess sets molded from bread, pretending a lack of scorn for the veneration of Communists and Catholics to the exclusion of the Jews. Nothing. *Judenrein.*

I went by myself to Freud's apartment. The good doctor had taken most everything with him when he and his family left, after much difficulty, for London in 1938. Now, instead of Freud's furniture and statues, there were black-and-white photographs of his furniture and statues all along the walls, roughly where the real objects had once been. A binder with multilingual pages gave the history of the absent artifacts.

I needed to use the restroom. I went to Freud's. It was large, like in an American house, clean white tiles. With a perfect metal trash basket for my American/Jewish/female unmentionables.

What do women want? Freud asked.

See above: a clean bathroom, a lined trash basket.

The Devil Shows You How to Use a Tampon
—*Megan Mary Moore*

The first time you bleed,
the Devil comes to see.
She knows life can find a room in you
and that scares Mom, Dad, and
every boy you've met. But not her.

She sits on the edge of the tub, not there to convince,
but advise. And as your fingernails grow redder
she warns you, they blame blood for ghosts.
When you leave this bathroom,
the burden is on you.

And after she shows you how to
push, press, and pull inside yourself,
she grabs your daisy print panties from the ground,
throws them in the trash and tells you to
wash the last bit of sidewalk chalk from your hands.

Transition

—Monique Hayes

Juanita's candy necklace, swinging above the menstrual pad, was almost empty after forty hours at the detention center. A three-minute good-bye from her parents hadn't aged her at all and now she was mulling over menses in McAllen.

Cafeteria ladies were supposed to be cordial, an "it's okay, baby" preceding the sweet comments they dished out to young, troubled diners. I'm only able to cook up one unfulfilling thought I keep to myself: why'd they have to send your mother back to Tijuana before your period came? I'm no great guest lecturer on puberty, a scooper of scalloped potatoes if anything, and timid about explaining tampons. I'd only given her the Kotex pad after I heard her sobbing in the stall.

I nudge my hairnet above my blonde bangs as Juanita opens the stall door.

"A few boys saw the red marks on my jeans," whispers Juanita.

I recall the squinted eyes of Juanita's mother Rita as she assessed the new ankle monitor above her thin foot. Border Patrol guards admired her swan-like neck before they dropped their gazes to the cloth strap choking her tanned skin. They didn't mind her exotic beauty as long as she knew she was foreign.

"They'll know I can have babies," continues Juanita. "I feel so gross."

When Juanita clutched her stomach in the cafeteria, there were a handful of wisecracks from my co-workers about the likelihood that she was with child at eleven. Even my social worker father clung to that nonsensical notion: Latina girls get pregnant early. I immediately knew it wasn't morning sickness but cramps because I'd wrinkled my nose the same way last Wednesday.

Juanita's pinkie traces the pad's wings like an infant touching the lines of a pacifier for the first time. I was raised by a single dad who had to be reminded by his barber that a latex pacifier had to be hand washed. There always seems to be a lack of knowledge wherever I go.

I could leave her there confused, something she must've been ever since she entered the chain-link cage with her cloud-patterned backpack. Juanita flinched when I gave her grade-A apple juice upon her arrival two days ago. She knew how to fit the straw into the hole but I did it anyway. I did it repeatedly as a latchkey kid. I've seen dozens of these displaced children make up their dingy mattresses and change their siblings' three-day old diapers. How can I soothe her with no straw in my pocket or without ever carrying a child in my womb?

"I don't wanna be a woman if it's like this," whispers Juanita.

Part of me wants to flee from the soiled sinks and locate an informative article on my iPhone, but her flushed cheeks freeze my knees. I thought about how I'd gone into the convenience aisle alone to sniff scented candles and fondle perfume atomizer bottles. It was all for show until I caught sight of orange-haired guitarist Greta Lilley, the only eleventh grader I knew bold enough to tell me about female anatomy. She'd also lost her mother and we discussed wings on the linoleum floor underneath rows of roll-on deodorant. The wings fit around you, explained Greta. They know your body; trust them to do the job. While Juanita could trust the article, it wouldn't really know her.

"Don't worry," I say. "Your body's just doing its job for five to seven days. My job is cleaning up after those boys. Talk about gross. Jello-covered pencils stuck in ham sandwiches?"

Juanita laughs, then covers her mouth.

"It's all normal, sweetheart," I add. "Why don't you see how the pad fits?"

After we're done, we leave the restroom holding hands. I let my sight linger on the gun of a Border Patrol officer, fingers on the barrel as a group of toddlers watch Hansel and Gretel peck away at the gingerbread house on the LED screen above the chain-link fence. The last candy rings of Juanita's jewelry leave chalky dust on my shirt when she embraces me. I don't mind the mess while I'm imagining her mother holding atomizers in a convenience store alone.

I readjust her necklace. "How about I get you something to eat?"

Paloma Wings
        —Katherine Hoerth

I wondered why maxi pads have wings,
and what the use of wings are
if all they do is hold you in place.

As a kid, I imagined a flock of them,
of maxi pads,
taking to the sky like startled palomas,

outstretching their white wings
and using them to get as far from me
as possible at that time of the month.

I thought that wings
were only used to fly away—
to touch the sky like Icarus,

who never had to wear a maxi pad.
Who would ever want to be grounded
in such a place, the delta of a river,

to collect the flotsam left behind
from the wreck of another month?
Because when you're thirteen,

you learn there's nothing worse
than yourself, a girl,
the red red red of you.

44 Songs to My Body
—Adura Ojo

Soprano

I'm filling up the kettle to make some coffee. Everything seems to be instant these days and I'm no exception to the default setting. Words forming in my mind asking for some space on my computer screen confirm that too. As the kettle fills up, so do my eyes. Syllables come in a sequence offering light to soothe all that aches within me, but then disappear with the suddenness with which they appear just before I get to my electronic notebook

1. To what do I owe the beauty of not pausing? Not for me, and certainly, not for men.
2. My body has been super theatrical with the hormonal drama of a host of perimenopause symptoms over the last eight years. I can hardly keep up: Chronic fatigue, depression, foggy brain, simultaneous hot and cold sensations, joint pain, mood swings and stiffness.
3. I'm done, except my eggs aren't going anywhere just yet, the sonogram said.
4. If only for the reason that men don't pause or are expected to pause at anything, can we as women have our name on this rite of passage that's ours to walk through?
5. We need a new name for menopause, like 'Queen Bliss' or something. (Queenepause would be great if it didn't sound like a disease.)
6. Talking about the menopause should be like discussing the weather; except when it rains we know it rains. We get the forecast. We prepare for rain.
7. Waiting. I'm always waiting.
8. Mum said I kept her waiting for three days and when I finally showed up, she needed help to get me out of her. The doctor was good. I own a finely sculpted skull.
9. Waiting. I'm always waiting.
10. I eat olives & guacamole to placate my inflamed body. I make love to it in spite of it.
11. Love is parachute, falling

12.   Parachute is love unfolding.

13.   I'm home with avocado in the same way water finds its place on the tongue.

14.   I'm unapologetic, chunky like guacamole. I sieve through prisms, minding the glass.

15.   Last August I woke up from a hysteroscopy in unbearable pain, relieved I was still alive. An hour and a half later with 10mm of morphine and enough Fentanyl, I was sufficiently stabilised to be wheeled back into the ward. Subject to results of a biopsy, the surgeon was happy she'd found nothing to be worried about.

16.   I say sixteen. Help a girl see herself for herself before she's sixteen.

17.   My sense of self, me-as- I-know-me—was gone in the puff of smoke that was my 40s. Social media, not known for its kindness, has flashes of light. Occasionally I'd find fragments of me on a blog or a Facebook post.

18.   At 51, the consultant gynecologist told me I was producing too much oestrogen. I bled so much in the two months prior to the hysteroscopy. I was given medication to stop the bleeding. She said: "Your body won't give up producing eggs and that's the problem."

19.   "It's just a waiting game now. Your body will give up (egg-making) eventually. That or HRT. But you go into HRT (hormonal replacement therapy) with your eyes open. You have to decide if you're comfortable with the risks of HRT, one of which is breast cancer."

20.   I'm to learn later from my research that the risks of HRT are higher for women like me who suffer from obesity. According to a Lancet paper, *Type and timing of menopausal hormone therapy and breast cancer risk,* published on 29 August 2019, obesity is an important risk factor for breast cancer.

21. The question is this: why are we quiet about the global nightmare for half the human population, of perimenopause and the menopause? Why are we in the dark? Why do we not warn young women about the menopause? No one warned me. According to NHS UK, as much as 8 in 10 women will have additional symptoms for some time before or after their periods stop. This can last up to 12 years. BodyLogicMD, USA lists 34 symptoms of the menopause including night sweats, memory lapses, incontinence, sleep disorders, mood swings, depression, and weight gain. The reality is many women like me have no idea what impact perimenopause can have on our lives until we actually experience it.

22. I look forward to the day my body and I would stop betraying ourselves.

Contralto

23. My garden is bush. I want to be a better gardener.

24. I'm not done. It's the fear of what to find or un-find, packing, yet unfurling.

25. Pruning, yet not done hoarding.

26. The sonogram revealed nothing. I continued digging, pondered the whys and where to go from here. My angry body became expert at hoarding the known and unknown.

27. There's a room untouched in my house ten years in the making...

28. Five foot six inches deep in manner of matter, my body is its anchor: it's the time warp room.

29. The monster I've known all these years is the same one I can't touch.

30. The doctors were worried it could have been cancer. The lining around my uterus is thickening instead of thinning. Apparently, the opposite is supposed to happen at my age.

31. I wish I'd been spared other monsters.

32. Lost somewhere in that time warp room are my passport, qualifications, investment certificates and anything of material value in my life.

33. In April 2018, I went on vacation to LA with my daughter and a close friend to celebrate my 50th birthday. I came back home and placed my passport in the time warp room.

34. I became someone whose identity was lost in a time warp.

35.   The time warp room has many nooks and crannies. It could be anywhere.

36. I'm in many places. It's a habit. I leave bits of me behind in places I like—Lipstick, a scarf, a notepad.

37. Some places are not so nice. They harbour smoke and lingering aromas like stale tobacco.

38. I theorise I've lived two thirds of my life. I panic about unrealised goals: unwritten memoir, another poetry collection, a longed-for 'naughty grandma' persona, Australia, Asia, travelling the world. I want it all now. My body gives me a reason to stop, catch my breath.

39. As much as I don't want to, I can hear my own ragged breathing.

40. My best friend Kay came into my bedroom to check on me as usual. We lay in bed together for a while. She held me soothingly, her hands caressing my back. I started to cry like I did just now while filling up the kettle.

41. I saw Kay ruffled for the first time ever at the hospital. I'd taken 90 minutes longer than expected to come out of theatre.

42. Kay is from a world different to the one I know. She's light. I play with her afro. The sun streams in through orange curtains, its rays reflected in strands of her hair curled between my fingers. Darkness did not take over her space in the world.

43. Is want a default of living? I last had a period in January 2020. Right now, my nipples are sore. Usually, it's a sign aunt Flo is on her way. I'm really hoping she'll just stay away for good.

44. 44...the year my life started to tangle in knots. If you think I sound like I'm talking while falling off a cliff and taking my shoes off at the same time, you'd be right. That's what it feels like in my body. Eight years on, I'm still trying to untie my shoelaces. I'm not done yet. I've been looking forward to doing me since I turned sixteen. It's time to tackle the time warp room.

Puce

—*Marty Head*

once i bled for months because my body is allergic to birth control, and when i went to the doctor because i was concerned and in pain, they told me it takes a long time to fade out of the system so even though i stopped getting shots i would still have symptoms and i shouldn't come back just because i was bleeding; the average period was four months long…when i got home my boyfriend had to ease me out of a panic attack; i'd never had one before and the knowledge that i was having one scared me as much the nameless fear swallowing my breath and when he finally got me calm he asked why, why was i so upset, it was only two more months, and yes it sucked, but i would get back to normal, and i couldn't tell him why, i didn't have the words, but more importantly, i didn't know, didn't know why the thought of months of blood hurt me so much i was seized by rings and reams of encompassing terror, but i know now, so let's talk about dysphoria, and what it's like to be a non-woman isolated in a woman's body, and how every time i feel that slick red smear between my thighs i'm reminded of what my body can do, and how very much i do not want that burden, and how, and how—i did not ask for this; realizing i am nonbinary is a blessing and a freedom, but it does not erase my uterine curse; i am condemned every month to live a woman's experience, eternally, incorrectly, until the end of my days, period

Period Haiku: A Series
    —Kelly Westhoff

 # 1

Shit.
Out of tampons.

I was hoping I wouldn't
need more for nine months.

 # 2

Could this be my last

Mother's Day as a non-mom?

lemon-lime tree buds

Sigh. Another month.

Another disappointment.

I hate telling him.

3

my blood does not want to stay inside me

                    it
                 f   s
                   l   w
                    o

dark mornings

dark nights

4

gathering of friends

Should i order wine?

Will i hurt the baby?

i slip into the bathroom

find red underwear

HA!

There is no baby.

Eight Years Old
>—*Anne Finger*

I'm 69 years old, and it's been nearly two decades since I last had my period.

Yesterday, in the course of my bending forward to retrieve my cell phone from the floor under the kitchen table, the joystick of my wheelchair somehow got jammed under the table, and we all went flying across the room: the wheelchair, the kitchen table, me—out of my chair, across the floor, the power chair moving me and the table relentlessly forward. When it stopped, I waited a moment before clambering back into my chair, taking an inventory of my body—no, nothing hurt, nothing seemed broken. I did have a lump on my forehead. Back in the wheelchair, I used it to push the kitchen table back into place, checked my forehead in the mirror—yeah, that's a goose egg—and made a video call to my medical provider. No, I didn't lose consciousness; no, I didn't feel nauseous; no, I wasn't confused. A bit freaked out by the whole thing, but not confused. I was given a list of symptoms to watch for and told to ice the lump on my forehead. Then I called a friend to recount the adventure: "When I was seven years old, I would have thought this goose egg was the coolest thing in the world."

So many things had been cool at that stage of my life. Building dams and forts, planting my crutches in mid-stream so I could leap across the cold, cold creek without getting my feet wet and freezing, straddling the footboard of my friend Debby's bed, rocking back and forth against it, pretending to be the Lone Ranger riding across the plain, thrilled by the sensations coursing up from that nameless place between my legs.

Then my mother told me that I couldn't go around bare-chested anymore. "You're getting too big up top." How old was I? Seven, I think. Soon, my going shirtless was one more thing for me to get scolded about—along with picking my nose, chewing my nails, pulling off my scabs, forgetting to flush the toilet. (I was astonished at the way that grown-ups always remembered to flush. Was it true that I would someday be a grown-up, that my finger would never idly drift to the inside of my nose, that I would be able to resist the temptation of a scab?)

The booklet from Modess said that my body was getting ready to have a baby.

Have a baby?

I'm eight years old.

I didn't want a baby—dolls were OK, sometimes, but I could put them away when I got bored and wanted to go hunt in the dried grass for the papery skins snakes had shed or look for fossils in the rock pile next to the cornfield. From a big family, I knew one thing for sure about babies: you couldn't just leave them on the floor when you got tired of them and head for the rock pile. And, also: I'm eight years old.

I'm sure the word "vagina," didn't appear in the booklet from Modess said, and certainly not "vulva." Perhaps it talked about "the birth canal," which always made me think of the nearby Erie Canal, where mules had once pulled barges. I couldn't link that to the thrill I got rocking back and forth on the footboard of Debby's bed, pretending to ride Silver.

I didn't think "blood" when it first happened. It was dark brown, and I wiped the strange thick fluid away with toilet paper. But then it started to accumulate in the crotch of my white cotton hand-me-down underpants. I suppose "hand-me-underpants" makes my family sound poor, or at least hardscrabble. We weren't. My father was a college professor, but there were five kids in the family and before the age of globalization, clothing was union-made and more expensive, not throwaway. My mother used to inspect the seams when we were shopping for clothes, and sometimes pronounce, "It'll wear well." I showed my underpants with their strange stuff trapped on the crotch to my mother.

She took the box of Modess and the booklet down from the shelf in the closet of my oldest sister, Ellen, where it had been set to await Ellen's menarche, which hadn't yet arrived—nor had that of the sister between Ellen and me. Here was my body, once again, out of order, out of sorts, shameful, wrong.

I was nine the second time my period arrived, at Utica Children's Hospital. At my last clinic visit, the doctor, alarmed by my precocious puberty and the fact that I was growing taller at a ferocious clip had declared I needed to have surgery on my left leg, the leg everyone always referred to as my "good leg," to keep it from outpacing its bad twin. It couldn't wait until summer, when surgery was usually scheduled, so I wouldn't miss school. Perhaps the stress of surgery triggered a hormonal flood, perhaps my body was just getting down to business, but one day, when a nurse was lifting me off the bedpan, there was that telltale streak of red.

A few days later, another nurse was helping me with the cumbersome pads. There weren't adhesive strips on the bottom of the pads in those days—one wore an elastic sanitary belt, with toothed clips on the front and the back through which the pads were anchored.

"You're nine years old," she grumbled "and you have your period!"

It was clear I was at fault.

"My daughter's fifteen and she doesn't have her period yet." She said this as if I were an entitled cripple, pushing ahead of the worthy and whole, taking advantage of others' pity to snare what I hadn't rightfully earned.

I had no idea of how to put this into words, but I wanted to tell her: I don't want this. Your daughter can have it. I don't want the breasts and the hair growing in strange places, and especially this gush of embarrassing, stinky blood.

* * *

Years later, I happened upon a medical journal article which discussed the greater prevalence of precocious puberty in disabled girls. The article had been written a long time ago—I imagine we were described as handicapped. I felt flooded with relief: this wasn't just me, my strange, awkward, difficult body. It happened to others.

* * *

And many years after that, my future daughter-in-law told me about going to a red party. I thought at first a red party just meant that you had red placemats, and red velvet cake, and drank red wine or cherry soda. It was all those things, but it was to celebrate her friend's daughter's first period.

* * *

When my mother needed to buy Modess, she wrote it on her shopping list, next to onions, and apples, and milk, but she didn't write out the word in full. She wrote, M_______. It was that unspeakable.

Red Mirror Glaze
—Judy Kronenfeld

In our tiny T.A. office, Roger quietly conferred
with a pale girl who spoke in whispery,
quavering tones—when she spoke at all—
about her first essay for Freshman English,
Fall, 1965, on which he'd given her
an unenthusiastic B-. And I listened in
while trying to grade. My fellow grad student
and I were novices ourselves, though he was
a lawyer, now building a second career—
married, like myself, but older,
and a parent, and maybe more assured?

The conference concluded, the girl rose
and turned towards the door,
when Roger and I immediately saw
on the blonde wood of her chair, a swirl
resembling grenadine syrup,
or red mirror glaze for a cake. It seemed
like the residue of her self-doubt.
We looked up, but she was gone—
surely with crimson blooms
on the back of her thin skirt.

The blood on the chair: naked, plain,
bodily—from another story entirely,
unrelated to "Symbolism in Eudora Welty's
'The Whole World Knows.'" Not remotely
exotic, like menstrual blood collected
from virgin palace maids by the Jiajing Emperor,
in pursuit of the elixir of eternal life.
But ordinary and helpless
as a not yet toilet-trained toddler's
pee on the kitchen tiles.
Roger and I, on the way to becoming friends,
were snapped together by what we saw,
and on the edge of awkward laughter.

I wonder now, if the girl had the marshy,
slick feeling of failing protection, and for that reason
faltered during her conference, or was it only
later that she flushed with hindsight
about what she had left behind?
We felt unspoken pity for her embarrassment,
but oddly, perhaps, or sweetly,
were not embarrassed ourselves.
Roger went off to the men's room
for a fistful of paper towels,
and thoroughly cleaned the blood up.
And that was that.

All those decades ago, the curse was capricious
and leaky for me, too, especially when I wore
my ill-fated red-ticking dress—and my husband
had to walk right behind me to hide my shame.
Yet I don't remember placing myself
in that girl's unlucky shoes. I belonged
in the newly embraced academic hierarchy
Roger and I shared—and I ranked a clear notch
above her. As if I never bled.

Perimenopausal at the Punk Show
—*Marjorie Tesser*

In the dark depths of a secret cave, some swamp thing, an eel, perhaps, awakes from its brief hibernation. Cautiously, it stirs, then begins to emerge, nose first, hesitating, and then slithering, pouring down the tunnel with a slick wriggle. In line for Bad Brains at CBGB, I know I'm in trouble. The super-sized tampon I'd installed not so long ago is saturated, so full and heavy it is slipping out.

My youngest son, at my side, gazes up ahead of us at the unaccustomedly long line, looking for a friendly face.

"I'm going to go up and see if there's someone who'll let us cut," he proposes.

"Better not," I say." There's a huge bouncer up there and these people do not look like they'll let someone get ahead of them."

As if to prove my point, just a few people in front of us, a kid tries to weasel in, only to be told where to get off by a burly hardcore type with a buzz-cut and no neck.

This is one of the last shows scheduled to take place at CBGB's; the place where we'd seen so many great shows was closing. We've been going to punk concerts together for almost five years, since my son was nine. We knew a bunch of the regulars for those shows, kids who'd gotten into punk during its resurgence in the early 2000's, who would have been happy to let us in front. This audience was clearly older. There are thirty-year-olds in 90's t-shirts; even forty-year-olds in 80's t-shirts, fitting rather snugly. They are impatient to get in, not a happy group.

I feel heat; wet; another glop of something exiting. "You stay here and hold our place in line. I need the restroom," I tell my son.

"But Mom, they're not letting anyone in yet."

"I don't care," I say grimly. We're passing the Gallery, a side room where CBGBs has alternative, quieter acts, acoustic stuff, poetry readings; nothing on for tonight, that I'm aware of. I ease behind the line and crack the door. An acne-scarred six-footer in a muscle shirt, beefy arms upholstered in tattoos, raises his hand like a cop halting traffic.

"No one goes in here," he says.

"Please, I need the restroom," I begin.

"NO ONE," he says firmly, taking my arm to turn me out.

"Please," I say again, "It's an emergency. If you don't let me in, I'm going to bleed all over your floor." He turns pale, steps back, and points to a stairway, a hemorrhaging middle-aged female being an eventuality with which he clearly does not want to deal.

I'm in my early fifties. I'd had my first hot flash at a Pixies concert the prior year, a sudden prickle and then a rush of heat, and I swam through the crowd to the side, where I stripped off my sweater to sway in my tank top, glowing like radioactive, under the watchful gaze of a security guy on full alert in case I was planning to sneak into the area saw-horsed off for VIPs. But I don't get many of those flashes, which feel like power surges, and are actually pretty cool. No, I have only one real perimenopausal symptom. I, who always had the most reasonable of monthly cycles, have been bleeding daily for the past year.

It started with some spotting, then staining in between normal periods. Then the periods became more frequent, short couple-of day ones every two weeks. Soon, on most days there was some blood. As the year went on, the flow increased. I cycled through the spectrum of "feminine" products, from panty liners to "light days" pads to junior to medium tampons. On this particular day I was wearing the largest super tampon available, with the thickest maxi pad as insurance. And yet, my strategies were proving inadequate to the inexorable tide.

Inside the show, I'm in the spot I usually like, against the left-hand wall facing the stage, forward of the pipe whose insulation is half burned away, but it never seems to get that hot anyway, padded by all the stickers, maybe just dead like the rest of the place would soon be. From my spot, I've been checking on my son, and I've lost sight. He'd gone from stage front center for Dub Trio to slightly further to the right for Avail, propelled by the outer ripples and pulses and swells around the eddying pit. The moshers are a whirlpool, a shark circle, a ring of tigers. My son had seemed okay; I knew he'd adjust his position in a way that was safe. Only fourteen but he's been going to punk shows since he was nine. An intuition of wetness, warmth. I pull my long shirt down even longer, surreptitiously brushing the front of my jeans with my hand; has it gone through already?

Between acts, some skinny guy barrels through the crowd, yelling "I'm an undercover agent" and sits on my feet. I edge them out from under his bony rear and wiggle over a quarter inch or so, crowding the girl just on my right, her boob presses into my arm. He's yapping, to me, to this long-haired guy, to some guy in a baseball cap, but I can't hear what he's saying, the background music is loud, and I've still got my earplugs in. I just hear, "It's all good," as he fiddles with something. He puts his hoodie over his head; sporadic flashes from a lighter indicate some activity down there.

Yes, I definitely feel something shift. But I'm stuck, wedged like a sardine in a gallon vat of its fellows. The bathroom might as well be in India. Even if I could get around the makeshift wooden tower set up for video shoots—my son and I had braved its lingering odor of urine and watched Madball from up there one time and it was a pretty cool view—I'd still have to make it around the pit, past the stage, with its surrounding throng, past the back-stage area crowded with instruments and band members and their hangers-on, and down the long staircase to get to the women's restroom, where last time I'd had to corral the wayward stall door with my shoulder bag handle and hang on to it to keep the door closed; most of the other girls using the room had come with a friend who could hold the door.

Every inch of the club is packed with bodies now, people from the back pressing ever closer toward the stage; the show, at forty bucks a pop, has been sold out for weeks, and they were still selling tickets at the door, no point worrying about overselling, as this is CBGB's final week, and the first of three swan song concerts I'm to see. The guy on my feet is now stripping off his shirt. "I'm still skinny," he says loudly, to no one, "I've been doing this twenty-two years." On the back of his neck, a dark Cro-Mags tattoo. His aroma rises; sweat, testosterone, something chemical. His head is about level with my hips but he seems oblivious to my own predicament, thankfully.

I don't see my son. I think about whether I should try to make my way across to where he had been, or try to get to the bathroom and realize, no, we're jammed in too tight, you're fucked, you're not moving. The guy at my feet stands abruptly, folds his sweatshirt, and stashes it behind a pipe, carefully wedges his hat in, then turns and looks right at me. "I know you, don't I? You go to a lot of shows, right? Do you know me?" but I say, "Sorry." He sticks out his hand and says something like "Ratbone" and I say "Marjorie" and we shake. "I think it would be fun to tear down all that shit," he tells the baseball hat guy, pointing up at some overhead speakers. "That's punk rock, not this shit." I consider telling him to watch out for younger kids, but decide against engaging to that extent, and Ratbone launches himself out into the throng.

I think about what it takes to be into the same stuff for twenty-two years, to still be eager to get into the pit and fuck it up. Twenty-two years ago, my eldest was two and I was under a different moon.

I conceivably could have been doing this for more than thirty years; after all, I've been listening to music since before punk's inception. But in the 70's, punk's first wave, I'd been in law school, then working at a small firm engaged in an equal employment class action. It was David-Goliath, us against several major law firms, and we blazed with the fervor of crusaders, working round the clock three years straight. I lived in Soho then, but only got out to clubs occasionally, including CBGB's once or twice. Then I married and moved to the suburbs and had kids. During punk's second and third waves in the eighties and nineties, I was listening to Barney and Raffi, Teenage Mutant Ninja Turtles, the Ace of Base. Once or twice my husband and I made the effort to get a babysitter and come to the city for some "classic rock" dinosaurs crashing through town, sitting up in the cheap seats of a mammoth arena, the nostalgic essence of marijuana wafting up from the tiers below.

When he was fifteen, my middle son got a summer job; I ended up driving him every day. He brought CDs he'd burned of his favorite music, stuff they never played on the radio, fast, melodic, fierce, hysterically funny—punk. We started taking the kids to concerts; first the 2001 Warped Tour, then others: they loved the music, and my sons, ages fifteen and nine, couldn't travel very far on their own power. Then 9/11 happened, and shortly after that, a serious diagnosis for one of my kids. Our world had been upended, and we searched for something, anything, as a distraction. The boys decided to make a movie about punk. So then we had to take them to more shows.

A punk concert was the polar opposite of an arena show; intimate and friendly. We saw bands in dive bars, gritty little holes-in-the-wall with maybe ten people in the audience, in a converted Ukrainian dancehall in which there'd recently been a shooting, in a barn-like former summer camp, at CBGB's. And I fell in love; with the music, the honesty and power of it, the humor and cynicism and emotion and hope. I fell in love with the bands, believing passionately in their music, their message, and, also out to carouse, with the kids who went to the shows; sensitive ones, the misfits, the extra-tall or extra-round, boys that wore Buddy Holly glasses and wrote poems and ones in studs and Mohawks, girls with purple hair who made purses out of duct tape. And my own sons, watching them watch the bands, singing along with all their hearts.

Now I'm hemmed in and dripping blood in CBGB's, where I can only be two times more. Five years. My older two went off to college, my husband decided he didn't much care for concerts. But my youngest and I still go to shows. All in all, hundreds of them. Now my favorite places are closing and I'm bleeding all the time and it's feeling like an ending.

At last, show over, I thread my way through the loiterers downstairs to the venue's legendary bathroom. I do what I can but still have to tie my sweatshirt around my waist to conceal the evidence.

In the car going home, a dank mineral smell, like the beach at low tide after a storm. Me. My son takes off his sneakers, evening things out.

Red

—Nikki Marrone

Sometimes I leave the blood on my skin,
To remember that red is not the colour of violence.
And that I am not a victim waiting to happen.
This space between my legs is not a crime scene.
Red is not a blood-stained sidewalk,
It is not the cut of a prostitute's gown,
Sometimes I leave the blood on my skin;
For the ones who have no choice,
To remember those who wear it like war paint,
And to support those who wear it with shame.
This is no tear-stained apology.
Nor a problem to be solved.
This is a not something to be taken lightly,
Nor a burden heavily carried.
Sometimes I leave the blood on my skin;
To remind myself that being a woman,
Isn't something easily washed away.
To remind myself that being a woman,
Isn't unclean.

Bruise

She Learns
—Laurel Radzieski

By experiencing his not knowing when the thick color gushes. A small stream below her fish-swimming stomach between armored legs marks sheets and chests. Splatters on the far wall and drips in the toilet. There is a boat one takes when the faucet won't stop dripping. He puts her on it and dips his hands in the water until both are clear. The water turns sinister brown and tells the crowd to go back to shore. She sits alone in the boat as it swells with her excretions and the hot mud beneath her pooling fluid congeals until the rest of the world hovers above her as if separating from oil. She imagines a young girl with toes in this water nervous of wet hair and the cold frozen nipples below her nylon suit. Holds her breath and head underwater until it is too late.

Nancy Drew and the Mystery of Life
—Helen Ruggieri

When I was eleven, we moved to a town with a library. It was a revelation. These people would give you all the books you wanted, well, four per visit actually. You could take them home, read them, bring them back and get four more. The shelves stretched forever, every possible book. Thank you, Andrew Carnegie. I worked through the teen section within the year. I was voracious.

I particularly favored mysteries or adventures. There were Trixie Belden and the Bobbsey Twins adventures, but I loved Nancy Drew who was more sophisticated, more daring than the babyish Bobbseys. Nancy Drew could drive for one thing. She had her own car. She could pilot a plane and sail a boat. She was resourceful and (I hate to say this) plucky. She was sharp, useful, understood nuances, things just out of kilter. She could sense the disruption in the regular flow of life. I wanted to be like that—an observer of life attuned to the world, but apart, solving the mysterious events that went on out there in the world. I wanted to be able to solve the mysteries that plagued me, about life, about everything. And most of all, I wanted a roadster though I wasn't too sure at the time what type of car a roadster was. But if it was good enough for Nancy Drew, it would do for me.

Nancy Drew had all the luck, all the fun. No matter how I watched my neighbors, no matter how observant or nosey I was I could find nothing resembling a mystery unless it was sex. Everybody talked about it in riddles. You could tell a conversation was about sex because the pitch would change, the voices would get lower, the words become metaphorical. She's in trouble. She's in the family way. She's expecting. She's knocked up. This was the secret language only the initiated could understand. I wasn't initiated yet. If you grew up on movies made in the 40s and 50s, you didn't get the sex education you do now. When sanitary napkins were first advertised, we'd have to get up and leave the room in embarrassment. So the mysteries of the body were great surprises to us.

I was selling poppies on Memorial Day. The Veterans of Foreign Wars Post on First Street gave you a can for coins and a fist full of poppies and you went out and bothered everybody waiting to see the parade until you got rid of your handful. Nobody could walk down Union Street without a poppy. It just wasn't safe. Hordes of young girls would shake a fistful of poppies at you, demanding you buy.

I sold my fistful of those red paper flowers and went to take my coin can back. The women's auxiliary had a lunch set out for us— make your own sandwiches and pop. I had on a pair of red corduroy slacks with an elastic waistband. I didn't even have hips yet, at least not enough to hold up my baggy slacks. I had on a pair of bright yellow cotton underpants, my favorite pair. I'd gotten them for Christmas, and I loved them.

When I went to the bathroom, I saw they were stained a rusty color. I thought the color of my slacks bled through. I thought I was wet with sweat. It's hot work selling poppies. I didn't feel much like eating and went home.

I washed the stain in the bathroom sink. I knew I'd be in trouble for getting my pants dirty. She came in and asked what I was doing. I don't know why, she usually never paid that much attention to me. I got something on these pants, I explained. She came back with a belt and a box of pads and said to put one on. That was all. Later she gave me a copy of a book printed in 1904 that supposedly explained what happened to young girls. It created more mysteries than it explained. I was a woman, the book said, and so far I didn't like it one bit. I felt stupid with this huge wad between my legs and it smelled and I felt sick to my stomach. Not once a month, forever, I thought. What anguish. I wished I'd been born a boy. This was disgusting. Even Nancy Drew, I thought. Her too.

The book described the process and said it was commonly known under the various names of "the menses, the courses, the monthly periods, and being unwell. Although when woman's health reaches the ideal state she will menstruate without the slightest pain and with no thought of being other than perfectly well." It did rattle on, giving all those turn of the century cliches. I not only hated the process, but I hated the book that attempted to explain it.

The courses was the curse, another of those words I'd picked up in mysterious, metaphoric conversations. Now I knew what it meant and thought it was an apt choice of names. This was Eve's punishment for eating the apple of the tree of knowledge. God cursed her. Everybody. All of us.

The book droned on in the pompous, irritating, swill, I'd come to associate with instruction: "When the young daughter arrives at the age of puberty, this monthly function is a continual reminder, therefore, of her womanhood, and should be regarded, not with aversion, but as a proof that she is one of the class set apart by nature to be entrusted with life's highest and holiest responsibility—that of preparing, under wise guidance, for possible future motherhood."

I always had an eye for self-righteous, fatuous baloney when I read it. If that didn't make you want to throw up, the cramps would, but I only had cramps because I was unwell, didn't live right, had negative thoughts, etc. Right. I loved being branded a hysteric, a complainer who didn't live right, and had imaginary cramps. Little did I know. . . more would I learn as I was initiated into the mysteries of womanhood.

The advice went from bad to worse. "No cold baths, foot baths, or wetting the feet by wearing thin shoes as any one of these errors is almost certain to stop the flow." Wear your rubbers, wear your boots. You can't go out, it's raining! Swimming? Under no circumstances. Absolutely not. You'll die from femininity.

It was 1950. Nobody knew anything. Nancy Drew had never mentioned a word about this. She'd never even dropped a tiny clue. You began to carry a purse and took it with you every time you went to the girl's room. You would notice who carried one and who didn't and now you knew why. One small solution.

The girl's room was where you learned everything if you didn't get invited to pajama parties, didn't have older sisters, or didn't have a clue. Dorothy Kytel said in the girl's room that she was going to the doctor's after school because she hadn't had a period in five months. (I said to myself, why would she complain about that? I'd be thankful). She then disappeared from school forever, a legend in her own time. "She didn't know," the older girls would titter and giggle. Didn't know what? That when you don't get your period, you're preggie. Preggie? Having a baby, baby. Oh, a clue.

Well, Nancy Drew might have made the connections earlier than I did, supplying the missing link, but she had more practice solving mysteries than I did. The book hadn't quite made certain connections clear enough for me. There were certainly some holes in the information, some big jumps from the wedding to morning sickness. Rough going for the literalists of the world.

Other societies have rituals for welcoming girls to womanhood. They slap your face, hard, so you'll remember the day. They take you to the exclusion hut away from the tribe; they do a clitorectomy. They tell you not to look men in the eyes or to walk so your shadow doesn't fall on them. Perhaps we're lucky there is no ceremony because the models out there don't sound promising. Perhaps we could hang a bloody sheet out the window or send an Email to all the family: Emily has had her first period. You can now talk about sex in front of her as she has passed her sexual vocabulary test.

Are we so horrible postmodern that girls make this passage via television commercials or health classes in grammar school, having some inept and uncomfortable basketball coach explain the facts of their bodies to them. Or some sex crazed teenaged boy in the back seat of a car says, don't worry, nothing will happen.

It was not only the facts that I craved, but what it all meant. I suppose that's the mystery we all want explained. If we take evolution: well, first there was one amoeba, and work our way up, we eventually gather all the facts. But the mystery of it, the cultural shrouds we've draped around it, the metaphorical implications, those we keep trying to figure out with or without a roadster or a brother. Nancy, poised post puberty forever, never was brave enough to lead us into the adult world. I guess she's another one of those role models who kept us in our place: teen forever.

Accepting the passage which we make alone and often without information, we had to come to terms with cultural expectations, taboos, emotions, impositions, double standards, when we were still trying to adapt to the mystery of our own bodies. In 1950, what ritual could prepare us better than falling off the roof?

overripe fruit (larger than a quarter)
  —*Ashly Kim*

the room is sterile cotton—unstained.
smells like disinfectant.
until i sit there, my insides spilling out
onto all that unblemished white.
now the air tastes like nectar.
fear cartwheels down my spine as i tell the doctor—
the fruit of my body is larger than cherries,
larger than the reddest apple.
the pulp sits like a pomegranate inside my panties.

the usual questions.
how many pads an hour?
could you be pregnant?

there're tests—an ultrasound.
more crisp hospital sheets ruined.
i am an unclean nuisance in these halls.
but no one has an answer, or a sturdy basket,
for this red that tumbles out like raspberries.

the doctor shrugs and says,
you're a woman, right?
when life gives you so much fruit,
you should learn to make jam.

my discharge papers say:
no big deal, only overripe fruit

Pea

—Verónica Rodríguez

The body is a world
A giant world
A world of tiny chemical bombs
Wi-Fi communication
Hey chemical sister
You have a cyst
What is a cyst?
The size of a pea
But don't worry
It may go away.
But
Endo
Its cysts and/or growths
Though they may be removed
They will most likely grow back
Like Love. Chronic.

Stripping Away at My Allowance
>   *—Kellie Diodato*

—Polycystic Ovarian Syndrome (PCOS) is a condition both widespread
>   *and lifelong—wreaking havoc upon a woman's reproductive,*
>   *endocrine, limbic, digestive, and metabolic systems—doctors and*
>   *specialists are still unsure of the exact causes.*

Man picked me a grim
rotten apple. Too many
bruises, extra seeds.

Cross: I am woman
'til hair mushrooms on my chin:
a weed, then. Not mum.

We trade. Synthetic
pill meets counterfeit blood run—
some small, lab rat hope.

Since I could not cast
my hip bones towards hourglass
I cut and I carved

forty pounds from me.
A cup size a half-ring size—
soul for ovary

still bruised and seeded.
But what dear exterior,
cool, soft, taut pink skin.

Walking malfunction,
what secret does my surface
hide? So kind you asked:

since I may never
conceive, I ripped open the
rind: crushed seeds to pulp.

A Perpetual State of Should
—Limi Marie Bauer

Having my period has always been living in a perpetual state of should. I should have said something to be more prepared for when it came. My mother shouldn't have yelled at me when I asked her to buy supplies for me. She shouldn't have suggested that I use toilet paper in that way, and I shouldn't have taken what she said to mean that she feels that she resents the burden of my being. I should have used more toilet paper—a diaper's worth. I shouldn't have been so shocked to see my own smear of blood on that yellow, plastic, standard issue chair in my 7th grade classroom. I'm glad I listened to a should that had me lagging behind my classmates so I could wipe it off as best I could, so grateful that my Catholic school girl's tartan skirt was dark enough not to reveal what had happened.

I should have told my friend right away when I returned her jeans with the stain in them, my mother urging me *you should call her mother so they get washed right away you should tell her what happened.* Calling her mom felt deeply confessional. I couldn't figure out why. I looked at my mother and thought how she should call the other girl's mother and then how I shouldn't feel quite so intensely about something so normal. I should be able to talk about my period. Shouldn't I?

I should have been gentler with myself in that girls' bathroom when my first tampon got stuck on my hymen. I should have had my friend waiting for me tell our teacher I had a medical issue, and I needed a minute. I should have thought about the pain of what tugging on skin might bring later that day. *You shouldn't have used tampons at all,* my mother said. Those tampons were hers. I should buy my own with the babysitting money I probably should be making more of. *You should call that family and see if they need you this weekend. You should find more families to babysit for.*

I should wash that spot out right away before it stains my clothes.

I should use only cold water when I wash out blood.

I should wash it again until it really smells clean.

I should be more careful next time.

I should use longer pads.

I should use pads with wings.

I should not get the cheap ones because these wings always crumple and stick to themselves.

I should stop hating my uterus.

I should count the days so I know when it's coming.

I should have done that so I knew when I first got pregnant that time.

I should know how long my cycle is.

I should teach my daughter about that. She tells me there's an app for that. I should have had a party for her when she first got her period, but she said that was weird and I spent the money instead on period underwear. That way she shouldn't get any blood on any chairs at school or anywhere else. I hope.

I should use a moon cup more often and I should find a way to get used to using one. I should have locked the door when taking out my moon cup that time. I laughed as hard as I was horrified at my little son walking in when he said moon cup wasn't as good a name as "body catcher."

I should stop wishing for menopause. I should remember how that comes with hormonal imbalance and I should find out if that mean all the madness of puberty because it feels completely hidden or reduced to jokes about hot flashes or sneers about dryness. I should loudly push for the concept of aging as a woman to stop being considered the unofficial 8th deadly sin. We all should let us bleed, let us bear children the way we really do, we all should let us put our cycles down without a deep fear of the normalcy of being replaced. Now in my forties I wonder of the women close to me older than me how much was menopause and how much was her phoenix moment of rising out of her own bullshit of the exhausting hustle for belonging.

I should advocate more loudly for a woman's right to a day off when she has her heaviest flow. I should take a day off when I have mine. I should remind people how painful it is. I should loudly say that I am grumpy because I am profusely bleeding. I should channel this anger into advocacy. I should vote for increasing access to hygienic menstruation supplies. I should look into political candidates that would do something about this on my behalf. I should find out how that tampon tax even became a thing. I should expose those responsible.
A period
should be
a
totally
normal thing.
Putting all my shoulds down, just for a moment, I take a deep breath and refill the candy dish in my bathroom with that variety of tampons and pads. It's the crystal dish my grandmother gave me when graduated from college, and it's proudly on display. I think about the next time a friend is over and she's got her period. The crystal dish whispers *you get your period and I get mine and maybe you're wondering if you should look around for my supplies or if you should use toilet paper. I'm telling you I've got you covered. You should take as much as you need.*

Junior High Rites
>—*Betsy Mars*

Under our jeans we wore elastic belts
slung from our hips, then so lean,
belts clipped with slack-hanging pads -
white flags of our fertility as we changed

for PE. In the halls their outlines
so thick, impossible to miss—
red cape under clothes, a target
for bullish boys to charge.

We swept them aside,
dodged both bull and matador,
tried hard not to get gored.
They teased,

drew first blood,
a trickle at first, then a line
as we bled out
what might have been a life.

The Big Change
  —Katelyn Shinault

No one tells you how
the worst part isn't the blood.
It's the changing men.

Bobsie Showed Me How to Insert a Tampax
—*Vicki Iorio*

Her father was the head of psychiatry at Pilgrim State
he approved lobotomies while he ordered lunch

She shouted out directions to me
through the closed bathroom door

When the Tampax slid in, and stayed in place
it was a summer vacation victory

Never again did I have to smell dried blood
in my Kotex soaked underwear

Bobsie was a college girl
the next summer she came home with a baby

She never told me how she got that baby
but she did show me how to insert a thermometer
to measure ovulation

My first birth control

Transvaginal Ultrasound
—Lynn Melnick

I try to make a joke to the nurse tech
about the dildo-cam, and I don't know if it's my delivery

or what, but she won't smile. I've been through a rape kit,
my body a crime scene, apart from itself so

I've spent enough of my life disconnected from joy.
And I am fine! Just middle aged! I deliver clots each month

clearing out until I'm empty. I text my friend
who has been with me even before blood first stained

my polka-dotted panties. I say, this could be over
and I think I'd be okay with it. I google *you'll miss it*

when it's gone and what comes up is democracy, office life,
magazine subscriptions, song titles, dresses on sale, summer.

When I worked in an office, a coworker kept a box
of tampons she no longer needed prominently in her workspace.

To seem spry, she told me. I sometime lifted one like I used to
lift bin candy at the grocery. Summer is just weeks away

and I'm already mourning how brief it will be.

Maroon

Blood
      —Virginia Chase Sutton

I am sick of it. And it is everywhere—my body expels in gushing waves.
Rivulets down my legs, spoiled underwear, clots as big as my fist.
Droplets spattering the bathroom floor, unable to make plans lasting
longer than half an hour during the day because of the deluge. It has
been going on for over a year, but I have been too scared to seek
medical attention. I am exhausted all the time, but somehow manage
to find a new gyn who listens to my story, says *no one should have to
live like that* puts me on hormones as an experiment to *jump start* my
regular period. Out one night, the bleeding stops at last, and I stand at
the bookstore register, counter piled high with merchandise. I feel a
familiar drop in my body, my uterus ready to flood, race to the
bathroom. I am leaking blood, my underwear and slacks already
stained a violent red. Back at the doc's the next day, he says *a
hysterectomy is in your future but let's try a D & C.* I flinch in fear as he
pats my hand. At the hospital I go under, stop worrying about the
bleeding from my vagina. At last, stop worrying about what he might
find. I wake, hazy as he explains *your uterus is very enlarged. My
instruments could not reach the top. Blood vessels up there have lost
their ability to contract, that is why you pass such big clots. The only
solution is a hysterectomy, but we can wait until your teaching
assignment is over.* Both lucky and unlucky. It means I am back to giant
pads, heavy flow tampons, sleepless nights, waking suddenly, off to the
bathroom 3 or 4 times each night. Waking I find wet, soaked towels I
place to protect the sheet and mattress. I tell my husband, but he does
not think it is serious, though I have a gnawing sensation. It increases.
By morning, blood is everywhere. Weeping, I call my best friend. *You
must see the doctor. You do not have a choice* he says. I argue but he is
firm. Stopping 3 times to change, once there, the doctor touches me
with the speculum. *You just lost 20 cc's of blood* he says. *Get fixed up as
best you can. I need to send you to the hospital for an IV treatment to
stop this bleeding.* Carefully I ease back into period devices, get dressed,
sit on his stool. He returns. I stand. Blood pours. It has never been like
this before. Puddles bloom at my feet, strange giant flowers on the gray
carpet. Grabbing my arm, he lifts me, tosses me back onto the table. He
dashes out of the room. Soon I dimly hear a wailing siren coming
closer, know it is for me. Four paramedics appear, cannot raise a vein

for an IV, though the doctor does at last. *I will meet you at the hospital* he says, and I am dragged through his waiting room, filled with pregnant women, women of all ages, and small children. In the ambulance, not a word is said, no reassurance. I feel strangely euphoric, carefree, amused these men are embarrassed to discuss a case of menstruation gone wrong. At the hospital, I cannot sit upright, have lost too much blood. My husband and the doctor appear at the same time. *We cannot wait for the hysterectomy; we need to do it now* the doc says. I nod. *No* says my husband. *That limits our options.* The doctor is shocked. And I am shocked. I know my husband wants a third child to go with our 2 daughters, but I am 35 and am unable to go through another pregnancy. *I am telling you this as if she were my own wife. She must have the surgery or she will bleed to death.* Chastened, my husband nods agreement. I have a temp of 102 degrees. *I hate to operate on someone with a fever, but we must do it now* the doctor says. In the pre-surgical room, he appears, an angel or a cloud, all in white. It is the anesthesia talking. Then I pass out. He operates, cutting me from navel to pubic bone. It leaves a long and painful incision, but I am alive and grateful. Later I ponder how I always thought if I lost my uterus, I would mourn it, then eulogize it. It did work hard during 2 difficult pregnancies, producing now healthy grade-school children. In pain, back in bed beside my husband, I can sleep through the night. I do not grieve my missing organ. I bless it and celebrate. I still have my ovaries with another 100,000 miles on them. No doubt they will take me through decades with natural hormones. I am a survivor, thanks to the doctor, and my best friend who saved me as blood slipped down my thighs. How I cried, worried, body almost shut down.

Ritual of Purity
       —Patricia Thrushart

When she bleeds
she is banished
to the shabby huts,
the bitter hills
scattered
at the snowy height
of the world.

"Touch her and
a tiger will come;
the house will catch on fire;
the head of the house
will get sick."

I'm happy to go there,
she says.
I don't want my parents sick.

She is forbidden to look
at her brother.

She sleeps with the snakes,
with unholy smoke—
she dreams of her father,
who fears the taboo far more
than her death.

Braided Women
  —Kaylin Margaret

   A foot half-heartedly kicks my leg, pulling the ceiling into view when I open my eyes. A twist in the back of my neck wakes as well and I tighten my eyebrows at the pain, rubbing the anger out with tight fingers. I droop my head to the side to look at who did it. Idha sleeps deeply, maybe even deeper now that she's kicked me awake. She's got high cheekbones that mush in on themselves when she digs her face against her pillow, like she is tonight. Her dark hair falls all around her face like an extra blanket, brushing against the dirt floor.

   The first night in the cowshed is always the most terrible. My body cramps and bleeds and turns itself inside-out, and Idha is always restless the first night she arrives. Her brain needs to readjust to the cowshed every month, and apparently the only way it can do that is to jostle me awake. She tends to sleep curled up next to me rather than sleeping next to her mother. I guess Idha spent her first nine months kicking Eenakshi, so now she kicks me instead. At least we don't have to share the cowshed with the cows. A new barn was built for them, so they sleep there now.

   I pull my blankets tighter around me, stuffing them around my neck to keep the heat in, but my mind is up and the ground is hard. And now, I'm aware of the heaviness of the wet cloth between my thighs. I throw my blankets aside, not caring if it wakes Idha, and walk unnaturally to the door as if my legs haven't woken up. I'm more worried about waking Idha's mother and the baby swaddled next to her, so I quietly pull my shoes on over my socks. I'm gentle with the door.

   It's cooler outside. The moon is whole, and this place takes on a new face when I see it like this. Far up the path tucked against the green shelves of the mountain, the buildings of the town lose their vibrance at night, like the blood's gone out from underneath its skin. They look like stacked, misshapen children's blocks from here. The stars bunch up over it all, almost beautiful enough to make me forget about the slipping between my legs. The crickets creak at me as I pass around the shed towards its backside, the dipped spine of the valley stretching out next to me, trying to get my attention.

I pick the fire poker off the ground. The fire has long gone out and the embers have lost the blush behind them. They have been reduced to charcoal and red pinpricks that flare up when I touch the poker to them. I'm not sure what time it is but the chill that sews deep into my clothes tells me that the sun left long ago and won't hurry back. The fire gasps at new air and I stand next to the little red cooler we use for nights like this.

I bunch up my long skirt around my hips, stretching down the waste-band of my pants. I pull the heavy cloth out of my underwear, and it sags over my fingers like a limp organ. The wad drops into the empty cooler with a wet thud. The slow mumble of the river drifts up from further down the mountain, but I don't want to go alone to wash the cloth right now. I shut the cooler tight and grab one of the boiled and dried pieces of fabric off the line. Dipping it into the bucket of water we keep next to the fire, I scrub off the blood that has stuck to my thighs. After throwing that in the cooler as well, I wrap another cloth into a rectangle and wrestle it past my skirt, my waste-band, into my underwear.

When I return to the door, I can't get myself to open it. Blankets do not make the ground more forgiving. Idha will keep kicking me, and I do not feel very forgiving tonight either.

I leave the door to my back and the whole valley, soaked in blue, lays stretched open in front of me. I walk. When the ground begins to dip, I take off down the hill and let my feet beat the earth, shredding through a tall night. My hair catches wind behind me, lashing out like it can hardly keep up. I am a thin knife through a thinner veil. I am speeding towards my forbidden friend. I am laughing.

Just when I feel that my legs will run on ahead of me, I lean backwards against my motion, slowing down before I reach the planks of the fence. I put one foot up and toss myself over, heading towards the back wall. I can already see her, laying there in the grass.

I walk right up to where her heavy breathing pushes on the blades. I move to her side and plop myself down onto her big back. The warmth of her body breathes up into mine. The strong smell of the barn rises off her.

"If I have to be awake, so do you," I say, and pat her sides with my feet. She rocks her head from side to side, shaking off my voice.

"Come on you big cow. I know I woke you up,"

Bibi heaves deeply at my accusation, flexing the muscles of her back beneath me. I get off of her and sit down next to her big head. She looks up at me with those half-lidded, black marble eyes that show my reflection in them. Round face. Long black hair. Wild eyes.

"The thought struck me..." I tell her, "I could feel you wanting me to come see you."

She huffs hard at that, and it means, *I could have gone without the visit*. I nudge her tough, brown shoulder with my foot.

"What, you're all about tradition now? I can't come see you on my period? I thought we were rebels," I giggle. I pet her velvet ear and Bibi closes her eyes again, shrugging off my words.

"You're a terrible listener." I fold my knees against my chest, hold them close, and scoot closer to my friend to steal her warmth. I look back at the cowshed, small against the mountain now. Like I could crumble it between my fingers. I stretch my neck and it sounds like rocks grinding against each other underwater.

"I am *not* a cow." I say it so small and put my face between my knees.

"Salmee!"

I hear my own name like a dream in my ears. I don't know how much time has passed but the sky has not changed when I haul my head off my legs. Idha's mom is walking towards me and I don't pull myself up. My brain has not yet reconnected to itself.

Eenakshi leans her body as she comes up to me, counterbalancing the baby on her hip. She looks beautiful, her long hair swinging opposite of her motion. I don't even process that she might be scolding me.

"What are you doing out here?" She asks, stopping in front of me. "You can't be touching the cattle right now, you know that."

I feel my eyes open now, feel the weight of Eenakshi's dipped eyebrows.

"I just wanted to see her, I'm sorry," I garble out, getting to my feet. She takes my arm in her spare hand. Something about the darkness makes her glow brighter. After a moment of watching my quiet face, her expression shakes itself loose. She crouches, pulling me down with her and releasing my arm. She whispers to me as if there's someone who could hear us.

"Maybe just this once won't hurt," she says, and pets Bibi's big nose. The baby breaks himself loose with gentle, chubby hands and Eenakshi lets him go. He kneels by Bibi's face, puts a tiny hand on her head, leaves it there. Bibi's eyes stay shut, ignoring her committee of midnight visitors. Eenakshi's defiance turns my brain to mush a little. It lights me up. I glow like her.

"And anyways," I say, losing my whisper, "even if we do make the cows' milk go bad, I don't care. If all we get is boiled rice on our periods, that should be all everyone else gets too. Then they'll see how terrible and... and stupid this all is."

Eenakshi stands up, and I go up with her. She picks up the baby, sticking him back to her hip.

"You shouldn't think like that, Salmee. We all have to take care of each other." She begins walking back to the shed, guiding my back with her hand. She dips her head down to my ear, speaks quietly.

"But I agree."

I mirror her, put my arm around her back too like we're braided together. She's one of those women who feels much bigger than you, who makes you feel small in the scheme of how grand she is.

"Idha is lucky to have you as a mom," I say. I guess she finds the discontentment in my voice. She hums a little in response.

"Your mother is a good woman," She tells me.

"She's a pushover," it spills out of me, and Eenakshi doesn't say anything, but she pulls her arm from my back. I scold myself, get smaller inside myself, I feel the cold where her arm has left. I pull my own arm away. Our steps fill the silence between us, soft padding as we come to the fence. She puts her baby down on the other side, climbs over, picks him back up. I don't climb over. I don't want what's on the other side. Her face turns to me when she notices the absence of my steps. The baby yawns into her neck.

"Salmee?"

"The girls in Kathmandu don't have to leave *their* homes for a week," I say, "*their* mothers don't make them," and her face falls a little.

"All mothers are different, that doesn't make some mothers right and some mothers wrong. They're just... different. It's different here." Her voice doesn't believe it.

"No it's not. A girl in my class doesn't do it anymore. Her mom is a healthcare worker now, she said her mom had them stop doing it."

My fists hide in the pockets of my skirt. I can't tell what comes off Eenakshi's face. She fidgets with the baby, needlessly adjusting his weight on her hip. He slumps into her shoulder. I don't know if she's sad or angry with me. She looks like she's trying to learn something about me. She'll learn nothing if she keeps looking through me, far past me, to somewhere else.

"And why do you have the baby?" I say. Eenakshi doesn't know what to make of that.

"What?" She asks.

"If we'll 'make the cattle's milk go bad' just by being around them, why hasn't your milk gone bad? Why do *you* have to take him here, to take care of him still? Shouldn't someone else keep him while you're here? To protect him from you?"

She tightens her grip when I say that, guarding him with her body, and I can tell I've hurt her.

"If your mother is a pushover for making you come here, then so am I for having Idha come. Am I a bad mother, Salmee?" There's a venom in her voice that you can only tap into once you've hurt somebody. Our faces match one another now. Squinted eyes, pursed lips.

"No," I whisper. I don't even know if she can hear me, just that she can see my lips form the word in the dark. It cracks my ribs open, the fact that I've hurt her. It makes me think of every time I sat in her kitchen, her hands in my hair, trimming the ends of it. I wonder if I've undone every moment we've ever shared.

She sighs heavily, loosening her grip on the baby. "I'm not tired," she says. "Do you want to come wash the cloths with me? I hate leaving it for the morning."

I unroot my feet and put myself over the fence, walking up the hill beside her. I wonder what she's done with her anger. Has she left it behind us? Has she tied it up into a tiny knot to put deep inside herself?

I don't lift my chin. I don't speak. But I do feel her big hand return to my small back, and I hope she left the knot behind.

I Met a Guy at My Rich Friend's House Party
  —Ada Donnelly

We went back to his place
I ate the food his mom made while he complained
He said he wanted me to go bike around with him and his friends
He said we could all piss off old people and then bike away very fast

I told him I didn't think it was very nice
It was more so that I couldn't ride a bike
He was insistent on going
His mom told him he should stay in with me, as I was leaving
   tomorrow

She went to the beach
He told me I had to make an appearance, so I reapplied my makeup to
   make said appearance
He didn't introduce me to anybody and it was painfully
   awkward
It became more awkward when we ran into the popular kids from my
   middle school

We went back to his house, into his room
He kept asking if I wanted to watch porn with him
Every time I said no
Eventually we settled on watching season seven of American Horror
   Story
He kept masturbating
It made me so uncomfortable I'd have to pee
Every time I peed I'd change my tampon out of force of habit
I ran out of tampons so I had to start using his mom's

The thought of her finding out/asking me made me more nervous
I would end up needing to use the bathroom more
She came home so her son cooled it on the incessant masturbating
She went to bed around 10

He and I were both still in his room
He started kissing me
The kissing wasn't the worst, even though he was terrible
He told me he wanted to finger me

It was less like he told me, more that he started trying to do it
I told him that I didn't want to because the last person who had
          done so had also done some
pretty terrible things to me
I explained to him how I associated the two together
This did not make him stop

Every time he moved his hand down I would move it right back up
I realized what I'd previously said would not be enough to make this
          man stop
I had to give him another reason
I told him I was on my period

He told me I didn't have to lie about being traumatized
I told him it was all very real
How nice it would have been if it was not all very real
Oh, how nice it would have been if my then boyfriend cared more
          about my safety than he did
some blood and tissue

No Apology
  —Amy Small-McKinney

Naturally I disliked monthly bleeding
received it grudgingly until

a boy threw me on the ground as if I were his skipping stone
and my creek dammed shut and silent

and shaming was a gun pointed toward a future I didn't want
and a woman shouting scriptures pointed toward a future I didn't want

until fluids seeped down my thighs
      my ankles
        and the seed's remains sank softly into a
        toilet's mouth impartial
and accepting

I welcomed back my blood with *thank you thank you*

and again my body belonged
   belonged to me

The Body Keeps the Score
—*Erica Bodwell*

As if in a dream, the body keeps the score—
Nurse says, *You have to relax, dear*. Does he know,
the one who leaned in the doorway?
My prayer goes here.

Nurse says, *Relax or it won't work*. Doctor
shakes his head, *You college girls*. Slides a needle
in my arm. My prayers narcotic dreams—
would the boy say, *sorry, sorry*, would he stroke my hair?

We college girls are so wild. At sea with vodka, sex
and prayers—would he recall
my name? Dream: he holds my hand. Nurse says,
ok, it's done. Prick of blood where needle was,

my prayer he never knows. Walking campus
in a dream, vodka goes down easy.
It's done, I'm back to one.
Familiar pain where a body was.

Like a dream, the trees are greening. Summer
and I'll leave this place. Doctor said, *Be careful*.
My grief my twin that walks with me,
the body keeps the score.

Flesh and Blood
>   *—Deirdre Fagan*

Trying to have babies, I peed on sticks,
First ten days a month,
Then, for an entire month.

"Irregular" avoided pregnancies
I wouldn't have wanted.
Irregular sent me to the clinic for tests.

Irregular is how it started,
A month shy of my 15th—
I might have been sterilized

When the quack low-income doc
Put me on pills for elderly women
to stop it, I later learned.

That's what they tried to do,
Did sometimes do, to the poor,
To the marginalized or unwanted.

I tell my daughter some girls
Are sent to huts in their yards
To wait out their periods,

And harm happens there,
Sometimes death. But
I also don't want to frighten her.

Blood is not what's scary, I tutor.
It's not the blood,
It's what some do about it.

Some men pass out,
While their wives give birth,
And yet, their wives give birth.

Some men try to pass legislation
That says what women can do
With their own bodies, own flesh and blood.

Some of these same men are afraid
Of blood, of flesh,
Of buying tampons, of buying pads.

These men who can't bear the sight
Of blood
Are still trying to bleed us.

Of our lives, our choices,
Of the lives only
We should choose.

I am 50 and still feeling the pain of ovulation,
And yet, I have no uterus.
You are only 12 and don't yet know.

My own late eggs, waiting since pre-birth,
Thelma and Louise themselves into my abdomen,
While I hold you in my arms.

You, who are just beginning. I stroke your hair,
And wish for you only what you want,
Only what you choose.

I wish for you,
None of your blood
on their hands.

La Mancha En Mi Alma
   —algae

1.   <u>La primera mancha</u>

Sir, puedo ir al baño?

                                             I don't know, can you?

                     Como te explico?

              Is there orta frase to say,

                 "Ya estoy crecida.".

Sir, I need to use the restroom.

It's important.

                                             How important?

Pienso que me manche.

2.   <u>Y las consequencias</u>

                        A stain

                 Caused by the dark red

         Historia that flows through my Gualmar bought underwear

            Hidden, though, by my dark denim skinny jeans.

                   Tengo miedo to go home

                   A home that's not home

                 Una casa que es una prision.

                A place where I am told como guardar

My secret garden.

The cramps were not what scared me.

Blood did not scare me.

That was part of growing up, acting tough.

No more playing fútbol with the boys on the streets,

No more licking paletas jokingly,

No more hanging upside down guelita's naranjo trees,

No more being silly little me.

3. <u>La inocencia: perdida</u>

He stood before me, luces de color brillando across his skin.

Guapísima.

Heat masquerading su sudor as a discotheque ball.

Bella.

Hands gripped my hips as though they belonged to him.

Amor.

Pecho contra pecho.

Vida.

Pressuring me further back.

Dime que me amas.

But I don't.

    And back.

        Como yo te amo.

But you don't.

    And back.

      Como debíamos de estar juntos.

We will only last tonight.

   When the act was finished, he shortly left,

   And with him went my innocence.

   Then there I stayed nested in my bed,

   Con la mancha en mi alma.

Goodbye, adiós.

People Keep Telling Me About New Mexico in Lubbock
     —Catherine Ragsdale

*—Lubbock, Texas is 294 miles from a clinic that provides abortion
services*

When people call out here
big sky country and I open
my legs to it really it's big
nothing big quiet moment
                    and I say

skipped missed waiting
the red in the dirt here
is red for the same reason
as blood
        oxidized iron. I tell

no one for a while and wait
then I tell the ones who would
drive me, over the phone and they
say, well

let me know when we need to go
to New Mexico. Well, I tell the man
I barely know I'm waiting for rain;

I say his name to him and spread
easily like before; I hold him
in the pit of my cunt; if I bleed

he'll thank me; he thanks me
for telling him now; for making
him wait too; watches me
drink a beer; it's dry out here

parched, red with dirt not slick
sapped red, crimson. Nothing
grows here but everything
has to grow.

Written In Blood
        —Limi Marie Bauer

You know how I knew Lady Macbeth was crazy?
All bitches know how to remove blood.

Blood. Moon blood. Mood blood. Running down my thighs blood.
Blamed PMS for personality swings
then outdated it like "hysteria"
Why have we not started testing how much
loss of stamina
loss of functionality
loss of being myself is intertwined in
my own loss of my own blood?

How does being in chronic pain
and smiling through it
not make you
the *strongest*?

The song says diamonds are my best friend and yeah
but so's my IUD.
Except when I bleed.
When I'm cramped in its vice and the blood is held until it
gushes.
Better stay home that day and
just *bleed*
and wash and bleed and wash and bleed and wash and bleed and wash
I watch the water of the sink and
swirl my blood
with my finger.
In a past life I was afraid of its power
its color and by past life
I mean past decade
when I didn't know the magic that is me
and the message held in my cells.

Messages that stretch my roots across continents and say
my blood belongs here.
The blood of everywhere is the blood of nowhere and
I read about a time when we gathered in a tent
and told stories and smelled spiced oils
and stayed away from others
as we bled.

My blood says I'm not with child.
My blood says I'm nourished enough to let go of this that no longer
    serves me.
My blood says I was born with double x's.
My blood says I own the house that creates life.
My blood says this too shall pass: these years, this pain, this power will
    fade.

When the blood drains from my cheeks and I no longer bleed
[when every child I could have carried has passed through me and
    down my legs]

When I no longer bleed

and I am left in peace

a deafening silence where

"my body my choice"
is no longer about the hotel at the base of my abdomen
but about my life support, my healing, and
my
own
damn
sacred
blood

Strawberry Moon

We Realized the Moon was Connected to Our Bleeding
—Liza Wolff-Francis

that the moon would not kill us,
but calls to us every month
like a battle cry from a shy lover
who our bodies cannot resist.
Every month she pulls us to her,
lays us down with full regard
for the magic our wombs hold,
for the edges we reach in her light.
When we emerge from the cave,
throats raw from our echo and song,
we see the moon full,
as if it filled its glowing belly
with our blood, then backed off
again from its hunger.
The faith of the moon's cycles
rest inside us like we were moon rocks
tumbled upon the earth
blooming, like life.

Check, Mate
—Lauren Rheaume

When we were in high school, Christina C and I were always afraid our period products would fail us. I didn't yet know about the usefulness of pantiliners, even while wearing a tampon, so I dreaded the day when I'd go to the bathroom and realize there was now a dark red splotch on the back of my clothing, for all of high school to see. That, and neither of us had yet mastered the art of figuring out when our periods would arrive in the first place.

I imagine the first conversation went down like this:

"Hey, class is over, you ready for lunch? Why are you still sitting here?" Christina asked me. Students were up, leaving the room, cracking jokes, already creating the din that took over the lunchroom.

The response came in a whisper and a leaning in, "I'm worried I started my period and it leaked," I said, with a scrunched up mouth and pushed-in eyebrows, not yet sure if it's okay to talk about this *gross* subject with this new friend.

"Oh, okay, well, here I'll stand behind you and just check as we walk out."

And that was it—the agreement was made. All we'd have to say to each other was "check" and we knew the other wouldn't be obvious about it, she'd take her time, but she'd tell you if you had something to worry about.

One time, I couldn't even muster the word, we were in mid-conversation, and my face flushed with blood. It must have been a higher stakes situation: the boy I liked was nearby, or I had a presentation. But Christina knew. She checked. I was fine.

We didn't always have classes together, but when we saw each other in the halls the agreement was intact. Sometimes I think about the amount of time I spent staring casually at another girl's butt in high school. I realize now that I didn't have an agreement like this with any other girlfriend. I haven't spoken to Christina in many years, probably 15 at this point. I wonder if she remembers this ritual, this vulnerability we shared.

Pushing Rivers
      —Jan Chronister

Full July moon
pulls at oceans
ovaries—
fluids flow.

Do all women menstruate at the same time?
Probably not—
we would have noticed by now.

On the Rag
  —Abigail Elizabeth Ottley

My grandma had not much to say. They called it on the rag.
Polite girls were *unwell today*. They called it *on the rag.*
Old linen scraps and folded cloths were all the help they had.
Each night they'd scrub the blood away. They called it *on the rag.*
My mother, though, when her time came said she was rather glad
to celebrate her *Lady Day.* They called it *on the rag.*
A cotton wad with loops and pins. A sanitary pad.
A goblet for her Beaujolais. They called it *on the rag.*
The age of peace and love was mine. For lusty undergrads
rain sometimes interrupted play. They called it *on the rag.*
Some lads, though, went adventuring as far as Stalingrad.
A taste for *filet de rouget*? They called it on the rag.
A rose is sweet by any name but isn't it just sad
what images those words convey? They call it *on the rag.*
French tongues, it seems, are spiteful. More De Sade than Galahad.
A woman there has *Les Anglais.* We call it *on the rag.*
Some Germans speak of *sauerei, a nasty mess* is bad.
In Italy, *bagaglie. We* call it *on the rag.*
But chief among the names I've heard there's one I'm pleased to add.
Say *carrying a rose bouquet.* Don't call it *on the rag.*

The Drop
>   *—Jennifer Schomburg Kanke*

Alice Ann, unafraid, approached the searing plastic and metal of the monkey bars. The three of them did everything together, and that included this. Kira thought she was afraid. Erica thought she was afraid.

I ain't afraid.

The others were already comfortably swinging upside down from their knees and the blood had not yet begun to rush to their heads.

Then get up here.

Hidden from Ms. Behr's eyes by the old oak in the middle of the playground for at least a good ten minutes at a time, the monkey bars were the sixth graders' preferred site for make-out sessions and fistfights, which gave Alice Ann and her friends a limited window to play on them. As fifth graders, they could be booted at any moment and no one would come to their defense.

Kira knew Alice Ann was afraid because she wanted to be the teacher's pet, even though Erica and Kira had decided they should all aim for being cool instead. They had been told from day one at Bradford Sinks Elementary that the monkey bars were for *hands* only. Penny drops, moon swings, and the ultra-challenging sloth slip (toes only) were expressly and vehemently forbidden, though nearly everyone from the third grade on up had tried them at least once during the lawless country known as The Weekends. Alice Ann and her friends were the first girls in living memory to attempt it during school hours and with a teacher not thirty feet away. Should they be caught, Alice Ann's status as smart and innocent good girl would most definitely be in jeopardy. For Kira and Erica, the point was 100% *to* get caught. But if only one or two of them got caught then that one or two would have to become friends with Julie Sue and Natty who stole Frozen pencils from the Student of the Week prize drawer and had folders covered in questionable smelly stickers like burnt popcorn, dirty socks, and boy farts. The one not caught would be spared but would be known as a traitor forever. Kira knew this was what Alice Ann feared the most.

This was not what worried Alice Ann.

Erica knew Alice Ann was afraid because she didn't trust her own body. The bars were a full eight feet up from the mounded sand of the ground and last year, the Saturday before school ended, Sasha Green had slipped and busted her head open. She'd healed up nicely, didn't even have a concussion, but Erica knew the story haunted Alice Ann because she had been next in line that day. Even though she wasn't directly involved in the incident everyone came to her Monday at school expecting a full reporting.

"She slipped," was all she could offer. This had been a letdown, and everyone had told her so. Erica had only been a little mad at Alice Ann for not spinning a better tale. Sasha's fall could have been the trio's ticket to instant day camp fame for the summer. They could have cut in line for afternoon snack for at least a week, maybe even two. Her inability to milk the situation had landed them smack in the middle of the pack for the entire three months, neither day camp royalty nor teacher-clingers (which were most certainly different from teacher's pets). They had an uneventful summer and Alice Ann had liked it that way.

Erica and Kira had not. They knew they were destined for popularity, destined to make a mark before leaving life in the big kids' hall to be back at the bottom of the pecking order when they moved on to 7th grade at Anhinga Junior High. This penny drop was the latest in their schemes to solidify their social position. They had already attempted a few tried and true tactics, such as dressing up as unicorns for a week, picking the popular girls first in kickball, and being mean to Carlotta Henson. Punching down was not something their families would have approved of, but if it had worked, it would have been well worth it. It had not and they'd all lost iPad privileges for a week, except Alice Ann whose mother had grounded her, but then handed the device back after only one night.

Come on, quit stalling. Get up here, Erica urged. All three of them had to be swinging from the bars without a care in the world by the time the teacher made her next sweep of the grounds. They would smile and wave, say a cheeky and drawn out, *Hey, Ms. Behr*, it would be glorious. But it had to be all three of them. The friendship pact they'd signed in the second grade was very specific that their fates were tied. They would not be like those kids in the movies where one went on without the rest and then came around by the end of the film, realizing that friendship is more important than popularity. No, this trio got out ahead of that issue and determined that no one was allowed to advance without the others.

When Erica got an invite to Kentasha Simon's birthday party last year, she'd wiggled one for her pals as well. When Kira got invited by Amí Figueroa to spend the day at Wild Adventures, Mrs. Figueroa had to make space in her Odyssey for two unexpected butts. And when Alice Ann had scored a kitten last year when her cat hoarder great-aunt had passed away, she begged and pleaded until her mother got ones for Erica and Kira as well even though their parents had most definitely not said yes to new kittens.

Where one went, they all went, and that included hanging upside down from the monkey bars.

Hurry, hurry, she's on the move, Kira said as Alice Ann stood with her arms above her head, hands barely touching the last crossbar, muscles not yet tightened, not yet ready for the lift and fling needed to join her friends above her. She was afraid, but not for any of the reasons Kira and Erica suspected, though Erica was the closest. She trusted her body fine. Her arms were strong from swimming in the bay, her abs tight from hovering over decaying logs looking for skinks in the pine woods behind GapGap's house. To be honest, she'd never thought much about her body before. She wanted to do; her body complied.

I'm coming up, losers, she tightened her grip, got her legs around the bar, and eased herself into a hanging position without even knocking into Kira who was hanging from a bar near the middle.

Instantly the worry came. Had this been a bad idea? Did she smell? Did she smell bad enough for them to smell her? Kira was the closest and Erica was all the way at the other end of the monkey bars, surely they couldn't smell her. Would the pad her mother had given her slip? Would they notice the small brown spot on the inseam of her shorts? Surely not from that far away, surely. Was it even safe to be upside down right now? If all the blood rushed to her head would it include THAT blood too? Would she flood her brain and cause a stroke? She was too young for a stroke! Was she risking death just to elevate the group?

Get your waving arms ready, y'all, Kira could tell Alice Ann was about to bail and they'd come too far to not get their rightful glory.

Hey, Ms. Behr.

Get down, Ms. Behr shook her head and rolled her eyes. Had it been Ms. McKee they would have been in trouble. She was a first-year teacher and cared a lot about everything, but Ms. Behr was retiring next year and had seen it all already. The girls got down quickly after they were sure no less than half the playground had seen them. *A talking to, moving their clothespin from green straight to red, that should be enough,* thought Ms. Behr. No need to get the principal involved, no need to make more paperwork than absolutely necessary.

Once both feet were firmly on the ground, Alice Ann was relieved. Neither Kira nor Erica seemed to notice there was anything different about her. She'd wait until one of them started too, then she'd miraculously get hers. No need to stand out, no need to go it alone. The girls felt triumphant. For the rest of the day they walked the halls as queens.

Avoid Head-Standing
       —Sarah Kai Neal

when bleeding Yogi says
it goes back in when it's meant

to be gushing Meant to be cats
and dogs de parting

So she stands on ground half-Moon posed
Tipping over tea pot sings *Here is my handle*

and waits for gravity animals rain
Here is my spout She counts

each breath wishing to be
poured

string, susio from cup
  —Amy Bobeda

string, susio from cup
      slides across the table
       curdled, first milk, red congealing jello

  becomes our first words, smeared across our bellies.

   interno y fuera sonrosado
   las--------strings--------between----blood-----fibers
   like
   a leaf divining the bowl

   the ancients ground ochre
      smeared in fat sexualized
     la alma,
       simulates
        blood.

The 'sham menstruation' or Female Cosmetic Coalitions ritual and symbolism emerged to over attention of philanderer males targeting females who were imminently fertile. (menstruating) whole coalitions adopted a strategy using cosmetics to scramble information of fertility. Using red cosmetics, females signaled their resistance. – Camilla Power, *Early Human Kinship*

The Birth of Motherhood
       —Sarah Dickenson Snyder

My mom told Anne and me
in the upstairs TV room before
the addition that changed our front

door from Central to Elm
giving us a family room
and a color TV.

The three of were us huddled
near the rabbit antennae.
I remember

talk of monthly blood
and something about napkins.
Mostly I grimaced or laughed

making it hard for her to speak.
Nothing came out
quite right for me—

after our talk, when I saw girls
about two years older than I,
with a cut on their knee or arm,

I thought *that* was their period,
gave them a knowing look,
smug in my newfound knowledge

of women and their blood.
When it was my turn to see blood
as I wiped myself in the junior high

bathroom, I knew about vaginas
and menstruation by then,
knew to stuff some toilet paper

in my underpants, run home after school,
open the front door to hear, *Hello?*
and yell, *I can have a baby!*

The Second Positive
  —Julia C. Alter

On Monday you were a single grain of rice
in a spoon. On Sunday, a sesame seed
with a smiley face. On Saturday, I peed on plastic
when I realized I wasn't synched with the new moon
or the full moon either, sat up all night in the knowing
wind, eating cashews under the sugar maple
at 5 AM. I imagined how many weeks
before you'd be the size of a cashew,
curved and raw, a question mark.

Today I am wearing my riot grrrl tank with the baby
deer in a flowerbed: *My Body is Not for Your Consumption*
in pink print across my chest, already two aching gray mountains.
Suddenly untrue, my body's on the starter block
to be consumed by you.

A website tells me I will gain three pounds
in my breasts alone. I marvel, the idea
of my milk exotic, luxe and sickening
as white chocolate. I examine my panties for
weeks after the tests, still looking for red
whenever I sit on the toilet. I become a trembling
woman in a dark bar waiting until last call
for someone she already knows
has stood her up.

First Blood
  —Carol L. Gloor

I hung the sheets on the clothesline,
the ones from the guest bed
my granddaughter slept in,

and saw the two stitched places,
trying to hide the folded red wounds.
She found the sewing kit.

I knew it was time, granddaughter,
from your breast buds and sudden height.
It is not *the curse, the friend,* or *the rag.*

The small fist in the body
you were born with has grown
into a blood layered room,
ready for a baby.

I cannot know how
it will be for you,
except it will last
about forty years.

Pay attention to it.
Learn its ways.
You will not know
which one is the last.

Crimson Tide

Seasons of the Ladybird
—Susan Darlington

Ladybird Spring

The dust of sun-baked red heat
shimmers with the blackness of shadows.
Each day has stretched out the same this year
as the ground has become parched
and reservoirs have revealed the village lives
that were flooded in their creation.

Into this dryness only ladybirds bloom.
Swarms cover the entire side of buildings
and rose bush leaves sag under the weight
of yellow eggs that cluster on the underside
waiting to hatch into a stillness and silence
that's broken by a cry:

the sound with which I enter the world.
The rent in the air attracts one ladybird
that lands on my blood-streaked belly.
"A good omen," says the midwife.
Her voice startles the beetle, which opens
its wings and leaves its shadow in a birthmark.

Ladybird Summer

The green of the nettle was a swarm of red,
sun-torpid ladybirds wandering from plant
to budding plant as they hunted for shade
under an alder that creaked with ring growth.

I plucked metamorphosis soft insects from leaves
with puppy fat fingers and put them in a tin
that was fragile in its sharpness with orange rust,
flakes of paint coming off on my downy pink skin.

Under my guileless eyes they circled and slipped
on the corroded sides of metal and when dusk fell
I placed the lid on the tin, stored it on a shelf,
and climbed between the white sheets on my bed.

In the morning, when I removed the cover,
I found stiff, motionless beetles cast in ruby
and when I made my bed, the linen was stained
with the iron-rich silhouette of a ladybird in flight.

Ladybird Autumn

Nettles have climbed back to root.
Alders have stopped to rain leaves.
And inside my house I've hoisted laundry
onto the rack to dry in front of the oven:
35 sheets for 35 years of ladybird summers.

The chaste white linen drips out the time
onto the scratched hard wood floor
and as I reach across the cloth for a mop
I notice that twin-cycles have again failed
to erase the stain of ruby beetles in flight.

I stretch out for the nearest swaddling cloth,
rub it between scarred thumb and forefinger,
and when I pull it taut to see the smear
there's blood on my skin and the insects
have tucked their wings under their elytra.

The tap gurgles as I turn it on, hot water
gushing pink and then clear as I wash my hands.
Steam condenses down my cheeks in tears
and as it lifts the beetles clean off the sheets
I know that I've lost all of my children.

Ladybird Winter

I collected wooden pallets for the ladybirds,
stacked them in the sunspot in my garden
next to the decaying rocking chair on the porch,
and packed them with dry leaves and straw.

I waited until my back doubled over,
my eyes became opaque blue marbles,
and the orange of my hair paled to white
but no ruby beetles appeared in the nest.

I searched for them in the corners of the house,
emptied out cupboards and looked in the folds
of musty linen and still wrapped, unworn clothes
that were bought for my never born daughter.

But among the memories that had been stored
in rusty tin boxes, that flaked dream saturated paint
and that tore at fingers until they spotted red,
all I found was a ladybird's dried husk.

The Stranger at My Underwear Drawer
—*Jodelle Marx*

Standing in the doorway of my bedroom, I interrupt the woman sifting through my drawers. "You're not going to find any."

At the sound of my voice, her hand hesitates over a wad of polka dotted fabric. *Dang it, she found my Dotties.* Dotties: my pet name for my favorite pair of childish, overworn underwear. At this point, they rarely leave my drawer, except for their monthly outing on my heavy flow days.

We pause in thick silence, me staring at the woman's neatly fastened bun and pulled-up collar. Her, leaning over my underwear drawer and quietly calculating what to do next.

"How did you get in?"

"Jimmied the lock on the bathroom window." Her voice is flat, matter of fact.

She is roughly my same age, early thirties, shoulders tipped forward in a breast reducing slouch, body stiff with uncertainty. In this day and age, she probably expects me to pull a gun on her, but I prefer to solve this peacefully.

"All I need is one pad, and I'll leave." Her body hitches as she exhales.

"I'm not going to tell you where they are; I'm not that thick."

"No," she agrees calmly. "You are. . ." she reaches forward, past my Dotties and lifts a newer pair of bikini cut, the crimson color of empowerment.

As she leans to the side, the hall light from behind me, catches the tag sewn into the seam. "No, not thick at all, quite petite, really."

"I am not thick," the word slices heavily, "as in, I'm not dumb enough to tell you where my pads are."

She drops my red underwear and turns to face me resentfully. "Well, who *is* thick these days?"

When I was a kid, my parents talked of their parents struggling to stay thin. Food used to be cheap, full of sugar and fat, and wrapped in clingy plastic, available any day of the week. Now, we receive pre-portioned, boxed food on our doorsteps once a week—or at least those who still have doorsteps do.

Standing in the nicked doorway of my bedroom though, food

is not the necessity driving tonight's' attempted theft. This woman is here because her body bleeds. She is a stranger, here to steal my pads.

I close my eyes.

"You need only one?"

"Well, two should get me by." The ransom for my solitude has gone up. "I'm barely hanging onto my job, and you know what happens to women who bleed through."

I nod, picturing the stains on my Dotties.

In the push to move away from single use plastics, tampons and pads became an environmental target for not only being packaged in plastic but being composed of plastics. With an increase in demand for organic pads, tampons, menstrual cups and discs, companies jacked up their prices. Meanwhile, legislators were touted as "nature's heroes" for passing laws to tax single use menstrual products. Community support organizations that usually provide free menstrual products to food banks and health centers, could not keep up with skyrocketing prices. Suddenly, millions of women turned to old practices, lining their underwear with rags that could be washed each night.

Judging by my house, which I have all to myself, the woman at my dresser probably has my financial status pegged as a cup user— she's right.

Like everyone who grew up with single use products though, I keep a store of pilfered pads that I haven't needed in years. "Where do you work?" I ask.

"The papermill."

"You been there long?"

"A few years. I weld—er, I used to. I mostly do mechanical stuff now."

"Have you noticed a decline in production yet?"

"Oh yeah. They're laying people off left and right."

I nod in solidarity. "I had a friend who used to work at the papermill, years ago. She worked twelve hour shifts and always had stories about sneaking pads and tampons into the restroom. This was before the new laws, of course."

The woman nods back, seeming to understand where I am going.

A smile softens my face, "She used to walk around all day, with a pad in each cup of her bra and a tampon in the middle, so that she had them when she took her bathroom breaks."

We both let out a huff of laughter and I continue my story,

"She was lucky, she had a pretty regular period that she could plan for. One day though, it came early and when a colleague saw her bleeding through, she was reported for 'unprofessional conduct in the workplace.'" If the woman standing before me is working twelve hour shifts on rags, without the ability to switch them out, she must be bleeding through.

With three cautious steps, I am standing shoulder to shoulder with her, both of us visually inspecting my underwear. Gravity draws my right hand to the polka dotted cloth. Our conversation stiffens as I shift the snagged satin of my Dotties to my left hand.

"Do—uh, do you work?" She asks.

Instead of answering, I pinch one corner of the wrapped parcel and open my palm so that the underwear unfold. Two tampons roll into my right hand and I shake it again. A pad clings to the fabric with static electricity, then falls into the drawer.

The woman shifts from toes to heels, realizing that she has asked for two thirds of my possessions.

"Uh—er." Her mouth fumbles open and I clasp my hand around the tampons.

One is a cardboard tube with a string dangling from one end and a wad of synthetic cotton poking out the other end. When the panic about plastic products first blew up, cardboard tubed tampons were advertised as plastic-free. That is, until some products were exposed for their chemical content and plastics in both the string and the cotton.

The second tampon leaves more of an impression in my mind as I squeeze its slick green plastic edges, contoured to slide in easily: a relic of luxuries past. Plastic tampon applicators were the first to go.

In the drawer, the pad lays neatly folded in thirds and wrapped in a soft crinkle free sleeve.

She avoids eye contact as I glance at her. "No one has many these days." We breathe. "You know how to use tampons, right?"

"Um, yes?"

I close my eyes, press the cardboard tampon and pad into her hand, and pick up my Dotties to reconceal the plastic tampon.

"I'll make some calls. Come back tomorrow."

The woman breathes deeply.

I gesture to the hallway, "Use the door next time."

Ode to My Menstrual Cup
—Raye Hendrix

No covenant in my blood, no
saving grace, no disciples
waiting to lift you to their lips
and drink, but still—small goblet
of my body—in your own way
you are holy: savior
of my underwear, protector
of my jeans, thanks to you
I do my laundry and the whites
are white as snow. You,
the only cradle I will ever own,
cradle of the children I refuse
to bear, collector of the debt
men say I owe this world
as a woman, I bleed for you
the way I'd bleed for any lover.
I fill you with myself and I am free.

CW: gender dysphoria, self-harm ideation,
mention of sexual assault, surgery

Chris & Crampus: Besties Since Evacuation Day 2015
—Chris Talbot-Heindl

At Age 10

You get your first period.

You aren't terrified or confused like the characters in every teen show
when they get their first spots. You were prepared for this; you dreaded
this. Laura Ingalls Wilder Elementary School gym teachers saw to both
when they awkwardly gathered all the fourth graders in the room of
carpeted bleacher steps where the chorus typically practiced. You sat
with your peers — who were also assigned female at birth by various
obstetricians across the world — guided there silently, by gym teachers
who couldn't cover their discomfort.

And just like the little video said — because the gym teachers were not
prepared to speak on it; they pressed play on the district-approved
educational video and looked mortified by its contents — you know
you need a pad or a tampon now. You can't stand the idea of touching
yourself and the bits that don't feel like they belong to you, so when
you find the tampon box first, you hunt further in the cabinet under
the sink for your mom's pads.

At Age 12

You need to use your first tampon if you're going to the pool.

You're terrified. You don't know enough about your own anatomy to
know what can happen if you screw up the process — you don't know
which of the adults who fidget the second menstruation is mentioned
you can ask — but you assume it's bad. You've read the box directions
repeatedly. The last time, you did it with your mother present, asking
her questions that she was reluctant to answer. Her discomfort with all
of this is palpable.

You ask her to wait outside your room while you put it in. She's uncomfortable there too. You tell her not to go anywhere. *I want you here in case something goes wrong.* You don't know anything about what specific menstrual products are made for or how to communicate how little blood you actually have during your period so when you put it in, it feels like your insides are being scratched. It's painful, but you assume this is normal, and don't want to call out to your mom. You get in your swimsuit and emerge from the room to your mom's relief.

At Age 14

You start hormone replacement therapy.

You don't understand the urgency; after all, it's only irregular periods, but you are excited to be *trusted* like this.

While you have no interest, you know that having your very own hormone prescription means that you can have sex and not get pregnant. You feel like an adult being trusted with this responsibility, even though you have no interest. Adults always assume teenagers do, so they must believe you are responsible enough to handle it.

At Age 16

You can't stand the way you look anymore.

You can't name it specifically and it will be three more years before you'll know what *trans* means.

After nearly two years of hormone replacement therapy, your body has changed. At first, it was gradual and you barely noticed. But then, you went back to school with fully developed breasts and a feminized face.

Gone are the days you could stealth as a boi or as confusing, which is what you've always preferred. Gone are the days when people would call you *young man*, and do a double-take, confused and unsure of where to go from there. It always gave you a thrill when that happened. But it never does anymore. Instead, you have perfect strangers chastising you and telling you to *act like a proper young lady,* something you know you never were.

When people hear your chosen name, instead of just calling you it, they now ask what it's short for and what your *real* name is. Everything feels so much more difficult now. And what for? Regular periods you didn't want anyway.

You begin to dream about cutting the whole mess out of your body and chopping off your new breasts. You know better than to tell others about those dreams. Your Catholic upbringing doesn't allow for variations like this; you found that out when you came out as queer two years ago.

At Age 20

You are in Grand Central Station in New York City with a full DivaCup.

This type of cup is specifically made for high cervixes, but you don't know yours hangs low and angled and this is the only type of menstrual cup you know about and the only kind available at your local food co-op. It's uncomfortable when empty, but when it is full, it is unbearable.

Although you are fully in boi mode, wearing stained black Carhartt jeans, and a brown hoodie, with your hair buzzed at ¼ inch, you have to use the women's bathroom for this.

The line is long and you start your wait. You see a white woman scoff and angrily eyeball you as she leaves.

The next thing you know, you are being yanked out of the line and out of the bathroom by a cop. The white woman is standing outside with her hands on her hips and looks haughtily proud of herself. *You found him!* she announces to the cop who begins to question you.

After you explain what you're doing in line for the women's closed stalls — where no one can see anything anyway — and show your ID which misgenders you, he lets you go. No apology from either party. You are mortified and the adrenaline from the encounter begins to deepen into a full-blown anxiety attack. You leave the Station with your full DivaCup sloshing uncomfortably.

At Age 22

You are bleeding profusely.

You've always had heavy flow days after you stopped taking hormone replacement therapy, but this is something else. The pain is excruciating.

You get one of your six roommates to take you to the emergency room. They do blood work. They are clearly not taking this or your pain as seriously as you are. From the blood work, they tell you that your estrogen levels are too low to be menstruating. They ask if you have had unprotected sex recently. You have. Ever since your sexual assault three years ago, you pretty much assume that if you don't have sex how and when your partners want to, they'll do it anyway. You feel stupid and disgusting when you tell them you have.

They tell you it may be a miscarriage, but it may not be. They don't seem too interested in finding out for sure and say that no matter what it is, their advice is the same: rest, relax, drink lots of water, take some iron supplements, take ibuprofen as needed, and use hot pads as needed.

You go home and spend the next three days bleeding profusely and fighting with your live-in partner until you tell him you don't want anything to do with him again. You move next door with your best friend. Far enough.

At Age 25

You are bleeding profusely.

It's one week after your tubal ligation and you were on the floor writhing in pain with the second worse period you've ever had. You call all the people you can think of, but by this time, you live by yourself, so when you can't reach anyone, you drive yourself to the hospital.

They seem rather annoyed to have to call in a technician on a Saturday morning. She seems rather annoyed to be there when she arrives with her hair still wet; you wonder if that's why the transvaginal ultrasound hurts so very, very much.

They tell you that you had an ovarian cyst rupture, which caused the extreme pain. They can't explain the heaviness of the bleeding because that's unrelated. They don't seem that interested in it. They tell you to go home, rest, relax, drink lots of water, take some iron supplements, take ibuprofen as needed, and use hot pads as needed.

At Age 31

You got an IUD with progesterone to deal with your heavy periods.

At this point in your life, you are experiencing 14-day periods and losing so much blood. Iron supplements aren't doing enough anymore.

It's the first or second most painful experience of your life; the endometrial biopsy to figure out if the fibroids in your uterus were painful, but short. The IUD felt like an eternity with pain so bad, you thought you were going to spontaneously shit.

Your gynecologist assures you that this is the next best step for you and it should either regulate your periods or make them stop altogether. You pray to whatever is out there and listening that they stop. You've had enough.

At Age 33

You let out a sigh of relief when your gynecologist says that he will perform a hysterectomy.

He says you've been through enough and he doesn't want to put you through ablation. *Let's just get rid of it*, he says. At this point in your life, you are experiencing 21-day periods with 10 days off. You can't hold a job anymore. You are temping, but in the last temp job you had, your DivaCup shot out of you when you got up from your desk chair. You were also wearing a Glad Rag with an insert and a folded hand towel, so it wasn't as bad as it could have been, but it was hard to clean up in the bathroom.

Your friend who is a reiki massage therapist and an herbalist — who gave you yarrow root and more reiki sessions than you can count to try and battle the pain — says you shouldn't get the hysterectomy because that would be *removing your womanhood*.

You cry a little, hoping that's true.

Age 35

You take photographs with your uterus in the park.

After your hysterectomy, your gynecologist told you that you would have been in the emergency room in a few months if you hadn't scheduled it when you did. The IUD was rubbing against the fibroids and a newly formed cyst — which was causing all the pain. If the IUD had punctured the cyst, which it eventually would have, that would have meant an emergency hysterectomy.

You were surprised when your gynecologist said you could keep it when you asked, provided you signed off that you would be responsible for it; after all, it is a biohazard. You promised him a Flat Stanley photoshoot, but it's taken you nearly a year and a half to get around to it. You're making it worth the wait with several themed photoshoots.

You took a two-week staycation to make a tiny bed with a uterus-patterned blanket and embroidered pillow, crocheted a stuffed uterus for yours to cuddle with like a doll, sewed a jacket and crocheted a hat, molded a clay Kegelcisor that you painted bronze, and molded a pair of clay skates and helmet that match your own for your photoshoot.

The uterus doesn't look like a uterus anymore and more resembles chopped ham with large growths. It had to be cut into dozens of pieces since they had to test the fibroids for cancer, but all the outfits and props make it obvious, for your gynecologist anyway. The only discernible piece to your non-medical eye is the cervix, so you shake the Tupperware until it settles visible towards the front. You make a whole zine using the photographs to show him that since your uterus is no longer trying to kill you or giving you gender dysphoria, you're now best friends, and send it to him as a thank you for giving you your life back.

The whole thing feels like something you can joke about now. Legitimately. Not like how you laugh about painful things in a self-deprecating way and feel the sting when others laugh with you even though you clearly invited it. And you also don't mind if they don't laugh with you now — this is cathartic for you.

You make up irreverent inside jokes, like naming your uterus *Crampus*, your remaining downstairs mix-up a *pocket pussy*, and you put the finishing touches on your zine, which you cheekily name *Chris & Crampus: Besties Since Evacuation Day 2015* with the tagline *Inseparable (figuratively, of course)*, and laugh at your own cleverness and from pure, unadulterated joy.

The Curse of Eve at the Damascus Gate
    —Lorette C. Luzajic

On my last night in Jerusalem, I felt that familiar, insistent tug at my center, felt the ribbons of my ovaries begin to heave and knot. My mouth was stuffed with kosher cabernet and a fat cigar, me with Dad and Jim.

Their wives were long past bleeding, and I was unprepared. It had been months since I'd had the monthly visitor. I felt thirty-five years fall to fallow, fell back into fourteen, the last time I'd asked Dad to walk with me to find a store where I could find tampons and pills. Dad was the guy who had always been practical about the body—he liked to stand clear of germs but took our periods like a man.

"Oh, that's still going on, then," he said, matter-of-factly, and took my hand like I was twelve, led me down the twilit corridors of the Holy City. We'd only landed in Israel ten days before, but it was like we'd always been there. I was slower, fattened by perimenopause and a bum thyroid, and all those cartons of shiraz. My knees were already dissolving under my weight from arthritis, and Dad was spry and fast, pulling me ahead and holding me steadfast at the same time.

The man in the small pharmacy did not speak much English, and I didn't know how to say *Tampax* or *nonsteroidal anti-inflammatories* in Arabic. It was a surreal pantomime, trying to act out these specific sundries in a way that might be understood. Dad, gray and fuzzy, knees knobby in khaki shorts, bird legs in hiking boots, ropes of veins around and around those spindly calves; and me, pale and puffy like soggy bread, waving our arms in hopes the proprietor could read our wide-open palms. He passed us cigarettes, band-aids, something that looked like licorice, and mouthwash before closing in on the sanitary napkins, an *a-ha* in the flourish of his fingers when he presented them, *voila!* He grinned widely, all the wider for the gaps in his teeth, pocketed our shekels, and put the stash in an unmarked paper baggie. Daddy carried that small sack in one hand, the way he always carried everything.

Every other moment on that trip we took together, spring and offspring, was bigger than that one. We towered above the world atop Masada, we sipped the bitter cup at Calvary, raised our hands skyward after, in gratitude for life. We felt the winds of Armageddon, crawled into its bowels. We crouched at the waters where the loaves were multiplied and men who could not live by bread alone were fed fish. We ate those fish, too.

But at the end of it, it was the relentless, cyclical persistence of the everyday that reminded us of everything that matters, what all that stuff was for, anyways, what it was about: how the clock is always ticking. How, if you're alive, you'll bleed.

Grandmother's Marital Bed
    —Carey Taylor

mess of sheet, flake of skin, lunar blood, dried semen

bowl of red

mess of sheet, flake of skin, lunar blood, dried semen

bowl of red

mess of sheet, flake of skin, lunar blood, dried semen

bowl of red

mess of sheet, flake of skin, lunar blood, dried semen

bawl of baby

mess of sheet, flake of skin, lunar blood, dried semen

bawl of baby

mess of sheet, flake of skin, lunar blood, dried semen

bowl of baby

sheet, skin, blood, semen

bawl of baby

skin, blood, semen

bawl of baby

blood, semen

bawl of baby

bawl of baby

bawl of baby

Riding Crimson Tides

—Traci Skuce

I am fourteen years old and in high school. I don't have my period, have never had my period. What I do have are braces, and legs so skinny there's no difference between thigh and calf except for my bony knees. I read *Are You There, God? It's Me, Margaret;* I send prayers and incantations into the darkness, summoning my hormones, my nascent uterus, to do *something*.

All the other girls my age complain about cramps and get out of gym class; they roll their eyes and moan. "I'm on the rag," they say. And I nod solemnly, as though I understand, as though I am a member of this mysterious tribe—with its symptoms and language and privilege. But really, I've only studied diagrams of an incorporeal uterus in Health Class.

How it feels, how it actually *is*, I don't know. But I believe it's the key to a world that opens to other worlds. The making-out world, for example. For too long, I've stood as a spectator at school dances. Beneath the swirling disco-ball and during "Stairway to Heaven", I felt my wobbly longing and watched other girls make-out with the boys. Except once. Back in grade eight, when I dared myself to kiss Gord H. with tongues and everything. Mid-kiss, during the dizzy part of the song, I peeked up at him. The kiss wetter, sloppier than it looked on all those episodes of *Love Boat*, making me wonder if I was doing it wrong. And I was. His gaze was rolled towards the ceiling, not in ecstasy, but in a kind of resignation.

A year and a half later, I wince at that memory and blush every time I pass Gord H. in the halls. I'm positive that once my period comes, I'll be released from this suffocating prepubescence and all its ignorance. When it comes, I'll slip into another dimension. I will know how to talk with boys and flirt. How to move in close and kiss them with such astonishing mastery, I'll leave them jangled, breathless, falling at my feet.

***

The spring and summer before my twenty-fourth birthday, I work as head cook in two different tree-planting camps. At the first camp, south of Prince George, I have an assistant with a four-month-old baby named Levi. Every morning, after breakfast is over, she plunks him into his baby swing, where he swings contentedly as we putter around the kitchen trailer, mixing batters, simmering sauces, chopping a million carrots. Occasionally he fusses, so his mom scoops him up and breastfeeds him. Or I lift him into my arms, carry him outside and show him the sky. I love his fuzzy head, the back of his neck, his tiny pudgy fingers looping through my hair. Some moments I look at him and think, *I'd like one of these*. But I pack that thought away, return to the kitchen, get busy cracking eggs.

Early July, I move to another camp in Northern Alberta. My period arrives without fanfare at the beginning of the contract and is over within five days. I don't know about the surge of luteinizing hormones, only those long-ago Health Class warnings about having sex mid-cycle. I'm not on the pill, though I have been, but it prompted such unruly crying jags that I stopped.

In these northern reaches, light lingers all night over the wispy forests. I hear talk of virgin meadows, though I never see them. Mostly I see the inside of the cook shack, counters checkerboarded with sheet pans and stainless-steel bowls, and an unprecedented amount of attention from young men. Up until this point, my sexual experiences have been mediocre, hardly the beguiling encounters I'd imagined in my teens. My last boyfriend treated sex like a mild allergy, and the one before that left me numb.

But under the magic of these twenty-four-hour days, I'm seduced by a young man who opens the door to shared sexual pleasure. Intoxicated by it, I float through my days, spiraling away from worries of pregnancy, convincing myself I'll be fine.

***

Forty-four and I've entered the long labyrinth called perimenopause. My brain becomes clouded, my muscles and bones dragged by the tidal whims of unseen forces. Most days I feel like a mythical woman, condemned to live in the perpetual fog and dim light of the underworld. The ferritin measures in my blood are chronically low. I buy dozens of supplements that promise to lift me back into the land of the living—liquid iron, evening primrose oil, B-vitamins, dong quai.

My periods become unruly, unpredictable. Once, in November, I drive down to Victoria for a writers' conference. It's the third day of my period so I think I'll be fine. But between panels and workshops I dash to the washroom to change soaked pads. Any iron stores I've managed to accrue since my last period vanish. My cells running on fumes.

Before the evening readings and despite the grippy cramps in my abdomen, the gritty ache in my eyes, I walk and walk. Then I stop at a Thai restaurant and bump into a former women's studies professor of mine. I approach her and, since it's been twenty years, re-introduce myself, remind her I was pregnant in her course about Irish women, had a crawling baby in the one about reproductive technologies. "Yes," she says, "I remember." She goes on to tell me of her retirement, her newfound interest in Tai Chi, a trip she'll take to Italy in the spring. All I want is to talk about this bleeding, ask her why, in all those women's studies classes, we never discussed it. Instead, I feel the pressure of a massive clot at the opening of my vagina. "Excuse me," I say. "Good to see you." Then I jog to the washroom, mincing my legs and clenching my pelvic floor. When I sit on the toilet, an amorphous blob drops from my body. Deep red; almost black. The size of a big and boneless fist.

***

The summer before I'm fourteen, my mother is forty-four. I've paid little attention to the number of times she lies down in a day. Or to the speed with which the bathroom trash fills with discarded pads and tampons wrapped tightly in toilet paper. Or even to the announcement that she's scheduled a surgery for the beginning of July, because my sister and I will be at camp.

While I'm rigging a CL14, while I maneuver it out from the dock, while I pump the rudder and ready the sails, a surgeon slices open my mother's abdomen, pulls back layers of muscle and tissue, removes her uterus and one of her ovaries.

In my thirties, when I interrogate her about this hysterectomy, she will say, "I just couldn't protect myself anymore!" She'll never mention the word *blood*. Never say, as I will come to experience, that she woke up too many times in the night, sheets bloodied and stained as though someone had been murdered.

That summer, though, I don't think much about the surgery, don't think about what she does with my brother as she convalesces, or how helpful my father, four years into a five-year affair, can possibly be. Instead, I cut out magazine pictures in the camp craft room, stick them onto construction paper and write in bubble letters: *Get Well Soon!* Then I go on to describe an elaborate camp game I played the night before, and wax poetic over a session of late-night star gazing, the velvet sky crammed with constellations.

When I return home, she's doing all her regular things—laundry, gardening, cooking, and even three days a week back to work. Several times I'm in the kitchen rummaging for snacks and I hear her on the phone speaking to one friend or another. "It's not like I'll need it anymore!" she says, again and again.

I begin to imagine her uterus discarded, like something once useful. A plastic bag say, emptied of its groceries, set adrift on one lake or another, heading towards the endless ocean.

***

By early August, my period has not showed up. Still in Northern Alberta, I convince myself the long daylight hours must've prolonged my cycle. Only a few days late and nothing to worry about until another full week goes by. Then the contract ends, and I drive with my new boyfriend to his parents' house just outside Edmonton. We sleep in the basement and I'm more tired than I've ever been. Truth swells and takes over: I've never been *this* late before. So, I take the morning after pill on the off chance that it'll work. I spend an entire night vomiting. No blood comes.

We leave for the coast and camp along the way. As we approach Victoria, shame slinks around the edges of my awareness. I feel stupid. Caught out by my own body. I *knew* this could happen, but I didn't fully believe it. "Let's not say anything to anyone," I tell my boyfriend. "Not yet."

Back on the Island, I uphold my status of the newly-in-love—with my friends, my boyfriend, and even with myself. He's manically excited, and in those moments after mind-blowing sex, he says he's never felt this way before and he'll marry me if I want. Because I don't want to disappoint him, don't want him to love me less, I don't suggest an abortion. Instead, I pray for miscarriage, for my body to bleed.

***

When I go to my doctor about the heavy bleeding and low iron scores, she suggests an ablation and an IUD. The ablation's a simple procedure, she says, a day surgery involving anesthesia and a heated balloon. The balloon is inserted through the vagina and inflated to cauterize the uterine walls. Then, because they might as well, they install an IUD to prevent the lining from rebuilding.

179

"Because you'll always be losing," she says. "Whatever iron you absorb. You'll always be in a deficit." She refers me to a gynecologist, though it'll take months to get in, and tells me life's too short to live with such low iron.

When I leave her office, I bawl. To undergo surgery, to cauterize my uterus, my *womb*, feels like betrayal, like I've failed my body and all my natural beliefs. Still, the supplements and diet changes, the herbs and yoga practices, haven't worked. My energy is depleted, dredged up from the marrow in my bones.

I call my mother. Since the only woman on the matrilineal line who's kept her uterus is my mother's younger sister, I ask when she finished menstruating. My mother tells me she'll confer with my aunt and let me know. Two hours later a text comes back: fifty-four.

Despair and anger swamp my heart. Both useless, I know, but several friends of mine have finished bleeding at fifty, and I've been expecting the same. "Ten more years," I say to my husband. "I can't."

So by the time I get into the gynecologist and he offers me a new drug that stops your period for six months, I accept. "It's a total game-changer," he says. "Bringing down the number of hysterectomies by the hundreds." After four months taking it, my iron levels restore, and I feel better. But at month six, I wake up with hot nerve pain running down my arms. For days, I cannot sleep. I go to the walk-in clinic with the drug insert and the doctor there says my pain and the drug are unrelated. She suggests I'm depressed.

Over the next weeks, I see three alternative health practitioners who each, separately, believe my liver is responsible for the pain. I stop taking the drug and follow protocols to 'cool' the heat in my liver. My periods return, somewhat tempered, but the pain takes months to subside. A year later, I learn the drug has been recalled—too many women ended up needing a liver transplant.

***

The spring before I turn fifteen, the just-in-case menstrual pad at the bottom of my bag is flecked with granola bar crumbs and pencil shavings; it's stained with a garish blue in three places. Probably I will never have to use it. As other girls skip into the verdant field of womanhood, I'll become a freak frozen in a forever prepubescence.

Around mid-April, I return home after school. Four-thirty and my mother is already out of her work clothes and transferring clean plates from the dishwasher into the cupboard. She stops when she sees me, tells me she had to pick up my sister from school. I open the fridge for grape juice, pour myself a tall glass, sip and ask why. All I really want is to drop into the couch and fall under the spell of sitcoms—Happy Days and Three's Company. But my mother lowers her voice and attempts to gentle the news. My sister, not quite two years younger than me, started her period that afternoon. During gym class.

Grape juice sours and sticks in my throat. A cyclone twist through my chest. My sister. My *younger* sister—who gets better grades and wins athletic awards, who memorizes her piano pieces while I still plink mine out. My sister has now beat me even at *this*.

My rage towers—propels me upstairs and through the bathroom door. My sister, wet-haired and naked, half cowers and clutches the tub. "I don't want it!" she says. "I don't even want it!" Which feels like a deeper betrayal. "You want it? You want it? I'll give it to you."

***

After my son's birth, my period goes on a twenty-two-month hiatus. In its absence, things happen. The relationship with my boyfriend erodes and disintegrates. I move to another apartment and finish my degree. I befriend K, another single mom, and we become each other's lifeline. I sign up for welfare. Plus, I get a subsidized membership at the Y—where I put my son in childminding and start taking yoga classes.

In the classes, menstruating women lie over bolsters while everyone else turns upside down. It's the first time I've noticed the menstruating body treated with such care, and I almost wish I'd start bleeding again. Also, there's K, whose period returns when her daughter is nearly a year old. "My moon's back," she says. Images of a full and silvery moon spring to mind, and it takes me a moment to realize she's speaking about her monthly blood. I've never heard this expression and fall in love with it. The body attuned to earthly rhythms. The sacred sisterhood. The *moon*.

I read a book about natural fertility. I go to a naturopath who praises my commitment to breast-feeding and says nothing of my waifish weight. She advises I take a daily tablespoon of flax oil to balance my hormones and encourage my menses to return. Every spoonful makes me flinch, but I endure it until a wave of cramps come. I'm almost thrilled at the first sight of blood. Now I can start charting my cycles. Plot my basal body temperatures on a graph. Assess my cervical mucus. Now that I'm bleeding again, I can lie over bolsters in yoga class, and align my body with the phases of the moon.

But something else happens too. Impatience flares more easily than I remember. A deep hunger for sugar. My blood is thicker, more crimson. And gravity bears down on me—full force.

***

In my late forties, I rescind the term 'moontime' and call it bleeding. "I'm bleeding in earnest," I say to my husband, who has been witness to these menstrual runarounds. The months my body doubles down and bleeds twice, the months it lasts over twenty days, the months when I declare I want a hysterectomy, that I finally *get* my mother. These followed by the lighter months or the long stretches between bleeds when I'm convinced I've figured out the formula to bleeding less. "It must be the hibiscus tea," I'll tell him. "It must be the acupuncture. I'm nourishing my yin."

The truth is: I feel poorly counseled. In fact, it's often all my friends and I seem to talk about. "All I ever heard about were hot flashes," one friend says. "If it were only hot flashes. I could handle hot flashes." But it seems no woman, no wise grandmother ever took us aside and cautioned us of the myriad of other symptoms. The elusive sleep, for example. Or the potential monthly rise of sharp headaches and joint pain. The free-floating anxiety and the varying degree of depressions. The exhaustion. And the simple true fact that this world does not love or support the aging female body.

Part of me hopes my periods will end soon. For my fertility system to close shop. Part of me hopes that once my periods stop, I'll experience deep relief. No longer will I lose so much iron. No longer will I need afternoon naps.

Another part of me knows not to hope too hard.

***

Two months after my sister gets her period, a rusty stain appears in my underwear. A sense of elation. *Finally*. It's here.

My mother hugs me, congratulates me, then tells me to change the bathroom trash after my period ends. If left too long, my bloody pads will stink.

That night, as I lie in bed, a menstrual pad wedged between my legs, I feel anointed, initiated into that secret club of womanhood.

I believe in its magic and my own transformation.

I believe beautiful things await.

Scab

After Post Menopausal Spotting
—Cindy Veach

I go to the hospital for a look around—
to measure my lining and the walls

inside my walls. The technician tells me
to reach beneath the scant green sheet,

grab the baton, help guide her
then let go, let her drive—back and forth,

up and down, reaching
into my farthest reaches—

sacred space that held my kids
when they were just a speck

until they grew out of me.
It's quick, ten minutes—

done she says pulling out her instrument
plunging it into a bucket of blue disinfectant.

And now I see, really see, how we are
both entrance and exit.

How we take in, take in, take in
and then are cast off. Incorporate and are parted.

Swallow and are emptied. Suck in and are vacated.
Say *come in* and are departed. Accept and are left.

Open up and are forsaken. All that enters
leaves. The doorway without door. The verge.

Period

> *—Susan Ito*

Mother-Daughter Movie!! Saturday in the West Ridge Multi-Purpose Room—All 5th Grade Girls and Their Moms Invited!!! Exclamation points had exploded all over the pink mimeographed sheet. I handed it to my mother as we sat at the kitchen table eating our after-school snack. The white squiggle of frosting on my Hostess cupcake seemed to squirm as she scowled at the notice. Her metal stool was lower than the rest of our kitchen chairs, making her chin droop close to the table's edge. She hunched over, frowning at the paper, then reached into the neck of her blouse and yanked at her bra strap, a gesture that I hated.

"You know about all this, don't you?" She shook the flier at me.

"No." I stared down at the table, my cheeks burning. What was I supposed to know?

She barked out the words. "Something is going to happen, this year or maybe next. You're going to start bleeding."

Bleeding? The room started spinning. I hated blood. I stared at the Bank of New Jersey calendar, at her small slanting script marking my father's return home. If he wasn't traveling so much, I wouldn't have to bear this alone.

I sat on my hands, terrified. She went on, saying something about cycles, and this bleeding thing that would happen to me every month for the rest of my life. It reminded me of a word I just learned: *Hemophilia.* My tongue felt huge in my mouth. I picked up my hand and examined the unbroken skin between my fingers. I had never noticed any fifth or sixth grade girls breaking into uncontrollable bleeding. Why was it only girls who were invited to the movie? Did this happen to boys too?

"Do you mean—" I swallowed, hard, and the dry chocolate cake stuck in my throat—"That if I cut myself, I won't be able to stop bleeding?" I imagined tearing the wrappers off an entire tin of Band-Aids, that they would be absolutely futile, and I would end up drowning in a puddle of red. It seemed like a lie.

She blinked, startled. "No. Nothing like that."

Relief. "Then what IS it? Like throwing up? Like a bloody nose?" I had had one of those at camp. The nurse had given me a lump of ice wrapped in a brown paper towel, and I spent the morning walking around with my face tilted up toward the sky.

She shook her head, looking exasperated. "Enough silly questions. They'll explain it in the movie." She stood up suddenly, and the metal stool scraped the kitchen floor with a terrible grinding noise. Then she clattered down the basement stairs to the laundry room, and I heard the washing machine lid bang against the wall. Something about this movie, this blood thing, my questions, had sent her down to do angry laundry.

I didn't bring any of it up again.

On Saturday, the fifth graders from my Girl Scout troop sat near the front in one row: Jane, Shelly, me, and Theresa. The mothers sat together in the back. Girls throughout the room were giggling and calling out, "Where's the popcorn?" Then the janitor came in and twisted the window blinds shut with a long hook on a pole, then switched off the bank of light switches near the door, and the multi-purpose room went utterly black. We gasped in the darkness and a few sharp little shrieks shot up to the tall ceiling. Then the movie projector whirred to life, and the screen showed the movie title in swirling pink script: *The Menstruation Story*. The audience went suddenly silent, and I could see through the side of my glasses, a sea of wide-eyed, upturned faces. We watched as a cartoon girl's body transformed from a lollipop-head on a stick into an hourglass. She smiled with utter delight as her top half and her hips ballooned out. A soothing, hypnotic voice spoke over a curved picture of a uterus, the fringed Fallopian tubes. Fallopian, which sounded like "elope," another dangerous, fugitive word. It made me shiver.

The movie depicted a little cartoon baby growing upside-down in a pink uterus, which miraculously stretched to the size of a watermelon. Beside me, Shelly groaned and pressed her palms to the front of her jeans. *"No,"* she whispered. The movie reassured us that this would *only* happen when we were married, and ready to be mothers. When you are a young girl, and you are not ready for a baby, the nourishing blood just slips away.

So there was the blood. First, I had to digest the idea that unborn babies drank blood. That was horrifying enough. And then I watched the cartoon blood, flowing out of the uterus in a happy little river. And where was the uterus, again? And where did it come out? I suddenly clapped my knees together and blinked up at the screen.

I took a quick inventory of the girls around me. Janey was

smirking behind her hand. It was funny to her, somehow. Shelly looked bored, as if she'd known all about this for a hundred years. Theresa, at the end of our row, had her head between her knees in the don't-faint position. The girl next to her was patting her back in sympathy.

I peered back to where my mother was sitting. She was on the aisle, not watching the screen. There was something in her lap – what was it? And then I knew: she had taken a crossword puzzle booklet out of her purse and was squinting in the dim light, working the letters into their tiny squares with a pencil.

My mother had been married, ready for her baby, but that baby never came. She had told me over and over, how she and my father had waited for ten years. The explanation was that she couldn't *have* a baby, so they had to *get* one instead. I never truly understood the difference, not until now. I tried to imagine the pear-shaped organ deep in my mother's body, empty and dark like a prune.

The final credits. *Brought to you by Walt Disney and Kotex Corporation.* The movie rattled to its end, and the free end of the film flapped out of the projector, leaving a bright white square on the screen. The lights were switched on, the blinds were raised up, and we all blinked in the bright afternoon, a little stunned. Mrs. Crevier, the Girl Scout leader, stood up and passed out little booklets and Kotex sample boxes. My friends and I ripped them open, staring sickly at the narrow diaperish pads, the springy white elastic belts with their metal teeth.

"We have to wear these things for a whole *week?*" Shelly made a choking sound.

I tried to imagine it but couldn't. One week out of every month for how long? It felt like two hundred years.

All the mothers but mine huddled around the refreshment table, shaking their heads and laughing. They all seemed to be talking at once, and I caught pieces of their stories as they floated over our heads like confetti. *Curse. Aunt Rosie's Visit.* They were giggling in a way that made them seem suddenly very young.

My mother wasn't laughing or talking to anyone. She clutched a bulging paper napkin, filled with pink and white pinwheel cookies. One by one, I watched her eat them, practically without chewing. I dreaded the thought of watching her wolf down all the cookies until there weren't any left. Before I could do anything, she caught my glance and raised her hand, waving the flowered napkin. *Come on.* She jerked her head toward the door.

The ten-minute car ride home felt as if it took all night. She seemed to be grimly driving at a speed of about five miles an hour. She didn't say anything and neither did I. I huddled against the car window and carefully studied my "Very Personally Yours" booklet, with my name written on a sticker on the front cover. I inspected the science-book pictures, the smiling girl with the hourglass body, all the strange terms. When we got home, I stuffed the sample packet into my underwear drawer and we didn't mention it again.

The next day, Janey, Shelly, and I launched an intensive search in each of our homes, looking for hidden menstrual stash. In the dresser drawer of Shelly's older sister, we found a small box with individually wrapped cardboard tubes, strings dangling from their ends.

Shelly's voice was low and trembly. "You're not going to believe it. But my sister actually sticks these things up her... you know."

We blanched, shaking our heads. *Not us.* Shelly held up a pair of the big sister's underpants with her fingertips, and we could see the shadow of blood, a light-brown flower in the crotch. "It never comes out," she intoned ominously. "No matter how much you wash."

We discovered that Janey's mother used the same pads that we got at the movie, a big boxful shoved under the bathroom sink. There was a little yellow plastic bucket next to it, with a few smears of dried blood.

"Gross," we all hissed together. It was like the site of a human sacrifice.

My house was next. This was so great, like a strange, disgusting scavenger hunt. My mother was in the backyard garden, harvesting tomatoes into paper bags. She waved at us as we ran into the house from the driveway. Janey stood by the back window and kept watch while the rest of us raided my mother's bureau, the hall closet, bathroom cupboards. We found nothing. Tentatively, I lifted a pair of her large, silky underpants up to the light. They were spotless. We all looked at each other. Was it possible that she didn't Do It?

Shelly shrugged her shoulders. "That's why you're a*dopt*ed. My mother said your mom went and picked you out at an orphanage, because her body didn't work right."

My face twitched into a red scowl. "That's not..." but then my voice faded away into my throat. I really had nothing to say.

Shelly and Jane continued talking, their voices buzzing over me. Suddenly all they wanted to talk about were the stories they'd heard from their mothers, about pregnancy and childbirth.

"My mother gained like a hundred pounds when she was pregnant with me," boasted Janey.

"Really? Well, I was born feet first. That's why I'm so good at dancing." She gave a little shuffle-tap in her sneakers.

My knees felt all rubbery and I sat down hard on my parents' bed. I stared at the pressed flowers in the small gold frame on my mother's nightstand, counted each petal and tried to think what to do. Finally, I said, "We have Mallomars," and they followed me into the kitchen, and started talking about something else.

Several months later I woke up to find brownish-rust splotches in my underwear. Here it is, I said to myself. I took the Kotex sample box out of my drawer and unfurled the white elastic belt. I spread the instructions out on my bed and read carefully, threading the tails of the napkin through the little metal teeth. Teetering on one leg, I stepped into it. It felt strange and thick between my legs. I pulled on my underwear and then tried every pair of pants I owned. I was convinced that I could see little bumps and ridges in the mirror. I tried on a half dozen dresses and finally picked a plaid jumper because it was loose and hung far away from my body. I put on two extra pairs of panties and a thick pair of woolen tights, even though spring had nearly changed to summer and some kids had even begun wearing shorts to school.

At recess, I tried to run on the playground but the feeling between my legs was sticky and uncomfortable. I went into the bathroom and checked the pad. It was completely saturated, squishing with blood, and there were sickening stains all over my thighs, my underwear and my tights. I checked the inside of my jumper and was relieved to find it unmarked.

I went to the nurse's office and stood miserably in front of her desk.

"I've started my period. But I think something is wrong." I chewed on the inside of my cheek, tasting blood.

Her brows came together in a point above her nose. "Wrong how, dear?"

"The pad isn't working."

She let me go into her small private bathroom and gave me a

fresh sanitary napkin wrapped in paper. "Let me see the other one."

I passed it through the door on a bed of paper towels. She made a small noise and asked me when I'd last changed pads.

"It's the only one I have."

There was a long pause. Then she told me to put the new one in the belt. I met her in her office and she sat beside me on the gray vinyl couch. Her eyes were stormy blue behind her gold-rimmed glasses.

"Dear, is this your first period?"

I nodded. She told me then that I was going to need a lot more than one pad per period. "You'll go through a whole boxful each month."

"Oh."

She stood up and got two more pads from the cupboard. "These should last you until you get home. Then you'd better tell your mother."

I didn't want to tell my mother. I went home and washed the soiled underwear in water so hot it nearly scalded the skin from my hands. I used the last sanitary pad from the nurse that night, and then I constructed homemade bulky napkins out of toilet paper squares. The metal teeth on the belt tore right through them, so I taped them to my panties. They lasted about half an hour each before soaking through. By the end of the week, I was exhausted from the effort of hiding. I was tired of trying on a dozen outfits each morning, desperate to find the least revealing things I owned. I was anxious and fretful from washing my underwear in the bathtub as I took a bath in blistering water, leaving my skin lobster red from the waist down. Still, four pairs of panties were irrevocably stained, and I buried them in the trash underneath a chicken carcass.

During one bath, I heard the knob rattle from the other side. My heart clenched in my chest. My mother called in to me. "What's taking so long?"

"Nothing. I'm washing my hair." And then dunked my head underwater.

When I emerged pink on the other side, my wet underwear stuffed into a ball in my bathrobe pocket, she was standing in the hall. "I don't like it when you lock the door."

"Why not?" I made a face.

"Something could happen to you, and I wouldn't be able to get in." She was peering at me with a funny look.

"I'm not going to drown in the bathtub." I pushed past her into my room.

On the sixth night, the bleeding faded into a faint trickle. I lay in my bed and listened to my mother shuffling cards in her bedroom. She was playing solitaire, which she did every night when my father was traveling. Sometimes I would wake at three or four in the morning and hear the quiet whirr and slap of the cards on the chenille spread. I told myself that next time it happened, I would be brave. I would tell her. I would ask her to buy me a box of pads.

I thought about the cartoon baby, smiling and upside down, in the movie. I thought about that odd saying that had never made sense to me before, "Blood is thicker than water." I understood now that real babies came from blood. They thickened inside that dark red pear; they grew arms and legs and a heart. My mother had no blood for growing babies. She was clean as a whistle. Where, then, was I from? I fell asleep, dreaming that I was in a small wooden boat, adrift on a vast blue ocean. There was a mermaid, deep underneath the water, longing for a baby that had crawled onto land. I turned over in my bed like a fish and tasted the salt water wet on my face.

Getting It
> —*Judy Kronenfeld*

We girls were given the Kotex
brochures in fifth-grade Hygiene,
with instructions to deliver them
to our mothers. Mine disappeared
once in my mother's hands. Not
a word was spoken—
if the pamphlet couldn't be found,
menarche might not happen. We knew
everything that mattered in it, anyway—
though the diagram of the Fallopian Tubes
like crab pincers with caches of stolen eggs
might have been news.

We'd read *The Diary of Anne Frank*
and mourned, but also longed
for the "sweet pain" of womanhood
she described. Oh, the intense competition
for membership in the secret sorority,
the fear of being among those
not yet hazed! Even the metal hooks—
which fastened the ends of the Kotex pads
to those ugly elastic belts—
that we heard dug into the tender
spot just above the butt cheeks,
seemed less like mortifiers
of the flesh, than a badge
and pledge of some power
not yet fully understood.

My mother choked back tears
when my visitor at last arrived,
and kissed me as if I'd won
an award. Dad sat close to me
in a chair, while I writhed on the couch—
cramp-shocked and soured
on "becoming a young lady"—
and told me tales of valiant sisters
and old girlfriends
who triumphed over it.

Epistle For J With Blood-Stained Sheets
—Kara Lewis

I'll tell you the strangest places I've gotten my period: At the Lawrence, Kansas St. Patrick's Day parade, in acting class while attempting a New Jersey accent, at the Georgia O'Keeffe Museum, when I was in your bed for the second time. In a college literature class, my professor informed us hair holds metaphor. Before they die, heroines revisit the sites of their scattered strands. Blood must be the same. In a scarlet vision of the future, you buy me Super Plus Tampax, you confess, *I'm so cool with period sex*, like a self-proclaimed savior of third-wave feminism. Every month, my body makes a bed and sheds through it. Before I die, you lie waiting on a thousand identical, red duvets, a towel arranged over each one. My mom gave me a towel and an orange coin purse the first time I bled. A vagina is also a *coin purse*, a *penis fly trap*, *magic crêpe*, a *sin flower*, like O'Keeffe paints. How did you talk about me with your bros after? My friends insist when you freaked, it was all PTSD, my ovaries an insurgency and every woman's body a war. Before you, a battle raged between my legs for boys to win. Boys want blood on their sheets because *capitulate* and *copulate* sound the same. Show me a sword and I will feign breathless surrender. I wasn't a virgin, but you said I sounded innocent. I loved you guiltless, guileless. My phone died on our first date and I joked you could kill me. When I try to tell a joke, it always lands too close. We sat on your couch and you taught me horror trivia, how in *Psycho*, the killer stabbed a casaba melon because it sounded like skin. We were always an almost ripened, yellow thing to anticipate, then throw away. I tapped my fimbriae to your forehead to hear the hollow echo. After the dominant follicle grows to its staggering diameter, all the others just wither. That's what love after you is like — adult and luteal.

Firsts
        —*Marty Head*

i get
my first
period on
the way
to church

a testament
to how
godless my
body is
to become

First Blood
> *—Anne-Marie Oomen*

First time it came, I asked to play outfield,
afraid someone would see my crotch
if I squatted to catch, my position,

but in the open stretch of right field,
no one would see if I turned away to push
into place the wad of TP—my mom

had used up the pads—what we had
before tampons were common, so when
my *first blood*—what she called it—

finally came—long awaited, anticipated,
I had nothing to catch the flow, nothing
but folded tissue. In dust and heat,

it could not be helped; a slow stream
seeped into grasses beaten down
with wind and waiting, and as

the dark rivulet stained right field,
that pop-up fly arched up and high
but because I could not stretch for it,

thunked behind me in the dust. We missed
the easy out and lost the game. Did
my blood help the grasses grow? No,

what happened is that I felt alone,
separate from my team,
found I could not bear the shame,

and so left the field, left the tall reach
for that high ball, left all the girls
to wash myself and call home.

It would take me years to overcome
the muff, to catch a different fly,
to find my pride, to understand flow

was not blood, nor even that lost
all-girl team, but the way we stand
and let it come, water deserts, know our power.

Tested, or Infertility
     —Kelly Grace Thomas

I beg my body
for an answer. 28 days
of silence. The blood
tiptoes out of me. I wait in rooms
to enter more rooms. Charted. Tested.
If I write about it,
does it make it true?
Made my fear, gotta
sleep in it. Give birth
to locked doors.
Panic for a uterus.

         ***

At a writing retreat, over porchtalk
and Cabernet. I ask the other women
how they learned
their bodies. The silence, answer
enough. Together we trade
hard lessons. The midnight rain heavy
on every leaf. This shame we keep
in our pockets. Who can teach us what
we carry? Our apologies rolled
in toilet paper, in hotel trash cans and staff
meetings. These last few years
I chased deadlines instead of
toddler feet. Blame bricked me
here. Can't overachieve
biology. And now the risk
of *over 35*. The doctor says.
Staring at my ugly, ugly
ambition.

     ***

What if the blood stops coming
home? Science needs no applause.
In the restaurant a lady
coos the names of her children
soft as lavender. The man
reaches across the conversation
to prove what he's made.

***

I come from a handmade matriarchy,
still they altar what's absent.
The husband that left
like landscape. The uncles mean
as the wind. And now my mother looks
to me. The only one
still married. *Give kindness
an heir* she begs. Prays *pregnant*
during dinner table grace.

***

Dear something,
tell me what I owe.
I tend this plot
of empty labor.
Places I dug inside myself
for seed. A gust inside
a bankrupt girl. Lonely
window. Childless city.

Done with That
  —J. Lois Diamond

What do I do with
my tampons now
that it seemed to have stopped?
sell them at rest stops
dump them like confetti above the
menstruators at
Zucotti Park
turn them into drones and
target the Taliban
or plant them in the
window box I never had and
wait for a mulberry bush to bloom?

Kintsugi (Year of the Cervix)
—Nikki Marrone

To get to the clinic we must walk through the maternity ward.
My mother, baby, and me.
Past the place where she was born,
Only half a year ago.

Birth was a quiet affair-
A choir of singing water birthed by breath.
The midwife thanked me back,
Said she'd never had a cup of tea—
In the delivery room before.
Recovery was quick.
One stitch and a couple weeks of rest.
I've never been so proud,
My body chipped in china, lacquered up in gold.

Upstairs the nurse asks if I want a sheet to cover up,
I lay down laughing.
My dignity was left across the hall a while ago.
I'm used to being bare.
The surgeon places himself between my legs,
Electric intimacy.
My daughter pulls my mother's hair—
And sucks on packets of surgical swabs.
Handed to her like sweets.

I want to scream about duality.
Laugh at the absurdity of this irony.
This year my cervix can't catch a break,
From birth to being burnt.
I'm humbled by my body and how much it likes to grow.
To hold and to carry -
And how easily the blood can flow.

I have not been filled with gold trimmings,
Or cherished for my scars.
The years have not been kind,
To the chips in my soul,
Or the cracks in my heart.
To the babes that I have made.
Betrayed by my body,
Shame is a white sheet, stained deep ochre.
Memories processed and filtered red.
My womb is like a haunted house,
There're ghosts in there that like to scratch about.

It took four months to love myself again.
To touch myself tender,
In an art of resilience.
To remember that the whole world is made of cells -
And that CIN isn't sinful.
I'm learning kintsugi of the body is possible,
And that scars aren't just on the outside.
That blood is an ocean, a river, a raindrop,
A confluence of life and death.

It's on days like this that I am reminded,
That I am bigger than body gives me credit for.

When Your Flow is a Religious Affair:
My Menstrual Cycle as an Orthodox Jewess
—*Nina B. Lichtenstein*

It's possible that I know my vagina better than most other women know theirs, and it's not because I spend an unusual amount of time in there, but because for several years I observed a Jewish custom called *taharat ha-mishpacha*, or laws of family purity. This ancient tradition is one of the three pillars of the Jewish religious practice, which includes the observance of the Sabbath, adherence to kosher dietary laws, as well as abstaining from all forms of intimate relations during the time of menstruation.

A Jew by choice, I felt it was important for me to practice these rituals, because the more Jewish religious laws and traditions I took on in my daily life, the stronger I became anchored in my new Jewish identity. It was not the same for me as for my Jewish-born husband. He could eat bacon and go shopping all day on Saturday, and it would never compromise his Jewish identity and sense of cultural belonging. Rituals such as lighting Sabbath candles every Friday night, taking care never to use any dairy products when I prepared meals with meat in them, and abstaining from intimate relations —any sex at all, even touching — until my once-a-month immersion in a ritual bath that deemed me kosher again, were some of the cornerstones of my evolving Jewish identity.

The customary laws surrounding the practice of family purity do not just forbid sexual relations during the typical five to seven days of actual menstrual flow but extend another seven "clean" days after the bleeding and spotting ends. Of course, there are some very good reasons why this custom has remained such a pivotal part of the Jewish life and survival: not only does the time of abstinence typically end at the time of the month when the woman is the most likely to conceive (and by then both husband and wife are eager to re-unite), but it's believed that when couples develop ways to communicate and support each other in other ways than relying on physical intimacy, it will strengthen their marriage and partnership.

Nevertheless, my husband, who had not grown up religious, was not convinced when I suggested we should incorporate this observance into our marriage. I had to coax him to go along because it did mean a radical change from the sex-when-you-feel-like-it approach we had enjoyed in the early years of our courtship and marriage. Eventually he yielded because he saw that it was important to me. As if offering a consolation prize, I told him I was sure it would help prevent our sex-life from going stale.

Once a month, after my period ended and the requisite counting of "seven clean days" completed without incident, I would immerse in my Jewish community's *mikvah*, or ritual bath, as a ceremonial acknowledgment of spiritual and physical renewal, before resuming intimate activities with my husband. But, before I could make my appointment at the *mikvah*, I had to check myself internally for seven days after my period had ended, to make sure there was no spotting or bleeding. Special small and white cotton fabric swatches called *bedika* cloths are used for this purpose, that the mikvah lady attendant sold from a little wicker basket in the *mikvah* waiting room.

The instruction, printed on a piece of paper inside the packet, was to make an internal sweep of the vagina morning and night, and to inspect the cloth under a bright light for any discoloration. I had read and heard many stories from Jewish women who discovered both vaginal and cervical irregularities this way, and that lives were saved since early intervention had been possible. So, the ritual felt meaningful not only from a Jewish observance perspective, but from a point of view of sensibility of health and being comfortable with and understanding one's body.

For seven days, I draped the four by four square inch, white cotton cloth over my index finger and felt the soft walls of my vagina and the protruding uterus on top with its little dimpled opening under the tip of my probing digit. More than anything, this practice made me appreciate the elasticity of my body as eventually three, much larger than average baby boys passed through this channel.

As I carefully counted days and our physical reunion approached, I'd wink to my tolerant husband, "Only four more days, honey!" or "Just another two days!" I'd say, wiggling my eyebrows and flashing a complicit smile. However, one month, my years' long experience observing this ancient Jewish tradition was put to the test. I found myself in the middle of a delicate quandary or *sheyla*, involving my vagina and menstrual cycle, a rabbi, and his kindly wife. And that's not counting my husband who was patiently waiting in the wings for the return of our satisfying sex life and the gentle mannered older woman who was the *mikvah* attendant. This turned out to be a few too many people. I think what happened was a small trauma, if trauma can be measured in size.

The day it happens, I'm in my mid-thirties and we have three young sons, all born within four years of each other. Life is busy but good. I'm a stay-at-home mom, the CEO of the Lichtenstein Household.

My period is over, and I am tallying the seven days with no bleeding or spotting. I feel the urge at a visceral level to be intimate with my husband again, and when I shower I close my eyes and imagine how good it will be to have his hands running over my body. Lips, hands, breasts, legs, hips, and genitals tightly connected; our breath close and our union affirmed.

Two more days and I will call Judy the *mikvah* lady or *shomeret*, to make my appointment. After sunset on the seventh day, I'll make sure my hubby will be home with the kids as I scurry off in the dark (for discretion) to the non-descript white colonial on Main Street where the ritual bath with its small pool of running spring waters will symbolically render me "clean," again, for marital relations. Before I immerse in the *mikvah*, I plan to spend a good hour in one of the building's two full bathrooms, each with a door that opens to the small pool area. In the bathroom that is equipped with everything I need from Q-Tips to nail-polish remover, hair dryer and dental floss, I will soak in a warm bath, remove my make-up, clean and cut my toe and finger nails, brush and floss my teeth, and comb my long often knotted hair, making sure the teeth of the comb run smooth so that there are no obstacles preventing the water of the *mikvah* to reach and surround all parts of me, even every strand of hair. Once I am ready, I will ring a small buzzer-like bell mounted by the door in the bathroom, alerting the attendant to meet me pool-side. Before I descend the seven steps into the living waters, as they are often called, she will examine me, front and back, gently brushing her warm hands over my body to make sure no loose hairs remain, checking in between my fingers and toes for any hidden specs of lint.

One-two-three-four-five-six-seven; the water is warm and welcoming, the turquoise and beige tiled walls of the pool form a rectangular space not much larger than six feet by six feet, and once I stand on the bottom, the water reaches to just above my breasts. I've done it many times, yet each time I stand here is like the first; I feel vulnerable but safe, spiritually lifted, yet grounded in the practical steps of the ritual. I take an inhale and dunk under, bending my knees, simultaneously making sure my feet lift from the bottom and my head and hair are fully immersed. For a second or two, nothing touches me but the water in the *mikvah*, I am like an embryo floating and protected in amniotic fluid, ready to emerge into a new beginning. When I stand back up, Judy hands me a small cloth and I cover my head as I keep my hands crossed over my breasts, as if to ensure modesty.

"Blessed are You, Adonai, Ruler of the Universe, who has sanctified us with mitzvot and commanded us concerning immersion." I recite the blessing in Hebrew with my eyes closed. Then I immerse two more times.

"Kosher!" Judy exclaims. "Take your time to get out, sweetheart" she adds, knowing many women relish a few moments of quiet time to meditate or simply just be.

Like every time, I will emerge from the *mikvah* like a bride on her wedding night, blessed and eager to bring *kedusha* or holiness into the mundane of our everyday lives.

But wait a minute! Later that day, the fifth day of the seven clean days that I am counting, I notice a couple small brown specs, the size of lentils, in my panties. *Oh shit, say it isn't so.* I'm spotting. I check myself internally with the thin, delicate *bedikat* cloths to see if maybe it was just a fluke. But there is more. *Oy.* Oy is right. I call up the *mikvah* lady to ask her advice. She tells me to call the wife of the supervising rabbi, *the rebbitzen*, who will act as an intermediary to ensure anonymity between me and her husband, to ask him what I should do. I call her and as I hear her young children's voices in the background, she tells me that in order for her husband to make the appropriate ruling, he needs to see the spots. A wave of confusion mixed with mortification washes over me. I am asked to place the "evidence" in a zip lock bag in an envelope and drop it off after dark (again, for discretion) in their mailbox at their residence in our town.

I know this rabbi and his lovely wife. Their kids are in the same school as my kids. They have dedicated their lives to helping Jews observe Jewish traditions, and they both do it with kindness and wisdom. As I listen to the rabbi's wife giving me instructions, I sit in a time-worn red velvet wing back chair near the window in the den of our house, the door is closed. Far away I hear my children fighting and our two dogs barking, and everything feels so surreal that it seems the chair is levitating in the air. With me in it.

Outside the window, the birds flutter soundlessly in the overgrown rhododendron bushes whose green, leathery leaves press up against the beveled glass panes of the leaded windows of our house. I see their small yellow beaks open as they chirp eagerly – angrily? – at each other, negotiating who will have a turn next at the birdfeeder stuck to the window with suction cups.

My fingers feel prickly and numb and there's a buzzing in my ears. To be a bird right now and fly away. How liberating. My cheeks and neck flash hot and warm and I'm cold-sweating. I sit slumped in the hand-me-down chair, holding the phone against my pounding ear, imagining the rabbi examining up close the spots on my underpants.

Later that evening, the rabbi's wife calls me back. It's late and my kids are in bed, and my husband is still at work.

"So, my husband checked..." she begins gently. I take a deep breath and feel embarrassed again.

"Unfortunately, he says you will have to start counting the seven clean days again," she continues. "From the beginning."

The prickly sensation I had noticed during our first conversation earlier in the day returns, and it's as if I am not in my body, but outside of it. Shame and indignation fill both spaces, the ghost of me and the other me, weighing me down doubly.

"You are kidding?" I say and realize how stupid that sounds the second the words tumble out of my mouth.

"I am sorry," she says. "Are you normally regular?"

"Yes, like clockwork," I say, thinking how it will be possible to continue observing this *mitzvah* if this is how my body will behave.

"Well, hopefully, this is just a fluke," she says.

"I sure hope so," I answer, sounding more sarcastic than I intend. "Ok, thanks for your help. Good night," I say.

We hang up.

Feeling utterly flummoxed, I decide then and there that I will no longer observe the laws of family purity. I don't count the new seven days, and I don't go back to the mikvah again. But this decision also comes with regrets. I will come to miss my monthly pilgrimage to the white colonial on Maine Street, my quiet chats with Judy, and the excitement of returning home to my husband, both desired and desirous.

More than ten years later, when my husband and I decided to separate and I was moving out of our house, I discovered a packet of the little, white bedikat cloths in the bottom of a wicker box where I kept tampons and pads. I held the clear plastic Ziploc baggie in my hand, a delicate drawing of a rose decorating the front. With a sigh that sounded like it held the breath of generations of women, I tossed it into the trash. As I was about to turn to walk away, I paused for a split second and then reached in and pull the packet back out of the garbage can. I opened the lid of the wicker storage box and tucked the bedikat cloths back in with all my other feminine products. I wasn't ready to let go.

Today, it has been over twenty years since I stopped going to the mikvah. I am now post-menopausal and no longer have periods, so the "laws of family purity" would no longer need to be observed, even if I were to get married again. After my divorce, I eventually moved away from the town and state where we had raised our three sons and where I had lived for nearly thirty years. There, I had been deeply engaged in the Jewish community which also functioned as a protective wall around my identity as a Jewess. Leaving the place where I had done so much fostering of cultural roots, both spiritual and relational, has been both difficult and liberating. Although I'm still a practicing Jewess by most definitions, I no longer observe Judaism in the same strict way I used to in my younger days. Happily, it does not make me feel any less Jewish. I guess the Jewishness I was not born with has embedded itself over time in the fibers of my body and in the breath of my being, but deep down I know that it took all that to get here.

Warning Signs

—Toby Sturgeon Wilcher

It was early June, 1965. School had let out for the summer and the days were already hot. I would be turning nine later in the month. The year was not going well for my family. At the beginning of the year, my dad had the first of three heart attacks that would kill him within a month's time, leaving my mom to raise two sons and a daughter on her own. Sadly, it also left her hardened. I was the baby.

On this particular day, we had gotten too tired and too hot from whooping and hollering and running all morning, so we retired to the shade of the porch at my girlfriend's house across the street to play Barbies. I loved to play Barbies at Karen's because they had case after case full of handmade Barbie clothes and several Barbies and all her friends. I had a Midge doll with clumped and matted hair that I had found in someone's garbage can, but I made do. She was the trashy friend who was always getting knocked up. Sometimes Karen's big sister, Becky (and yes, their names really were Karen and Becky), played along with us.

Becky was of the ripening old age of 12, so you can imagine how much more knowledgeable in the ways of the world she was than we were. She was, after all, the one who showed us exactly how trashy ol' Midge kept getting knocked up. On this particular morning, I felt the sweat running down my legs, and my nether regions felt damper than usual. When Becky came out to join us, she took one look at me, pointed to my crotch, and said, "You started your period!" I looked in the direction of her pointer finger and saw the blossoming blood stain on my pink and white striped seersucker shorts and the tendrils of blood snaking down my legs. I screamed the blood-curdling scream of the damned. Becky said I must go and immediately tell my mom, and not to worry, she'd clean up the mess I made on their porch.

I ran across to my house where the only one available to share my horrible secret with was my 15-year-old brother. Knowledge of the female reproductive system was not his forte. In fact, I don't think he even had a forte or even a clue at that age. Mom was at work, so he said to call her. I couldn't. I just couldn't do that to her!

You see, most of us have heard about the Seven Deadly Sins; but from the time I learned to read, I knew about the SEVEN WARNING SIGNS OF CANCER! Thanks to a sticker from the American

Cancer Society that was stuck to the mirror on our medicine chest, I reviewed those seven signs every time I brushed my teeth. Number three on that list was "unusual bleeding or discharge." As far as I was concerned, what was happening to me definitely qualified for the No. 3 spot.

How could I tell Mom I was dying of cancer via phone? Me. Her precious baby girl. Dying of cancer just a few short months after she had lost her husband, father of her children, the love of her life. I could not make that phone call. So, my brother called her and told her I was bleeding from my cooch. Mom, who always swore she went through menopause in one day, the day Dad died, no longer kept feminine products around the house, so he was instructed to instruct me to take a bath and then put a towel between my legs. I spent the rest of the day curled up in bed, crying and thinking about my impending demise.

Later that afternoon, Mom came home and presented me with a turquoise colored box of Kotex and my very own personal sanitary belt. Picture a touching mother-daughter talk about all the ways my body was changing so that I was becoming a young woman with all the wonderful gifts a young woman has, and this is the part where the film breaks. The record screeches. The brakes squeal. Instead, what I got was, "Here. You'll need these once a month." With tears streaming down my face and my hysteria mounting, I tried to fling myself into her arms and apologize for having cancer and soon shuffling off this mortal coil too early. She grabbed me by my arms and said, "Oh, for the lick that killed dick! You are NOT dying."

Later, after reading the package insert, a habit I still practice these many years later, I taped two quarters to the order form (I always had quarters-my mother paid us a quarter every time we used a new word in context and fined us a dime every time we belched or farted. My brothers, who still think belching and farting are among the funniest things ever, never had two dimes to rub together when we were young), included a SASE and sent off for a booklet called, "Very Personally Yours," which sort of told me what I needed to know. That day, I swore that if I ever had a daughter, I would not be so mean to her when she got her period. And I wasn't.

Siren

And

—*Olivia Kingery*

I got my period
I say, *I've been waiting*
and worrying on it I say,
like my period is an expectant friend
who can't cross the creek soon enough,
and it's getting dark but they said
they would come and just as the light dips
low into the open mouths of trees,
the friend breaks through the horizon.

When I look down and a tiny blood clot
is dancing in toilet water, I say *oh no*
my blood clot didn't flush, and you are
working at a blister on your hand,
maybe with scissors or cuticle clippers
but definitely something sharp and I wonder
if it is as sharp as what is in me.

And I say, *how does that make you feel?*
and I'm talking about the blood clot
and not the blister and you know this,
and you say *like I'm glad it's not me*
and with full blistering pride, I say
I'm so glad it's me.

Monthly Torture
—*Claire Loader*

You joke and say we should never be trusted —
that anything that bleeds

for that long and doesn't die
could never be right. I imagine taking your flesh,

letting it hang by the weight
of its strange supremacy, slicing

the skin just so. We will see
after seven days

how much you should be trusted.
We will see if you have breath to jest.

That Summer the Blood was Almost
—Kelli Russell Agodon

too much, my period beginning
across the street from my mother's childhood
home, my family history staining

my A.Smile jeans, a family reunion
and for a while I felt shame,
felt *don't talk about this,*

and the boys I didn't want
to know, yet still I was pissed
how even menstruation included "men,"

a little older I walked through
the hallways of high school with a tampon
tucked behind my ear, unafraid

of what was happening below,
how my body was a marvel,
how you couldn't come at me—

I will bleed and live and you will bleed and die,
I said to a boy who tried to explain
how males were stronger,

each month the moon kept me
safe, each month I thanked God for the red,
knowing I could still walk into the world by myself.

Young Again
—*Andrea Askowitz*

One of my best friends called. We've known each other since we were 22. Now we're both 50. She said, "I'm freaking out. I need your support. I haven't gotten my period in two months."

I said, "Oh no. You're pregnant."

She said, "No. I'm starting menopause."

I said, "NO! *I'm* starting menopause!"

And then I listed my symptoms: Night sweats. Bad moods. Impatience. Anxiety. No sex drive. Overly sexed up. Hair's lost its sheen. Lack of focus. I can't remember shit.

She said, "We'll handle this." And then I was embarrassed because I remembered she was the one who called me for support. But she talked me down. "We'll get through this," she said. "What else can we do?"

I remember the first time. I was 13, two months shy of my 14th birthday. It was Tuesday, March 21, 1981. I was watching *Laverne & Shirley* when I got this vague, crampy feeling, like maybe I had to poo. I went to the bathroom and there was brown on my underwear. I thought I did poo. But then I couldn't figure out where the poo was coming from.

I showed my mom and she said, "That's your period." Then she gave me a pad the size of a submarine sandwich. For five days I walked around like a cowboy.

After third period, I took my backpack into the bathroom to change my pad. The pad was saturated. Red. And it smelled rotten, like guts and pennies.

I wrapped my pad in toilet paper and put it in the metal bin hanging next to the toilet paper on the stall wall. Finally, I knew what that metal bin was for.

I put on a new pad. It was hard to get it right. If I taped too high, blood could drip out the back. If I taped too low, the whole school would see the pad bulging from behind.

A few years later, my friend Robin said tampons would save me, but I couldn't find the hole. For an hour, she stood outside my bathroom and coached me through the door. I had a large box of tampons with cardboard applicators and a big tub of Vaseline. The instructions were open on the sink. There were two drawings: one of a woman crouching and another of a woman with one foot on the toilet. Her first and second fingers spread her labia. Lavender shading indicated the proper hole.

I went through half a box, trying both positions. Each time, I dipped the tampon into the Vaseline. My Vaseline had indentations the size of fingers.

After an hour, Robin opened the door. She pulled down her shorts and underwear, unwrapped a tampon, crouched down like in the diagram and without Vaseline, slid in a tampon. I was so impressed.

On my 23rd try, I got it.

I've had my period for 37 years and it's been a pretty good run. I've had cramps, but nothing debilitating. Though I've had some humiliating bleed-throughs.

According to the Centers for Disease Control and Prevention, women lose an average of three tablespoons of blood each period. For me, it's buckets. Three buckets.
I have a period to be proud of. My flow is so heavy, I can bleed through a tampon and a pad. More than once it happened in high school. One of my friends would say, "Um…" and I would want to die.

You needed a pass to get out of school, but I learned that if you walked to the parking lot with purpose, you could go home and change without anyone suspecting you of skipping. As I got older, I learned never to leave the house without a sweatshirt to wrap around in case of emergency.

What's cool is today attitudes around periods have changed. My fourteen-year-old daughter doesn't even consider humiliation. The other day, while we shopped for new sneakers, she bent over to show me her butt and asked me if she got her period. She hadn't, but she was wearing tiny white shorts, so I suggested she put on a pad just in case. She said, "Whatever, you'll tell me if you see blood."

So why do I love this bloody mess and why am I afraid to lose it? Because women are at our best when we're on our periods. I remember hearing that Chris Evert won Wimbledon while on her period. I think it was Chris Evert. I tried to Google "Wimbledon winner on period," but that information isn't easy to find. Whoever it was, Christ Evert, Steffi Graf, Martina Navratilova, I get it. I bet every winner of Wimbledon is on her period. I was always more powerful, more alert, better at tennis whenever I had my period.

But I'm not afraid I'll never win Wimbledon. And I'm only a little bit troubled by looking old. I don't mind the gray in my hair, but I don't like its lack of sheen. I don't like losing body functions, like that I can't get to that drop shot I could get to ten years ago, but those aren't my biggest fears.

I know from playing tennis that to be great at anything takes years of training. For the last twenty years, I've been training as a storyteller. I've written one book and got it published. But I've spent three years with another finished book and have not found a publisher.

I'm afraid I'm running out of time. Not time to garden and enjoy a cruise to Alaska, but time to think hard and well. I'm afraid that with less estrogen and progesterone coursing through my body, bathing my joints and soaking my brain, I won't be as smart.

No one disputes that a woman's hormones go haywire during perimenopause, the period leading up to menopause. And no one disputes that hormones are significantly lower after menopause. What is disputed is how these changes affect women.

According to Harvard Women's Health Watch, estrogen and progesterone fluctuations that accompany perimenopause can cause moodiness, lack of focus, and memory loss. Perimenopause can last up to ten years.

According to many articles, including one from *The Wall Street Journal*, spotty estrogen could mean spotty memory.

I know my thesis is problematic: I'm suggesting that older women don't think as well as younger women, a notion that could send women back to the kitchen. I know this is not true for some of our greatest thinkers and writers. There's Gloria Steinem, Alice Munro, Jane Goodall, Maya Angelou, Joyce Carol Oats, Ruth Bader Ginsburg, Toni Morrison, Hillary Clinton. There's my mom. I'm just afraid I'm not one of those women.

A few years ago, when my daughter was 11, on the verge of her own hormonal upheaval, she came into my room with bloodshot eyes. I motioned for her to sit on my bed. She said, "You forgot the name of the movie we saw last weekend."

That was true.

"And today, twice you forgot 'figurative language.'"

That was also true. I'd been helping her with an English assignment and couldn't remember the term "figurative." She was crying now. She tried to hold it back, I could tell, but sobs and tears broke through. She was no longer the little girl who cried freely.

She said, "I'm scared you have Alzheimer's."

I told her Alzheimer's strikes people who are much older. I told her Alzheimer's runs in families and that no one in ours has it. I told her, with confidence, that I didn't think I had Alzheimer's. I told her that my hormones were changing and probably affecting my memory.

How did I remember this whole conversation three years later? I didn't. I had written it down and found it in an old notebook.

So what do I do? Hang it up? Hope that my fear of losing my mind is all perimenopause-induced anxiety? Take hormone replacement therapy and risk breast or ovarian cancer? How do I age without freaking out that I'm losing my mind? I don't know.

Last night, while the family was eating dinner, I got this vague, crampy feeling, like maybe I had to poo. I went to the bathroom.

I came out of the bathroom with my arms held high. "I got my period," I said. "I'm young again!"

Bloodbath

—Alexis Rhone Fancher

blood when I fall asleep
blood when I wake
blood when I touch myself
blood where I ache
blood as a metaphor
blood as a lure
blood as a sacrifice
blood as the cure
blood on his penis
blood on my skin
blood on my pussy
when he sticks it in
blood when he kisses me
blood-bitten lips
blood when he fucks me
blood on my hips
blood on the sheets
blood on the spread
blood on my boyfriend's tongue
blood on his head
blood in my crevices
blood in my crack
blood on my new white jeans
blood on the back
blood on my lingerie
blood on his sleeves
blood when he finishes
blood when he leaves
blood in my panties
tossed on the floor
blood stains the nighttime
blood marks my door

**While PMS Binge-ing on Buffy The Vampire Slayer,
A Line from Episode 5, Season 5, Resonated With
What My Inner Aunt Flo Voice Likes to Say to Me
And Became a Sort-of Sonnet I Could Never
Find Anywhere to Submit. Except Once. *Bitch.***
—Juleigh Howard-Hobson

"Out for a walk. *Bitch.*"
Just go away. *Bitch.*
Fucking fuck off. *Bitch.*
Have a shit day. *Bitch.*
You make me sick. *Bitch*
Fuck you times two. *Bitch.*
Tell the whole world. *Bitch.*
Your point of view. *Bitch.*
You wrote a poem. *Bitch.*
Don't throw a fit. *Bitch.*
Hey what the fuck. *Bitch.*
Don't give me shit. *Bitch.*
Pick up a knife. *Bitch.*
I'll ruin your life. *Bitch.*

Black Bigender Blues
      —Mariah Ayscue

I sit here
bare chested.

Pink + Blue
Du Rag.

Red boxers.

On my period.
With the wings of this pad
taped all crooked.
Because it was never meant to fit.

my body
that is black.

my body
that is transgender

is vulnerable.
and never protected.

You see.

I have the
Black
bigender blues.

Because they
overturned
Roe v Wade.

And the validity
of my body
has been forgotten.

Or was it ever remembered?

I have the
Black
bigender blues.

Black
That is my skin.

bigender
meaning that
I am both
woman and man
simultaneously.
on the transgender spectrum.

And I have the blues because
the black is beautiful
and the pink blue white flags
that built my body
won't be protected
because it was never meant to fit into
your talks about reproductive rights.

I have the
Black
bigender blues.

Foster kids.
Adopted kids.
But, never birthing kids.

Because it is
Triggering
body dysmorphia
Triggering
gender dysphoria
Triggering
manic yellows
Triggering
depressive blues
Triggering
my bipolar disorder
that intensifies
with pregnancy

And what if the mood stabilizers
can't save me while the hormones
are ravaging my body?

What if it kills me?

I don't know.
But, I don't want to find out.

I know you say you're pro life
But, I don't want to die.

I have the
Black
Bigender blues.

And I don't need to explain why.
But, it needs to be said.

Because I should have
the freedom to choose
what happens with my body.

And I didn't choose
to be transgender.

I just am.

But you chose to forget
that men like me
can have abortions.

I have the
Black
bigender blues.
Because amidst this
overturn of
Roe v Wade

I am never woman enough to be considered a victim.

And never man enough to be
holding the coat hanger.

But, despite the validity of
my body being forgotten.

And your binary ideas of
what my body is supposed to be.

I am woman enough
and man enough
to be terrified.

How to Stem the Flow
        —*Laurel Radzieski*

Stuff the hole with cloth or cotton,
a Dixie cup that can be emptied
then rinsed. Insert orange rinds
(apply pressure) or dried herbs
(be gentle). Maybe try fine china,
a Ziploc bag, newspaper, wax.

Diva Poem
        —Freesia McKee

Corey has Donald Trump-themed toilet paper in her guest bathroom. It's a gag gift. She wants people to use it, but I must admit, the thought grosses me out. I have no desire for proximity to even his likeness. Donald Trump is famous. And isn't this what he's always wanted, his picture near thrones across America? Did he secretly think he'd never win? Each square's inscribed with the phrase "Countdown to 2020," a future we're hoping will change things for the first time. Corey and I are drinking white wine. Earlier, we climbed onto her roof to write poems as the sun sank past palm trees. I felt like a teenager. As an adult, sometimes independence still seems magical. It's completely flat on the roof; who knew? The Wisconsin roofs of my childhood were slanted for snow. Gravity always pulls down. I love being almost 30, though the voices of men sometimes seep through. I heard somewhere that DT thinks 28 is the perfect age for a woman, her *prime*, like a rib. How disgusting. Twenty-eight is the age I am now. In less than a month, I will climb another rung. Every age is the perfect age for a woman. In Corey's bathroom, I reached inside myself to pull out my Diva Cup—a name I've always found ridiculous, though not as bad as the word *pad*—to empty its crimson contents into the toilet. Without thinking, I grab several squares of Donald Trump's face—*Waiting for 2020*—as I squat over the bowl to catch every drop of blood. People who've bled know how to make special maneuvers. When DT's folded face turns red, I am still weirded out, wondering if the black dye is biodegradable, skeptical of whether they consider environmental concerns when designing gag gifts. Aging is lucky and magical. Someday, my period will be over for good, but not now at 28. The last male acquaintance who hugged me held on for a little too long. He was in his 60s. I love the Diva Cup because it's made of silicon and designed to be reused. I've read that in some prisons, menstruating people are forced to wash and reuse disposable pads because they're allowed only a few per period. Trans women prisoners are often locked up with men. Prison officials conduct strip searches to "assess" what parts people have under the seams of their pants. No prisons, no porcelain prisons, the bathroom as a gendered space with the president's face grinning up at the sitter, jeering into the back of the stander. Some states have laws about who can pee where, and some of the reverberating damage happens in high schools, like the West

Virginia principal on the news who told a student in the men's bathroom he wanted to watch him pee in a urinal to prove it. His gender, you know. The bathroom and the prison are sites of intentional violence and there should be no prisons, no stalls filled with DT's likeness except the one he himself occupies. No watching other people pee or bleed, no disposable pads soaked clear in the sink and hung up to dry like wet socks. No bloody mirage. My pink watercolor joins with all the others, through pipes and tanks and out to the sea when I step back out to join Corey in the living room. I am so free here: I can climb up a ladder even when I'm bleeding, walk openly from the bathroom to the kitchen to my notebook on the table next to a goblet of wine and a water glass, small ocean with ice cubes. Later, when I read Corey the lines about the man who wouldn't let go, she makes a sound initiating understanding. Neither of us wants to wait until 2020.

●

—*Danielle Bero*

I said no period
this month anyway
but still it came
and went
with grunts
and cramps
you uncrimped
the organs
with clots
of blood
from old
her's that
stopped off
at the bodega
and never bothered
to follow the crumbs
back to the
trap apartments
of harlems
& oaklands
& brooklyns & queens
& queens
I lay on
and into
who take it
and fight back
with a little
blood
I match
in my center
this month
I promised
I wouldn't
cry ugly

Cayenne

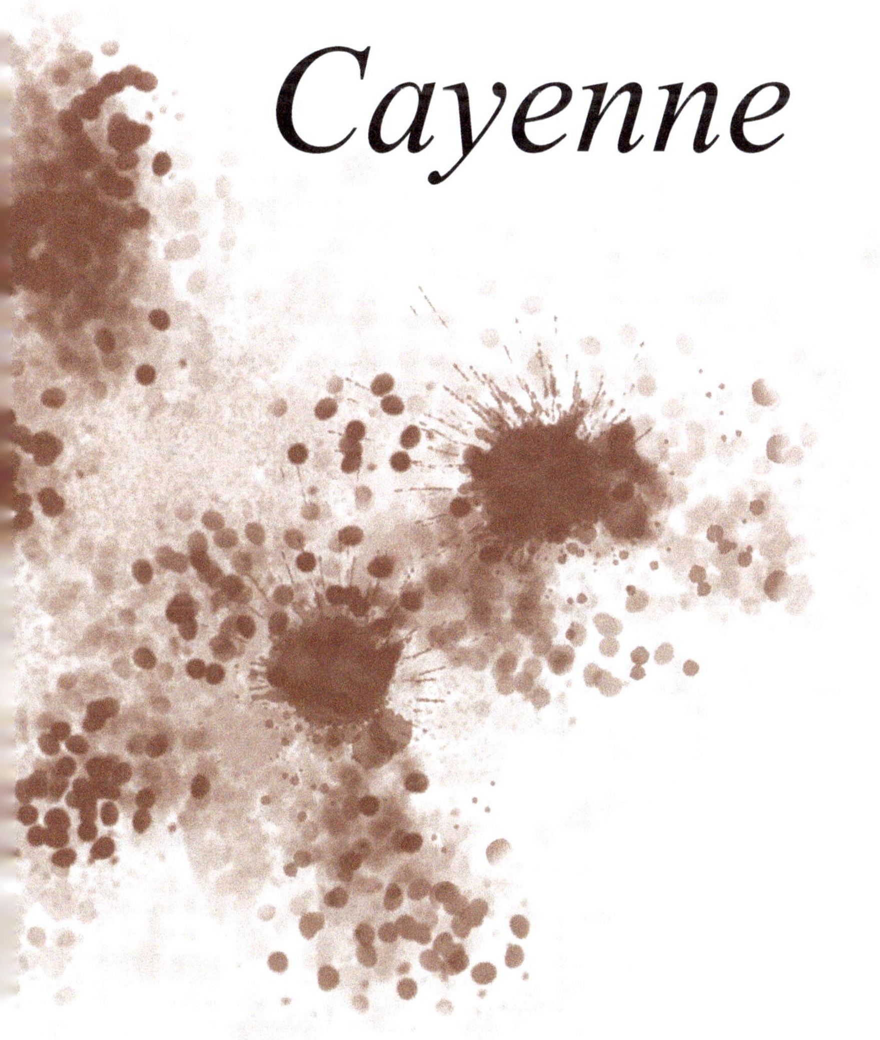

Witch, You Are Bleeding But You Don't Die
—Sarah Lilius

I remember the boys in high school that said, *don't trust something that bleeds for a week but doesn't die.* Scared boys become scared men who won't buy tampons in the middle of the day at CVS. I wonder how they're doing with wives full of children. Maybe I am a witch. Accuse me. Get out my cauldron that I keep in the garage. I'll add the herbs and a drop of blood. Stir it around until you call me woman. Call me history, ancient, someone as old as what my body does. Iron-scented, hoisted onto the wooden post, I am cleansed.

Supernova
>   —*Marti Mattia*

Just before your period stops
forever, you bleed and bleed
like a Red Giant

like Betelgeuse: climacteric,
luminous, wildly energetic
in hot decline.

Don't mourn. A dying crone-star doesn't
shyly draw the shade, doesn't blink out
like a switch. She brightens, bloats, spreads
sleeves of fire, licks the hospice dark
with mutant forking tongue, splits
the velvet curtain, spews
her shredded heart, rips off Orion's
arm and hurls it like a stick,
twists night to whitest day.

Below, on trembling, slow-turned earth, Oh!
how necks will crane! Oh, the billion waving hands.
Oh, the unfurled radium dreams as you,
the grand parade,
recede.

Scarlet
   —Chella Courington

Little Red Riding Hood
Runs through the woods
Happy I say
Celebrating I say
Decorated with red roses I say
Flo packs her bag
Falls off the roof
Sharks circle
Nile runs red
Noses bleed
Meralda has a nosebleed
Monkey has a nosebleed too
No sex I say
Playground's muddy
Ride the banana now
Drive the red car now
Slip me some lipstick
I need a tube now
Ruthie rotten crotch draws closer
I say good news
I say ride the rag
I say on the rag
O.T.R.
Bloody beast
Vampirito
Dragon time
Plague
PIP
Saint Menses I say
Ride the moon I say
Howl at the moon I say
Brown towel night
Black towel night

Bloody Mary
Hopping rabbits
Plum pudding
Cherry topping
Cotton candy
Drip drop
Dead rat
Damn curse
I say B. L. A. S. P.
Bleed like a stuck pig
Period.

To the Blood
      —Raegen Pietrucha

swirling in the toilet—
      a song to you
         in deep red ink spilling

      through sheets,
         acrobatic clots
            tumbling down a dark tunnel.

      To the brown bloom beginnings
         and ends, to the smell
            of the dead

      and what will rise again. To the counts
         of four and seven the women
            check with Xs

      by the moon, to the beat
         of the silent tune
            of animal lifetimes

      springing from their wombs.
         To the women, red-hot, burnt
            brown with desire,

      who house this power and say,
            "Yes, I will wait. Then, in one move,
               I will fashion the world."

In A School Full of Boys, Period.
        —Angela Gregory-Dribben

This is where I learned to wound like a woman,
in a military school full of boys.

To catch the blood and hide it away,
bury its shame in bleached chlorinated rayon.

Cloak its dog-calling guilt, its areola spreading, labia swelling,
hips swaying, a curse, a spell, a beckoning the boys in.

This is where I first learned to hold power alongside shame,
how to smile like I can't hear the whispers,

smile like I don't know how they will break me,
run just before they do.

This is where I learned not to leave the applicator in,
its length triggers a gag reflex, its plastic points pinch.

Its pinkness serves only as a reminder of the small girl still inside
meant to be discarded.

To bleed with purpose—capture life deep in my pelvis—to hold
a boy firmly within for a reason, for the family

my uterus will fail to create. Bleed as a woman, smell of iron, of
    wound,
to tear open a scab like clockwork,

set your watch by, marking of time and possibility passing.

Note: Hargrave Military Academy, located in Chatham, VA, accepted female cadets
from approximately 1979 to 2013.

The Only Red in the Room
    —Janalynn Bliss

The owner liked young men, boys
even, my companion told me of
the rich Frenchman who owned
the palatial Marrakech riad.
He was caretaker of the property
and took me to see it, keys in hand,
proud of an opulent place that was not
his, but was his for all those weeks
of the year when it stood waiting
for the man and his boys to return.

A large pool in the central courtyard,
palms and potted plants around it.
I tried to imagine the water they both
needed to exist in the scorching
desert sun, and I couldn't. A vast
kitchen, countless rooms, I tried
to imagine the hum of activity, busy
staff to bring it to life at the return
of the owner, and I couldn't.

We climbed stairs to the roof terrace,
sat close on an elaborately carved bench,
our quiet voices rising into the oppressive
heat of the August night. He kissed me
and spoke to me in Arabic and French,
marking a path on my neck with his
hot, soft mouth. I leaned back and saw
the stars glittering in the bowl of the sky.

On the pill that summer, I skipped
periods for months, so convenient
for traveling, and this unexpected affair.

In a room with ornate woodwork
and cool white plastered walls,
just one of many sumptuous guest rooms,
he laid me back on a high, soft bed.
My hot skin pressed against tiny mirrors
ensnared in the looping whorls
of embroidery on the sea-green coverlet.

His form was lithe, his skin smooth, and
I wanted to ask if the Frenchman had ever
had him, if that's why he had the job. But
I couldn't. He'd told me that he'd never
made love, claimed the only sex he'd ever had
was with a woman he had paid for the service.

She had taught him well, his patience
a contrast to his lack of experience. Or
was it the Frenchman who taught him
to hold back, to pleasure his partner?
Because he did, slowly, surely, tenderly.

The pill should've worked, but I'd been drinking
orange juice, fresh-pressed I thought,
but not—mixed with unfiltered water
my bowels could not hold. So, I shat
out the pills that should have delayed
my period, should have kept my cycles on
pause, should have left me bloodless, infertile.

Our thighs were slippery, his thrusting
had brought down my flow, bright
not dark, the only red in the room.
As we rose from the bed, magically
unmarked, still pristine, we entered a cobalt
and gold tiled shower and as he entered
me again, standing this time, blood gushed.

Sweat and slick juice from our sex mixed
with the red swirl around the drain, and
we grasped each other's wet bodies,
the Frenchman and the paid woman
forgotten. We were baptized in passion,
his first love-making a blood-rite.

Cult Classic
        —Anna Sandy Elrod

It never gets to me. Thick
gore, high-snaking score,

one cinematic sluice
of lightning or flickering

lighting. I have more
blood with the moon.

Dark as cherries in a tablespoon

of old chocolate syrup,
here is my first date

dress, featherweight, once bone
gray, now stuck to my thighs

and the nice upholstery
at this cafe.

I can't stop once I've started.

I turn this place into a scene.
I turn this place obscene.

In Defense of the Period Poem
      —Emily Perkovich

Tell me you're squeamish without saying
Lay down a towel first
Without saying
it smells funny
Without saying
That time of the month
Or
Anything that bleeds that long and doesn't die—
But
That's the problem, isn't it?

Anything that bleeds, anything that bleeds, anything that bleeds—

Tell me you're inferior without saying
you couldn't handle having to bleed,
And I'll keep wrapping this in sparkling bows
In sheer panties and clothes that you can imagine taking off
I'll paint my lips the color that scares you most
Because isn't fear so fucking charming?

Fear is a fucking luxury
And we don't have a choice in the matter
When the water crimsons
When the stomach clenches
When the clot sends us dizzy, light headed, bent at the waist
When the body rebels, miscalculates, ruins your whites
When the bleeding stops before we're ready
When the bleeding keeps coming even though we'll never be ready

When, when, when—

What, but art, knows how to elicit such discomfort?

Here's an artist's statement—
I'm done with
Reaching double fisted to stop the flow

Super Blood Wolf Moon
   —Raye Hendrix

I write a poem about the moon
& a man says:
   there are already too many poems
   about the moon

he confuses the cycles:
   menstrual
   lunar
believes all women bleed
when the moon is full

I tell him he's thinking of werewolves
   & he asks me
   if I'm sure

he tells me to consider the word:
   lunacy
its Latin root meaning *moon*

so how could we be sane?
   the hysterical moon
   is woman defined
by the man inside her

I write another poem about the moon
& a man says
   the old masters wrote her
   already

fuck the old masters, I tell him
the moon was never theirs

I am a menstruating werewolf
I will bleed with my mouth open
I will howl

Burgundy

all she needed was menstruation
>   —*Amy Bobeda*

confusing our blood with blood:

neglecting silicone cup for blade.

in the dream, the man punctures my uterus,

a knife through the door. I wake, fall back cramping.

Jesús murió por nuestros pecados, which always sounded like *pescados,*
filleting ourselves in original sin,
balance of red, unending,
la cruccifiction erased our need to bleed,
and yet she asks the sea of *red* continue–

so we bleed in streets, borders, neighbors gnawing our meat to return
her water to soil,
it must be misunderstanding–––

–––lost translation.

A Screaming, Bloody Mess: How I Learned to Be Loved on My Period

—Elena Aponte

I was Roberto Clemente the day I got my first period. As part of our year-end collective project, the fifth graders put on a wax museum to celebrate notable figures from history. Two of my friends were Elvis Presley and Sally Ride, respectively, but I asked to be Roberto Clemente because he was Puerto Rican royalty and I had not gone through ten years of my short Half-a-'Rican life without knowing who he was. I wore a ball cap and chewed gum, dressed in the approximation of a Pittsburg Pirates uniform, feeling bright and proud. My note cards were worn and sweaty in my hands. I'd memorized all my dates, all the names of my children, all of the steps that led me to hit 3000, the reason I was going to Nicaragua, why I had died. Yet, there wasn't anything that could have prepared me for this combination of events—spending the whole day embodying a man I had learned to admire and respect while battling my body's sudden assertion that I was now a woman.

What I remember most about this moment is pain, my little uterus now a clamping vice inside my body that made me run to the pink-tiled bathroom to investigate whether or not I was going to take the worst poop of my life. Instead, what I saw was the dark, rusty smudge of blood. Ten-years-old is young to have a period, but not as young as my sister, who was nine when she got hers. Mom and I had talked about this, that I might get my period sooner rather than later, but nothing prepared me for the shock of it being there. So, I did what any rational ten-year-old kid would do. I ignored it. I didn't understand the gravity of the situation until I was home, shed the armor that is Roberto Clemente and found a bright, horror film-red bloom of blood in my underwear. After confronting my mother, I started crying.

"Please," I said. "Don't tell Dad."

This moment is crystallized for me because it is the moment I understood, even as a little girl, that the men in my life would now find me disgusting and they would be unable to tell me why. I would be a screaming moody mess and thus, no longer knowable as a child. I would be instead, unfailingly, undeniably, a woman.

As I sat wearing my first pad, squirming around on the brick now affixed to my underwear (yes I used those awful pillowy ones until the winged pads won out as my preferred brand), I thought back to the videos we watched in Human Growth and Development class. All the mothers in those videos congratulated their uncertain daughters about becoming women. I thought about how we watched the same "learn about your bodily functions" video for the boys' side of the story and no one was sitting there congratulating them about an erection. I remember hearing the chorus of laughter through the classroom wall as the boys watched the video about menstruation. I felt slighted, sitting at home with ibuprofen pumping through me, wearing purple pajamas with sleeping puppies on them, hoping to feel like the woman I was promised I'd become.

I learned quickly that no one wanted to talk about having a period. I spent months paralyzed with fear that someone would see the bright green plastic of a pad sticking out of my backpack when I went to get one from my locker. I was terrified my friends wouldn't want to hang out with me because I could bleed. To my father, it wasn't my period, it was "are you on your...Thing?" I desperately tried to muffle the sound of opening a pad at home, lest my younger brother hear it and start asking questions. A few of my friends who didn't have a period yet would scoff at other girls who talked about having theirs, telling horrible stories about how someone's tampon fell out and you could see the stain on their white jeans.

It's bad enough to wake with a period, wake with blood on your sheets, blood that's probably ruined your underwear. And it not only fills you with self-loathing, but you realize you're unable to sit with your own body. It is alien somehow. Alien not only to you, now, but also to your friends who do not have a period, alien to your father who doesn't want you to be a woman, alien to the gym teachers who don't ask questions when you say you can't swim in the pool for obvious reasons. From the ages of ten until thirteen my period caused me so much anxiety I would wish like hell I'd never gotten one.

Eventually, though, I learned why people were so scared of it, why there were commercials of men looking ashamed when they bought pads or tampons for their girlfriends, why a women's shaving ad scandalized my father because they all trimmed little trees that covered the lower half of their bodies. It is the same fear that consumed me one hot summer day after my dog casually ingested a sanitary napkin I'd thrown away in the bathroom garbage. As Lexi stared at me teeth bared, hackles raised in a defiant mohawk as I begged her to let go of the remains, I realized this fear is twofold: not only has the dog consumed something that will either kill them or at least require a week's worth of vigilance each time they take a quivering shit in the yard, but they've also consumed your blood, your flesh, your body, and it's deeply unsettling.

That is why men are afraid of it, too—the unsettling knowledge of bodies as matter. A woman's body, especially, reminds us of birth and death and life. For many, it destroys a woman's body as an object of sexual desire. I think this is why the realization of having my period crushed me as a young girl: as I developed into a woman, men would start to notice me. Suddenly I not only had to deal with the pain of a changing body, but the knowledge that my body was suddenly attractive—unequivocally attractive, from what they made it sound like—and I didn't want that power.

It's so powerful in fact, that men have spent thousands of years trying to both control it and understand it. Once I learned that leading scientists in Ancient Greece believed a woman's uterus travelled around her body and caused various episodes of malaise, I realized how much men had no fucking clue what it was like to be a woman. And not only did they have no clue, they were also afraid.

As a teenage girl, punk rock found me. Though my parents encouraged me in my pursuit of writing of reading, and my mother was a powerful figure in my life, we were both still stymied by patriarchal constraints of familial expectations. I grew up in a household influenced—directly and indirectly—by Latino masculinity. Men weren't necessarily meant to be questioned. When punk music came along and gave me the tools to express myself, so too, did my desire to know my body and how to take up space using it. I loved how people were scared by the pictures of bloody Sid Vicious hanging up in my locker. I adored how women in this space could put on trappings of masculinity but also be completely feminine, like Debbie Harry or Patti Smith. I loved, loved, loved, being understood and seen and heard. I loved being angry.

Still, female rage wasn't even on my radar until I watched a documentary about the early punk groups of the 90s, hoping to hear snippets about Green Day. The most memorable part of this documentary, however, wasn't the coverage of Woodstock '94 (of which I knew quite a bit about already). It was Donita Sparks from L7, ripping out her bloody tampon to protest the way her band was being bullied on stage. I remember the grainy footage, the blurry form of Donita holding up her tampon (which was censored), a guitar strapped to her chest, thinking this was the most powerful, nastiest thing I'd ever seen. Nothing brings the deep-seated fears of men to the surface more than a bloody tampon. A woman bleeds. She does not exist for your enjoyment.

I've talked largely about my experiences as a cisgender woman, though I know for a fact there are women out there who have wanted to experience menstruation and are unable to, who conversely don't believe they need to menstruate to be women, and I completely agree. The experiences of all women differ, but we are united in the fact that our bodies are powerful as much as they are contested. For a long time, I believed that I would have to accept that men would always find this aspect of my life as a gross hindrance to their view of me as the perfect person. That said, I realized that some of the men in my life weren't really educated about the subject (or didn't grow up with sisters). A few were genuinely curious to learn about women's bodies and women's issues in general, and I was happy to tell them what I knew from my experience, pausing a few times to delight in their quiet horror as I described crippling pains and the heaviest flow before I went on birth control (you can't quite take that shock-value punk rocker out of me).

There's a recent moment about this very subject that I keep thinking about. It's a sort of simple one, really, but significant regardless. There's a feeling you have as a woman committed as you are to the cause that you're scared of falling in love with the wrong person, a person who might somehow usurp the power you've hoarded for yourself like a dragon who breathes white-hot feminist rage. What you may not expect is to be in a grocery store some day with the person you love and they casually ask you, while balancing boxes of popcorn, sour gummy worms, and fried chicken in their arms, if you'd like to keep a box of pads at their house. As if it is, and always has been, that easy. And, because they really do love you, because it isn't even an issue, because they love your body and everything about it, it *is* that easy. For me, who spent a sweaty, miserable afternoon pretending to be Roberto Clemente as a child simply to ignore that she had gotten her first period, I wish that moment for everyone. It feels good to be disgusting, angry, and feared, but it feels better to be loved, recognized, and treated like a normal person. My only regret is that it took me so long to find out what that feels like.

Gift for a Grown-Up Girl
—*Christina Myers*

I'm 11. My best friend has no breasts, and she's several inches shorter than me, her gymnast body small and boy-ish. She has curly hair and a cool older sister who asks if we want to try a cigarette one night during a sleepover (we do, and I pretend not to cough standing knee-deep in the prairie winter snow). Despite my best friend's lack of obvious girl parts, all the boys are dazzled by her. I try to learn her magic but can't.

I'm 11. I have these breasts I don't want to have. They stand out, literally yes, but figuratively too: I'm one of the only girls in a class of all boys, and taller than almost everyone. We're in a gifted program, and I am pretty sure I have landed in the wrong place, the least gifted of everyone. Except maybe in the category of growing. I spend a lot of time with my shoulders hunched forward, to hide my height and my chest.

I'm 11. My mom takes me to Sears to get a bra and my face is hot, my fingers tingle from squeezing them into fists. I block out most of the memory, but we find the right thing, somehow: a simple white training bra with a little pink rose between the cups-that-are-not-really-cups. I stuff it into my drawer when we get home and continue to wear tank tops and big sweaters.

I'm 11. I have a moss-green dress, with purple dotted pinstripes. It has puff sleeves, just like Anne's dress when she goes to the Christmas ball with Diana in Charlottetown. My mother made it for me, and she tells me the neckline is called a "sweetheart." I say sweetheart over and over in my head, my new favorite word.

I'm 11. I have fancy white shoes and soft green tights, a hand-me-down miracle. They match the dress *just right* and in a week I get to wear the whole outfit to a wedding. It's a second cousin twice removed, or some other kind of relation, who happens to have transplanted to the same province as my mother. I don't care whose wedding it is. I have a green dress with purple dotted pinstripes, puff sleeves, and a sweetheart neckline. I have shoes and tights that match. I am counting the minutes.

I'm 11. Wedding day. The house is full of relatives, and my three younger siblings. Enough noise to wake an elephant from a coma, but I sleep late and then wake with a jolt, sitting upright before my eyes are fully open. I feel strange. Warm and sore, like I have a fever maybe. I need to pee. I go to the bathroom and when I pull up my nightie and pull down my underpants, my heart stops. My breathing stops. Everything stops.

I'm 11. First thought: I had an accident. It's brown-red, like old bricks, like the dirt on Prince Edward Island where we went the summer a few years past. I'm too old for *this kind* of accident. I am horrified. Second thought: I'm dying. Something is wrong inside of me. I am sick and I am dying. I am horrified. Third thought: This is my period. My period just started. This is what a period must be like. I am horrified. Fourth thought: I need my mom. I need to call to her, from the upstairs bathroom, while she is busy wrangling relatives and loud children, and I need to make it sound urgent enough that she will come but not so urgent that it draws anyone else's attention. I am horrified.

I'm 11. Mom sorts me out. No problem, she says. She hands me a Kotex pad which is bigger than my arm, bigger than my thigh, bigger than my whole entire body it seems. She tells me how they used to have belts for these but now they stick right inside your underpants. It's much better this way, she tells me, upbeat like I just need to look at this situation the right way to understand how lucky I am. I want to cry but I also want to be brave – I don't know the word stoic yet but that's how I think I ought to be: stoic in the face of awful and unwanted new things. "Don't tell Dad," I say.

I'm 11. When I come down for breakfast, my aunts – in town for the wedding – are beaming at me. Here comes the little woman, someone says. I don't know where to look. I look at the wall. I look at my hands. I want to say: I'm not going to the wedding. But it's in another town, it's an all-day adventure, and though I'm old enough to babysit the neighbour children I know I will not get permission for this leave of absence.

I'm 11. I put on my green dress with purple dotted pinstripes. I puff up the sleeves, I tie the bow behind my back. I sit on the floor to pull on my tights, one foot at a time. I pull them up to my waist, and wiggle, feeling the unfamiliar bulk between my legs. I have to change it before I have an "accident," before there is a "leak." How long is that, exactly? I'm not sure.

I'm 11. We pile into the car, the boys have matching velvet bow ties on – one navy, one black. I sit in the back row of the van. I don't want to talk to anyone. Ever. We head south and I watch the flat land of southern Edmonton unrolling ahead of us. Eventually my Dad pulls off the highway and into the parking lot of a K-Mart. "Stay here," he says, as though there is anywhere to go.

I'm 11. My dad returns, bag in hand. He holds the package up over his head and hands it backwards to the next row, who in turn hand it back over their heads to me, a fireman's line of mystery. "Give this to your sister," he says. "It's a grown-up gift for a grown-up girl." Everyone looks at me—half of them with grins, half with confusion. I am on fire with humiliation.

I'm 11. I can see my dad watching in the rear-view mirror. Years later, I will remember this moment: he has made so many mistakes as a father, navigating foreign territory with a map that is damaged from the complicated and wounded life already behind him. But this day, he tries. He tries to know the right thing at the right time.

I'm 11. I open the bag. Inside is a box, and inside the box a brand-new cordless phone. A huge brick of a thing, with a long silver antenna that pulls out from the top. This is 1987: cordless phones are for movie stars, some futuristic technology from the penthouse apartments of rich people. But this one is mine. For me. For my room.

I'm 11. At the wedding, we dance and dance and dance. I'm a Solid Gold dancer. I'm Anne of Green Gables. I'm Margaret and I don't know if God is there but I feel like maybe it's possible. On Monday I will be the only girl with boobs in a classroom of boys who are smarter than me. I will be the best friend of the girl who dazzles them with magic. I will have to wear a pad to class and keep extras in my backpack. I will hide under my sweaters. But today, I dance with grown-up men who twirl me like a princess, and I almost don't even mind that it's possible to see the outline of my breasts through my green dress with a sweetheart neckline. There's a cordless phone in the backseat of the van, waiting for me.

The Drawing
     —Erin Wilson

Max Richter's synthesizer is using its blue notes
to rip apart the ten thousand pieces of the world
       into fragments of void,
while I pull away from the post office.

She has sent to me a pencil sketch of my body,
       made from memory.
I receive it on the day she is to lie on the white table,
       an open vault
to the doctor who will enter, plucking and probing.

There is a music to all of this, isn't there?

Today my own right side throbs with a white heat,
my panties speckling a Morse code that my doctor
will or won't understand,
       or will and it will be too late.
It's a naked draft of me, my face half enfolded in
darkness. Yes, half enfolded. And half bleeding out
       into starlight.

First There Was the Period
  —Karolina Zapal

The sentence had not come. That was a lie.
The sentence had come down to *woman*.

Then came the cramps that woke me
three times throughout the night, turned on

the fan, the light behind the heavy door,
the only door in my studio apartment

(the only wall protecting your dreams),
and sat me naked on the toilet watching

Shark Tank, while the white earbud wires
plugged my immovable skin to charge.

I typed out a text to a friend: *100% where
you were yesterday, unsure of what you felt:*

*whether you had cramps or were about to shit
or were only releasing a fart that would leave you*

*staring at the blue shampoo bottle as you tried
hard to breathe, breathe through the pain,*

but I deleted it because maybe we weren't
that close. Then came the other cramps

that bent me backwards forty degrees
in the passenger seat, pressed the crown

of my head against the leather, like rabbit pose
meant to evoke nostalgia for childhood

playfulness. 600mg Ibuprofen meant for
my wisdom teeth calmed the nursery

of my body, quieted it down before
it leaked like a silly roof, inattentive

to its duty as cover, so I went to shower,
first running my spotted panties under water

and hanging them on the sink to dry.
Then you walked in, wanting to brush

your teeth, so from behind the curtain
I joked, *Don't mind my underwear just hanging out.*

Then came silence I wanted
to bounce like a ball and the sweet

lampshade sheets that blocked it all out.
You turned to me, saying, *That was gross.*

I told you it was natural, and you replied,
Roadkill is natural.

                              It's still gross.

Then I had to say, *My vagina is not roadkill*
and swivel away like a spun-open door

before both of us backtracked,
apologizing for the underwear and blood

and for not liking the blood, for not fitting
the anatomy of our differences.

Raspberry
Tea

I, Chedipe

   —Cindy Veach

Hide and seek placenta—
gully washer, dream stopper
bleeding out
on cold tile—
and me
holding the clot
in both hands
saying *look*
I am undead
now I can suck the life
out of men.

Hymen

  —Erin Wilson

(I have entered into such a period of stasis and love with my children, such a low-lit and protected time that I dare not articulate too loudly for fear [for knowledge!], that we will, with a shudder, be violently delivered once again into astringent, brutal linear light. For now, we gather quietly in the red glow of late afternoon, which in early winter is darkness lit by familial warmth and lamps, something in the oven baking, something about to be cooked, stories floating all around us as desk-talk [homework, friends, pop culture], all the while the cat jumping up for affection between us. We are languor here together as though newly sewn again to womb, the heavy bulb of hymen, two beats before menarche cracks the door, peeks around the corner, and breaks the whole room — wide open — with movement.)

Surely, This Time
—Valerie Hunter

It is the spring of 1922 when Bertha realizes her monthlies have stopped. A baby? It's been so long—her youngest is eight—and she doesn't feel queasy like the other times, just tired and worn. She frets. Suppose it's not a baby? Suppose it's something wrong *down there*? It's this nagging fear that leads her to the doctor.

Once she's there, she wishes she hadn't come. Her English isn't the best, but even in German she doesn't have the words. After much stuttering and blushing, she simply asks if she might be in the family way.

She's not sure she understands his answer about the change women go through when they get older. Not because she's never heard of it before, but because she's only just turned forty, and surely that's not so old?

But she accepts his words. At least she's not dying.

A month passes, and another, and she knows the doctor was mistaken. It may have been awhile, but she still remembers how it feels to have a life inside.

She goes back to the doctor, and he confirms that yes, there's a baby, chuckling over his mistake as though it's humorous. It's not, but Bertha laughs with him anyway, because while the change is better than death, she guesses maybe a baby is better than the change.

Still, it's a shock. She had her first two children in less than three years after marrying Eb and had decided she didn't want to be one of those women (there were so many in the neighborhood) who always had a baby on her hip and a houseful of screams. So she'd asked around, speaking discreetly with a few older ladies she trusted, and she learned about herself in hushed whispers, how to listen to her body, how to know when it was safe to be intimate and when it wasn't. She had it down to such a science that she could even make Eb think it was all his idea. And though she did have a third child, three years after her second, one slip in eleven years' time seemed pretty good odds to her. Three children were manageable, especially now that they were half grown. She'd hate to be Mrs. Reilly next door with her seven, or Mrs. Giovinazzi down the street with—good heavens—nine!

Bertha has felt like an expert these past eight years with no baby, and now she can't figure out what she's done wrong; her body has played a trick on her. She accepts it, because what else can she do? Eb is pleased, even more so when it's a boy, as though the two sons they already have hadn't been enough for him and his "Sturm and Sons' Butcher Shop" sign. They'd named their first three children after relatives—Marius, Ida, Ulrich—but this new son Bertha names Gabriel, in hopes that he'll be angelic. He's not, particularly, but maybe he'll grow into it. Bertha gets used to the warm weight of him on her hip, and Ida dotes on him, convinced he is superior to any baby doll from the Sears Roebuck catalog.

Bertha's monthlies don't come back, which she knows is not uncommon; it takes a while, it always does. But still, Gabriel is nine months old now, and she feels more tired than when he was a squalling infant, and a little queasy.

She visits the doctor again. "Could I be...?"

He frowns his disapproval. "Mrs. Sturm, you've only just *had* a baby. It takes time for the body to recuperate from such things, especially at your age. Some women have a last baby right before the change, you know."

His words are a slap but she accepts them, because surely this time the change would be preferable to another baby. But her belly balloons again, and she knows, she knows. Or she thinks she does, anyhow.

She doesn't know it's twins until they arrive, two more boys. Their number of children doubled in less than two years, some terrible line crossed from manageable to unmanageable. If it had been just one, would she have been all right?

So much screaming—red, toothless mouths—so many nappies drying over the backs of the kitchen chairs on rainy days. Ida isn't enthralled anymore, though she'll still take Gabriel, leaving the twins to Bertha, her arms overflowing with them. She tells herself it will all be fine a few years from now, when they're older, out of nappies, but this doesn't help the day-to-day reality of now with three babies and the whirlwind of daily, mundane duties.

Her monthlies come back, erratic, just another annoyance in the long string her life has become. She turns away from Eb as much as she can, not having to feign exhaustion, but husbands have needs. She can't very well have him leaving her with a houseful of children. She may not be young or a looker anymore, but she knows how to do her wifely duty.

She's extra careful, so very, very careful to only ever give in to Eb at the exact right time of the month. But her body is nothing but tricks now, turned into something strange and unreliable, because here she is again, with her monthlies disappeared. She ignores it as long as possible—surely, this time it can't be true—but that doesn't keep her belly from swelling. She doesn't go to the doctor until she's five months along, and even then he doubts her, is shocked when he's wrong and she's right. At least the twins will be nearly eighteen months before this one is born, and maybe it'll finally be another girl.

It's not. A sixth boy. They've all begun to look the same, a blur of small, needy faces. She can remember the wonder with which she held Marius, her firstborn, all that limitless potential resting in her arms. She could look into his eyes forever and see a thousand futures, each one grander than the last.

When she looks at this baby, all she can manage to hope is that he'll sleep through the night and leave her in peace. He never seems to, though.

She puts Eb off indefinitely. He's looking gray and haggard now himself, no great catch. She doubts he can find someone younger and thinner and less tired to take her place. Really though, she doesn't care what he gets himself up to as long as he continues to bring money home.

But in a moment of weakness, she gives in to her need to be desirable. She's missed it, missed him, missed the one time she can feel like something other than a mother. Surely just this one slip is allowable, and she'll be all right.

She's not.

She doesn't see the doctor; there's no point. She's out of hope that she might be wrong and doesn't feel like being laughed at or pitied or stared at in disgust.

And then it's twins again.

Bertha imagines dying right there in the bed and leaving Eb to take care of them all. The fact that one of them is a girl does nothing to cheer her. It's too late to care.

After the first set of twins, she'd taken comfort in neighborhood gossip. Everyone had a story to tell about women having unexpected surprises, late babies, twins, and it made her feel less alone, less like a circus sideshow. But no one has a story for her now, not when she's forty-five with six babies in not quite five years. Now she *is* the story, a cautionary tale, a way to soothe someone else: "It could always be worse, you could be like Bertha Sturm."

She tells Eb outright that they are never having intimate relations again, and he looks abashed and strokes her hair in a way that he probably imagines is soothing but isn't. She can't be soothed, can't dream of a someday when there won't be nappies and snotty noses and hungry mouths because it is so far away.

Marius moves out west and Bertha can barely mourn; they need his bed. Ida marries young, and Bertha knows it's just to escape the house. She wants to tell her daughter how to listen to her body so she won't have a houseful of babies, but how can this advice be anything but a joke now? Ida will figure things out for herself, or she won't. Ulrich, the baby for so long, is the oldest at home. He goes by Ricky now, and Bertha barely sees him; when he's not with Eb at the butcher shop, he's running wild in the streets, a hooligan.

Years pass, as they do, and in the fall of 1932 her youngest two start school. Bertha sits down for what seems like the first time in ten years and contemplates that she will never have another baby. She's fifty years old. She tries to remember the last time she had her monthly, but she can't. It was irregular after the last twins, but she hadn't worried. Barring immaculate conception—and surely God would never be *that* cruel to her—there was no cause for concern.

She wishes, though, that there had been a little more fanfare, that she could point to an exact date to mark that passage of her life. It deserves a celebration. She figures better late than never and bakes a cake, tall and extravagant in these penny-pinching times. When the children come home from school and ask what the occasion is, she says, "Never you mind," and for once she cuts herself the biggest slice.

I Love You, But
—Allison Whittenberg

"How are you feeling?" she asked with a tentative air.

"Okay," I said, matching her tone.

"Are you ready?" she asked.

"For what?" I asked.

"My information," she said.

I nodded.

Denyce had a big smile as she continued teasing out the question. "Are you sure?"

"I guess," I said. Denyce had a way of creating what was known as a buzz. I had no idea what she was going to say.

She cleared her throat. "Okay. Here it is. You're pregnant."

"Come again?"

"You're –"

I cut it off before she could repeat it. "There's no way in the world I am."

"Are you telling me condoms don't break?" Denyce asked. "Or are you on the pill?"

A quick flash of the possibility went through my brain: the thought of having a border inside me stretching its limbs, kicking. Emerging after nine months and expecting me to push him or her in a stroller. I shook my head. "I am not pregnant. Where are you getting this from? I asked you about my period."

"And I looked it up."

"I didn't ask you to look it up. I asked you if something like that ever happened to you."

"Well, I must have misunderstood you because I looked it up and found out a period that is early is not a period period. It's a pregnancy." Again with the unplanned pregnancy? First from Sabine and now from Denyce.

"Who do I look like? Bristol Palin?"

Denyce looked at me deeply. "Before or after her plastic surgery?"

Under other circumstances that might have been hilarious but right then nothing was funny. "Denyce, you're way off on this one. It was a period period. Period. An early period or a late period is still a period, Denyce."

"Do you have Wi-Fi here?" she asked.

I gestured to the table in the far corner full of hands pecking away at their keyboards.

She pulled her laptop from her oversized bag. She made space before her by pushing the napkin dispenser to the side. After it loaded, she furiously typed away with her long, graceful fingers till she had an 'ahhhh' moment.

"Implantation bleeding," she said.

"I've never heard of that."

Denyce pointed to the screen. "It's right here."

"Implantation of what?"

Again, she smiled sweetly. "You're little bundle of joy, of course."

"Oh come on, Denyce." She flipped through the screen and read aloud. "Look, right here it says, 'a normal menstrual cycle can be anywhere between 21 and 34 days'."

"Okay. And?"

"So you said you just had one two weeks ago."

"What's the difference between every two weeks and every three weeks?"

"One week. Don't you see, Lizzy? You're using up all your eggs."

I didn't think hard with regret before saying, "That's okay."

"You say that now, but what about when you want to have a baby."

"According to you, Denyce, I'm already pregnant."

She closed her laptop.

"Maybe you ought to see a doctor."

"I'm not gonna make a fool out of myself walking into a doctor's office to say I think I'm pregnant because I'm --early."

She shook her head. "It's not a period, Lizzy."

"How do you know, Denyce?" I asked her.

"From what you said. Plus, you look a little flushed: that's a classic symptom."

"Everything is a classic symptom of pregnancy. That's why half the women of childbearing age walk around in a perpetual state of anxiety."

"Are your breasts tender?" Denyce asked.

"No!"

"I'm only trying to help."

"Thanks," I said. I glanced out of the glass wall. The sight of her hit me like a gust of cold air. "I don't believe this."

Denyce held my hand. "I know you don't, Lizzy, but these things happen."

Pregnancy Scare in the Pandemic
—Raye Hendrix

This time it was worse:
the failed prevention,
the late-coming
blood—or rather,
the absence of blood
where there should
have been blood—

because we made love
when any other night
we should have been
asleep, not sleeping
because of the sickness,
the absence of work,
the absence of work,
the abundance of time
trapped by an abundance
of walls, the absence
of open doors—

because what could we want
what could we need
more in isolation
than being together
in isolation, closed off
from the world
by sickness and
the absence of our sickness,
touching sunlight
through the window,
fingerprints on glass—

the bloodless panic,
no blood where
I should have seen
blood, the only doctors
left the doctors
who couldn't help me,
the only clinics open
not the kind of clinics
that I'd need—

the absence of sleep,
the absence of work,
the quarantine keeping
us in, or keeping
the sickness out, or
keeping the sickness in,
asymptomatic, or
keeping the potential
for morning sickness in—

the second week
of bloodless panic
in the third week
of pandemic,
the cruelest month,
isolated April,
the absence of coffee,
of liquor and eggs,
abortives that should
have been rationed
consumed in excess,
the abundance of fear—

then one night, suddenly
the midnight bleeding,
the late-coming
pain, or rather,
the failed unfailing
in excess, finally, the blood,
the abundance of blood,
the abundance of blood
where there should
have been blood,
blood even where
there should not
have been blood—

a wintering
        —jessamyn duckwall

for months now you've subsisted
on bitter bread, red wine, strong
sour yogurt. you bleed & bleed. why
don't you plug it up, keep the blood
in.   you should go gather
nettles, that should take care
of those moon holes on your face.
that ghost glow under your
skin. each day, prepare loose tea
in a heavy iron kettle—

like blood, tastes burnt.
your body is supposed to heal.
press soldier's wort to perineum.
a witch hazel bath,
you know. aren't you supposed
to exist on the moon, to spill forth
song from your navel, to light like
a breeze in the window.
no, no.   you're supposed to resist
the moon, staunch the milk light
falling from your womb.
in the cold, at night,
you take more tea for sleeping
& dreaming. it crosses your tongue,
that astringency, dries up
your mouth with its valediction,
burdens your throat with its hexes.

Don't Call Me Hormonal
—Eve Lyons

When my period is late
sometimes sex will nudge it along –

I call this *the intervention.*
My partner rolls her eyes

tells me how unsexy this is.
She's not wrong.

Sometimes sex is just procreation,
as queer people it's easy to forget this.

I spent most of my thirties taking
Chinese herbs and sitting

with tiny needles in my arms
hoping it would make me more fertile.

Cinnamon, I learned, is an ancient herb,
will help expel pathogens from your body.

In the end, it only made my period
more reliable.

Now that I parent an eight-year-old
who I never carried in my uterus

and my lining is still shedding,
but who knows for how long

I've come to resent that reliability
as well as the costochondritis.

How many centuries of modern medicine
and still doctors barely know

how women's bodies work.
A friend comes out as a man,

decades as a depressed butch lesbian
then menopause hit, he said *fuck this*,

decided he might as well transition –
he's never been happier.

Our hormones remain
as much a mystery to others

as they are to us.
Yet they determine so much:

Our deepest joys,
how and who we love,

when this blood that means we can create life
will come to an end.

Thirteen
> —*Ginny Lowe Connors*

Cake crumbs on the counter.
I have turned thirteen.
My skin is untouched, though zits
march across the faces of friends,
red hot, white-tipped complaints
they pinch, squeeze, dab with make-up
that conceals nothing.

In the last light of day, oak leaves
whirl down the street. Windows rattle.
Two streets over a blaring of sirens.

I have turned thirteen.
A new bra huddles in my top drawer,
strange contraption I'm supposed
to shake myself into. My mother says
why bother, I've hardly the need for it.
I've watched a friend walk into her new,
heavy-breasted life while boys punch
each other, leer at her, gesture.

Today the news is bigger than me, bigger
than any of us. A hurricane barrels our way.
Neighbors evacuate.

I have turned thirteen.
My friends bleed. Youngest in my class,
thin as the pause between lightning
and thunder, I am still waiting
for the changes I dread, I long for.
The lights blink off, blink on, off.

My mother sets a box of matches
on the table, three kerosene lanterns,
a thermos full of coffee.

Sis chatters nervously, swaying left,

then right, twisting her fingers.
Not me. I have turned thirteen.
But my innards cramp just a little
as my mother says we can't run from it,
the whirlwind hurling toward us,
trees falling in its wake.

Sentenced

   —Jessica Hudson

> *O, train me not, sweet mermaid, with thy note,*
> *To drown me in thy sister's flood of tears.*
> *Sing, siren, for thyself, and I will dote...*[1]

Hans should have written a sequel about an unnamed daughter of the air who aches for a body but eventually learns to love her insubstantiality and inhabit her translucency with joy. She'd learn to love the wind for its strength and buoyancy. She would have become an example to little girls around the world, telling them to forget about their bodies and embrace their breath, the ins and outs of their very beings.

The one thing they never mention is how itchy they are. We never see her treading beside her kelp bed at the end of a long day. We never see the mermaid after she drops her conches to the coral carpet. We never see her scratching her weary boobs.

> *Write your self. Your body must be heard.*[2]

After Gram and Grampa left in their big black boat of a Cadillac after a week's visit one summer, we found one of Gram's long creamsicle-colored fake nails on the carpet like a shed scale, white remnants of glue hardened to the curved inside.

I don't remember the color I chose or what we did after. I was a young girl, my sister eight years older than me. I only remember the singing of my cuticles as the manicurist pushed them farther ashore than they'd ever thought possible. I didn't know if it was supposed to hurt, so I didn't tell my sister.

Of all the pains, our fingernails bear some of the most precise: hangnails, torn cuticles, cut-too-low. My sister caught her thumbnail on the needle of her sewing machine in her Home-Ec class in high school. Our scales aren't as thick as we let ourselves believe. Just one piece of metal, sharp as a fishhook, and we are in pieces.

----

[1] William Shakespeare, *Comedy of Errors*

[2] Hélène Cixous, "The Laugh of the Medusa"

I had to cry and it was hard because
you can't cry when it doesn't hurt. [3]

In college, my roommate fell in love with Payne's Grey, a shade of blue that evokes sudden rainstorms and steaming London Fogs. We decided to code our days, calling our blue-but-not-sad, I'm-just-here days Payne's Grey Days. They colored me about once a month.

...a garden of red flowers...flowing blood...
knife-like pain...All of these images indicate that
the mermaid must be a menstruating adult before
she will be given a chance to realize her love...[4]

Carefree

That powdery smell of the narrow right-hand drawer stocked with pink squares, the folded white liners lying quiet and dry within, shushing each other when she draws one out, flicks open the lightly-sealed edges with salmon-polished nails, peels the slick covering off the sticky side. How tired her fingertips must be of that sticky side, the calloused pads of a mother's fingers laying the fresh liner on her underwear as she looks up at me, asks *what should we have for dinner tonight*, her hands moving by instinct against the pastel fabric.

Always

Before I know when it will come, before I have a smartphone and an app with a pink flower thumbnail, before I learn to save an extra in my dresser for emergencies, before I can even think of saying the word to my dad without turning red—I wilt on the toilet and wait for him to return from the store, budding chest folded over my thighs, menses dripping out of me like drops of dew slipping off a petal. Brave man, my mom says as she opens the new box and hands me a pad, its wings tucked inside the purple plastic lining. My petals ache.

Pearl

Every month a cavern opens wide within me and its walls echo: a buried pain cups bloody hands around its mouth and cries a hello! that ricochets off the insides of me for days. In the high school gym

---

[3] Zoé Auclair, behind-the-scenes featurette, *Innocence* (dir. Lucile Hadzihalilovic)

[4] Roberta Trites, "Disney's Sub/version of Andersen's *The Little Mermaid*"

285

bathroom, I reach for the string and it's not there. A bullet of cotton rappelled and fell within me. All I have to do is reach inside, yet even alone in a row of empty cubicles, I'm embarrassed to enter that dark space. Moving quickly, my blind fingers grasp the slippery tampon and retreat to fresh air, the white string dyed, dripping.

Thinx

The first time I visit my husband's family in Texas, I pack a pair of thick black underwear, the waistline topped with lace, expecting another sentence to end there. The park is hot and bright. We grin sunglassed smiles into his Canon. My black padded underwear sticks to my sweaty thighs, gorged but not leaking. During lunch at Pappadeaux, the girl at the table next to us dashes to the bathroom, caught off-guard by her own punctuation, the white plastic cushion on her chair covered in jean-brushed swirls of red.

L.

I awake to another statement pouring out of me: familiar cinching below my abdomen, the ruby corset I wear every month. I pad to the bathroom to protect my underwear for the rest of the night. Back in bed, curled like a conch, I hear her insistent whimper. The private tightness in my pelvis feels like the hand of a drowsy infant unconsciously squeezing my thumb like a lifeline tossed into dreamland. I hug my knees closer and picture her fingernails, soft and transparent like the wings of the giant lunar moth.

Saalt

When I was young, if I could have had a small cup and spoon, like the ones used for soft-boiled eggs, I would have been satisfied with those tongue-ringing crystals, so tiny, yet strong enough to balance their shaker tilted up on its bottom edge. When I pour out the little pink cup, I wonder how big this egg was, so tiny, yet strong enough to shake loose these garnets and rattle them out of me. Would those salt crystals seem like mansions to it?

Flex

There's not much room to grow now. What fits will fit, what flirts will flirt, what's still will stay. Only my fingernails and hair continue to change daily. When I flex my arms, nothing changes, yet I can flex inside and release an entire sentence, period and all. Flex again, pulling in, and the door closes, the disc sealed inside, propped against my bones.

U.
The shiny box of ultra-thin liners heralds the goal: barely there. Barely there when I'm wearing another product inside me, be it bullet, cup, or disc. Barely there yet enough to count the days. Barely there to catch the last faint drops, more rusty than ruby by then.

> *Our glances, our smiles, are spent; laughs exude*
> *from all our mouths, our blood flows and we extend*
> *ourselves without ever reaching an end; we never*
> *hold back our thoughts, our signs, our writing;*
> *and we're not afraid of lacking.*[5]

Is something still there even when it's swallowed by an ocean of itself? Are tears still tears under the sea?

Another college roommate and I decided to watch all of the Disney princess movies chronologically. When it came time for The Little Mermaid, she told me her mother could sing just like Jodi Benson, then proceeded to belt out Ariel's wish song like she was her mother reincarnated, a bit too loud but right on pitch. We shared a room for sixteen weeks. I never saw her cry.

> *I'm as soft-shelled out of water as in,*
> *but I'm trying not to be so out of my depth.*[6]

I had no problem learning scales on the piano when I was little, but I couldn't stand the repetition. At least my fingernails were always changing, always growing back after I bit them too low and they'd get hit by a four-square ball at recess and bleed. I think I've always known that change is the grace of a living body, its cycles, its scales.

---

[5] Hélène Cixous, "The Laugh of the Medusa"
[6] Nancy Carol Moody, "Mermaid Stops by True Value to Pick Up a Screwdriver"

What The Fibroids Said
—*Kristin Prevallet*

Sitting snuggly in my belly are seven fibroids,
and my body collapses around their weight.

The blood pours buckets from what is most open in me:
lost babies
          loneliness

                    beauty aging into wisdom...
                      but not without a fight.

The doctor's words lace surgical scissors into dire predictions;
she speaks sentences that are incised and drained—
she wants to cut them loose.

I seek out the witches.
They feed me nettles and red clover;
shepherd's purse, raspberry leaves, and wild yam.
They ask me to see my womb as a bowl filled with water
into which is blooming a singular flower.

They chant:

> *arch your back to the frequency rhythm pulse*
> *universal law of bell gong*
> *vibration perfection vibration*
> *arch back tongue out*
> *hhhhhhhhhhhhhhhaaaaa*
> *the divine unfolds that flower its roots*
> *absorb your blackblue blood*
> *into the core of the earth*

From the eye of the trance, the Goddess Sekhmet,
lion's head with human hands,
drinks wildly the fury of that blood
as it pours down my thighs and straight into her mouth.

Then, my fibroids,
the whole gaggle of them, start talking:

The first one cackles,

> *I hold the dead, those dear ones you cannot
> let go of, who are now taking up residence
> in your womb;*

The second cries,

> *I am carrying shards of rejection that you
> have wedged snuggly down here like
> slivers of glass hidden among grapes;*

The third is confident,   *I am bubbling your unexpressed anger into
a whirring pool for four, five, and six;*

And the seventh goes straight for my heart—
Finding it broken,
she sets about making a new one,
large as a cantaloupe,
that beats with the same pulse.

Sitting snuggly in my belly, seven fibroids hang
my body luminescent around their weight.

Clot

Seven Months Later
    —Chelsea Risley

She keeps a jar of fertilizer
beneath her bathroom sink –
nine parts water, one part
blood. As she douses her sweet
peppers and sunflowers, she
thinks of the little one that
slipped from her womb
when she wasn't looking.
Her peppercorn should have
been pineapple-sized by now.
She pours out her glistening red
disappointment, eager to grow at least
something from her emptiness.

Lochia
—Geula Geurts

discharge from the uterus after birth,
fr. Greek lokhus, an ambush, epithet of Artemis

After birth, the hunt begins.
Her hounds smell me, I swear.
Mucus, clots of blood, the inner dams of slime
& sludge fold out of me, a trembling heart,
the trail I leave behind.
My legs like deer anchoring down
in the mud, days, weeks
I wait for the dogs to collect me.
Under the cypress branches
I try to feed my fawn, her tongue
an arrow quivering through me.
How is my body still liquid?
A blank chase of moon,
another night rises.
They don't come, those mutts.
I am my daughter's prey.

Bloodwork
         —Emilia Phillips

This morning
my period arrives late
and sludgy. Ten years ago, I gave

birth to a bundle
of cells in the bathtub in the cement
block house—too early to have

known I was pregnant, too
young to feel relief. I carried
the miscarriage all night in gasps

between the tub and the mattress
we kept
on the floor. I buried

the sound of blanks
in my ear, some figurative
weapon raw

with desire. Whenever
I smell red
wine, I'm back on my knees

for communion, the church
always making me
think of sin, the position

my body found in the pew
after service while I listened to
my mother's footsteps

echo in the nave as she refilled the altar
vases with tap water

and then drank the rest of the consecrated

wine that couldn't be poured
down the drain. Yesterday,
without my glasses on, I saw a clothesline

from the car and saw prayer
flags. I want to belong
to some ritual of muscle, but not religion—

I'm genetically prone to high
hemoglobin, colonialism, and paranoid
depression with obsessive

tendencies. Somewhere in the dusty
filings of the state
of Tennessee are the names

of my mother's biological
parents: her mother unmarried,
her father already

with another family. Someday
I'll have to contend
with the fact that my body is a dead language

euphemized by razors
and denial. Tell me again why I should rise and dress
in the name of my father?

it darkens my jeans the color of red clay in a stream
        —*Kate LaDew*

and I tip the solo cup of dirty water onto my lap like it was planned
the self portrait blurs as the instructor of my sip and paint class
hurls paper towels like a president unsure of what country he's in
24 years since my first period and I'm still slinking away,
an emergency tampon up my sleeve, 75 cents in my pocket, a purse
        over my crotch
and a knifing pain inside that doubles me, hand on the bathroom stall,
head at my knees, eyes squeezed shut, sorry, sorry, sorry,
the human female's mantra even surrounded by women
in a place specifically designed for our kind
I blot at the stain with a toilet paper wrapped hand
wishing I could pinpoint the day like my sister always has
wishing I'd finished my glass of wine,
wishing I could walk back into a class I enjoy, a class I *paid* for
and shrug and point and laugh the way girls on podcasts tell me I
        should,
not certain, but relatively sure the laugh will be returned
because there is not one person here who doesn't understand
and knowing, instead, I will zip up my jeans, angle my purse,
only wash my hands if someone else is there
find my car and drive home with my hand under me,
hoping the polyester is dark enough to hide any stray blood.
as I stand and flush the red away from me my mother's voice is dark
        and deep
the way it always was when speaking of shameful things,
blending with my aunt's, my grandmother's, no one must see, not even
        god.
when I walk outside, wishing I could treat this the way other women do
wishing I could convince myself what I already know
wishing I could say the words menstrual cycle out loud
but mostly wishing I had a man to trace this humiliation back to
(the way I almost always can) I look up, where heaven must be, and
        figure, he'll do

Becoming a Young Lady: Theme and Variations
—Libby Falk Jones

I. You're a Young Lady Now, 1952

Men
   month
        (years)
   watery
     opening lower front
part
     -stru
blood leaves
     body (baby grow)
       men- period
(years) womb
   three to seven, opening
     spongy
       watery *men*
    a way
      front, lower
period body
lower front part
          three to seven
      men-stru
fluids month
   part/opening/flow
men- a way
      baby grow (years)
    organ
     -ate
        away
  word

II. Menstruation Is

a viable option for women today
at the heart of a major conflict
an unhealthy and unnecessary process

the last taboo
power
outdated and harmful

a very common problem affecting women travelers
dirty
a feminine issue

a defense against microbes that enter the uterus with incoming sperm
not something adults talk about among themselves very often
a momentous event in a girl's life

something women are supposed to be embarrassed about
not an illness
the destruction of tissue

a beautiful and divine thing
not such a condition that prevents a woman from performing
the most common gynecological complaint

termed as bleeding
a woman's rite of passage that signals her sexual maturity
house cleaning

III. In the Bathroom, 1954

I stand with Mama
by the wooden
cabinet, door open,
pink cardboard box
inside. I have read
the small booklet
Mama handed me
after school, pigtailed
girl in pedal pushers
smiling on the cover.

*You're a Young Lady
Now.*

Reaching into the box,
I finger a thick soft
white cotton pad.

How will I play
Capture the Flag
with *that*
between my legs?

IV. Menstruation Is a Flutist

of watery flypasts and a small analgesic
of blubber that leaves the bomb
a little at a tinkle
over a peroration of three to seven
deans. It comes from an original
called the valediction of wool
which is inside the luncheon parvenu
of your bomb. When you are married
and have a backlog, that is where
the backlog will grow.

V. Milestone

Thurs. September 25, 1958
Went to school.
In the aft. I went to Boosters.

Today I became a young lady.
I was sitting down in my slip
& I happened to look down
& I saw a red stain
all over my pants.

Besides that,
not much else new.

Bye!

VI. What They Said, 2011

Obsessing... surprised but excited... Left the periodless club... embarrassing... wanted my period soooooooooooooo bad... I stood up and did a little dance... I lied to all my friends... kinda scared/excited/freaked... worst pain ever!... i stuffed toilet paper... i was so nervous... i just about fainted...so grossed out... COVERED in blood soo nasty!... I was like what??!?!?!... "mom I think I got IT"... i was at church dressed in black (thank god) ... oh dang!!!... "arrghhghhhh"...white skirt with red polka dots... I literally screamed... I walked really strange for two days... staring at my butt... "what is that smell?"... so scared... i HATE it

VII. Hand-Me-Down

Once, she
forty-five,
me fourteen,
both surprised
by my new
period, my
mother gave me
her Kotex,
slightly spotted
with brown,
still body
warm.

Note: This seven-part poem explores cultural and personal experiences of
menstruation. "You're a Young Lady Now, 1952," plays with words from the first
page of the pamphlet of that title published by The Kotex Corporation (Chicago:
International Cellucotton Products Co., 1952). "Menstruation Is" is a selection of
Googlisms on menstruation, obtained in June 2020. "In the Bathroom, 1954"
"Milestone," and "Hand-Me-Down" are drawn from personal experience;
"Milestone" is a verbatim diary entry. "Menstruation is a Flutist" is an
N+15 variation on the beginning of the Kotex pamphlet. "What They Said, 2011" is
taken from "Period Talk" in *Girlspace* on the website of The Kotex Corporation,
where girls were invited to contribute their experiences and responses (the
website no longer includes this page).

Ode
      —Marty Head

I want to be excluded from the narrative of my body
this hallowed hollow set to a path I did not ask for
      nor ordain
Each month I grieve the fact of my potential,
the harsh seizures of pain that come in the form of
womanly blessings

Blessings indeed,
lo, a celebration of agony
the insides of me no longer belong to any kind of self,
rather an autonomous zone of aching

Aching is too subtle a word for the screaming spirals that
      rend through me
      bearing down and
out in stringy splatters,
The most delicate parts of me raw and strained under
pressure to expel ropes of gore

In the toilet, a latticework of blood,
thick chunks and gauzy swirls
My underside a rank jungle of rusty smears and
mats of hair

This is the chronicle I wish to dispel
Would that a curtain of sterility would descend on me,
fantasize about surgeries no doctor would perform

So rather, I perform body and gender,
dream of excusing myself from
this charade.

Wish Not < Want Not
  —Kellie Diodato

Last night my
self spread open.

I seized in pain,
and like a crazed

masochist I lingered
in the stick. Blood dribbled

down. Down and out, a dance,
a simple coveting, but one

horned and raging devil
hooked itself.

What kind of Lucifer
could coagulate;

would discolor the sky
birthed for itself

and slush upon my thigh?
The pain passed pleasure.

Left to loiter above the toilet seat
in a hinge, my fingers pulsing

the floor, the serpent kept spitting
a shellack, a reddish-brown finish

pungent of copper taunt
and poisoning, contorting until

I gave up on the thought of gravity.
He's my menace now, he

hums the familiar lullaby.
So go ahead, I'm listening to you.

The Other Woman
—Keily Blair

The story can start with blood. It can start with the knife running over my skin, drawing beads of it out from my body to quiet my thoughts. It can start with my teeth sinking into an ex-boyfriend in high school the moment he said he liked another girl. It can start with my hands throwing a chair across the room. Or maybe it can start with the blood, thick and red, flowing between my legs and pooling into the uncomfortable pads that coated my panties on each of those occasions.

That's the appropriate blood for this story, which begins with me sitting on the couch with my then-boyfriend. My bloated stomach aches, my hormonal migraine pounds in my skull with excruciating force. I wait until his fingers start to tap against the screen.

"Who's texting you?"

The words stumble out of my mouth like vomit—automatic and tinged with acid. My eyes are marbles—cold and hard, rolling at my then-boyfriend's expression when he takes the bait for the millionth time. He sets his phone down and turns to me.

"Amanda," he says.

Of course, it devolves from there. It's always Amanda. It's always someone from my boyfriend's little harem he calls "friends." My abdomen cramps as I shift in my chair. My smile is one of bared teeth, a wolf prepared to leap out and strike if he makes the wrong move.

The argument is pointless and lasts for hours. There is occasionally a raised voice, a dropping of the words "fuck" and "shit" in whatever chance we can get. Always, it ends with a bitter apology for my jealousy and a whispered apology for his anger.

And always, a few days later, I tell him the same line. And every time, it comes as a desperate plea. No, I wasn't myself. No, I'm not that horrible, jealous witch.

"I don't care if you have female friends. You know that. It was just my period."

I used to count down the days on my birth control pills. I'd watch the estrogen tablets disappear one-by-one, knowing that the other me lurked somewhere in the white sugar pills that made up the last week of the month. I didn't think much of the migraines, the risk I took to keep my body in control for twenty-one days.

My one solace was that it was predictable. Unlike my dance with my bipolar disorder, the game I played with PMS always had a beginning that started with the first drop in hormones. The cramps began like clockwork, the acne sprinkled my face. I'd buy the jumbo box of tampons at the store days before it struck.

Then I would try to remind myself that I loved my then-boyfriend, and he was not interested in other women. I would mentally prepare myself as though I was about to disappear, and this was my last chance to leave a mark on whatever beast would slip into my skin.

One day, after ten years of taking the pills, my doctor looked at the most recent questionnaire I'd filled in.

"Migraines?" she asked.

My brow furrowed.

"I've had them since I was a teenager," I said.

"You can't be on birth control pills," she said. "The combination of migraines and birth control pills leads to high stroke risk. We have other options available for you."

One numbing injection, one giant needle slipping under my skin, one splotch of purple flesh.

One birth control implant living safely in my arm.

I sit in my psychiatrist's office on his plush couch. My eyes are locked on the collection of water and oil timers seated on an end table in the corner. Most of them no longer work, but the childhood memories of my tiny hands flipping them over and watching the red oil drops slide through the water to the bottom of the timer are enough. There's a soothing sensation just by remembering.

He asks me the usual questions, unbothered by my lack of eye contact. Have you been taking your medications? Yes. Have you been getting enough sleep? Yes. Are you taking the fish oil? Yes.

There is no elaboration. My psychiatrist has known me since I was eight, has drilled his ideas into my hormonally imbalanced brain for most of my life. I know the volumes he doesn't speak by heart.

Have you been exercising? No. I'd like to weigh you. Okay.

Then he asks about the mood swings. He looks for situations or events as the root cause. Is my marriage going well? How is school? How is my writing? Everything is fine.

So instead, he ups the doses. Lithium. Abilify. Buspar. Prozac.

My cocktail of pills can only be adjusted so far—I've experienced lithium toxicity, and it's eerily similar to the stomach flu.

Not once does he ask where I am in my menstrual cycle. Not once is my issue anything besides bipolar-obsessive-compulsive-autistic brain.

There are many downsides to the implant. It has a tendency to rub the nerves in my arm the wrong way in certain positions, sending little electrical sparks up through my arm, shoulder, and beyond. It has zero effect on hormonal acne, so I break out like a teenager all over again.

Then there is the seemingly perpetual PMS. There is the glaring at my now-husband whenever he checks his phone. There are the hateful words I hiss when my head is throbbing and my eyes are aching from an oncoming migraine. There are the countless pairs of panties ruined by spots of blood. There are the tears shed when I'm home alone, and suddenly the world comes crashing down.

The rage is familiar. It mirrors mania in a way I understand. Nothing can quench it. Nothing can pull the red filter from my eyes.

Even the strong pull of depression is familiar. It pulls me down, and my limbs struggle as though I'm swimming in molasses, and there is no way to keep myself afloat.

I've learned that women with severe PMS symptoms often get misdiagnosed as bipolar. But where does that leave those of us who suffer from both? Does it magnify the symptoms, or simply leave it impossible for the specialists to figure out exactly what ails us? Am I striking the dog because I'm in a manic rage or because my hormones are out of whack? Am I bawling my eyes out over my "B" in my Psychology of Aging course because I am severely depressed, or is it because my uterine lining is shedding? Am I paranoid that my husband is planning to cheat on me because I am obsessive-compulsive, or does it have something to do with the menstrual blood and migraine headaches and the feelings of ugliness and self-loathing from the whiteheads littering my oily skin—

There is no longer a cute little colored chart where I approach little white pills that warn me of my oncoming mood swings. There is only a matchstick in my arm that aches and slides further from the insertion site scar with each passing month.

Coda

Impressions of the Bloody Vagina
—Liza Wolff-Francis

I am a woman bleeding.
Crimson blood like battlefield remains.
A wounded soldier. A hemophiliac
for five days each month. I am a sacrifice.

I bleed for life. Like a river that washes
the earth clean. Red gushes down my legs,
tangled and sticky in pubic hair. Sap
down my limbs. Tonight, its color

is of the rose on my dresser. Yesterday
it clumped like ketchup. I bleed
in the shower, watercolor red,
party streamers left in the rain,

shapeless splotches on a white porcelain
toilet seat. I am suicide blood. Squashed
strawberries. This blood camouflaged
in wine colored pants. I walk naked,

heavy polka dot drops on the floor,
stain dark blue underwear. Moon waves
pull and push this blood from me,
I bleed like an accident; this is no accident,

but a celebration. This is good grief.
I pry myself apart, blood on my fingers,
under my nails, draw a woman's symbol
with my blood, below my belly button,

on the outside of my womb. My bleeding
is like a calendar, the paper I have wiped
it with, a Valentine. This bleeding
is a feature of my body, an art form.

I bleed like no CIS-man will ever bleed.
My blood is scented. It attracts sharks
in freshwater lakes. This cut, this cunt,
this indentation in my body, ancient

petroglyphs carved into my caverns,
sugarless raspberry tea, red wine.
I bleed the poisonous round red berries
of fairy tales. Blood wax drip from a candle.

Red silk cord wrapped around my hips.
A hysterical woman, a sexual woman,
a witch. The cracks in the dry earth call me
to bleed. I bleed ritually. I ritually bleed.

This blood is a privilege, a gift. I bleed
for hysterectomies, for menopause,
for childhood, childbirth, and death,
glops of blood that look like bean fetuses

in a lunch thermos. I bleed for rape victims,
for abuse survivors, to call out injustice.
This blood is a tornado siren for change.
I bleed under my white dress, red

like the red of her bicycle seat.
The inner lining of my uterus on sun-dried
sheets. Blood the color of pizza sauce,
the color of burgundy red patches

on old blue jeans. I bleed like women
all over the world bleed an unspoken bond.
I bleed with the rhythm of the rain.
It washes my blood down my legs,

onto the street, into puddles. I will bleed
until there is a full moon. In tight blue jeans,
my clenched fist angry at this blood.
I hold my breath through pain.

They used to say women were sick
when they bled; I am sick. I dye my white
panties with spots of red turned
brown in the wash. I bleed

with the rhythm of the rain. My blood
puddles in the street, we jump
in the puddles. Sacred womanhood.
I bleed my own salvation. I bleed.

Contributors

- **Kelli Russell Agodon**'s newest book is *Dialogues with Rising Tides* (Copper Canyon Press) was recently named a Finalist in the Washington State Book Awards and shortlisted for the Eric Hoffer Book Award Grand Prize in Poetry. She is the co-founder of Two Sylvias Press where she works as an editor and book cover designer. She lives in a sleepy seaside town in Washington State on traditional lands of the Chimacum, Coast Salish, S'Klallam, and Suquamish people. She teaches at Pacific Lutheran University's low-res MFA program, the Rainier Writing Workshop. www.agodon.com / www.twosylviaspress.com

- La mancha en mi alma is an excerpt from **algae**'s undergraduate creative thesis, and the piece discusses the cultural shame that periods bring from the Mexican perspective and how one is forced to become a woman overnight, leading to the hypersexualization of the self or by others. algae (they/them/elle) is currently pursuing a master's degree in Latin America and Latino Studies, and their work has been published in The Eckleburg Project, Fudoki Magazine, and in Folkways Press' anthology *We Are Not Shadows*. They love grapefruits and can be followed on Twitter @writer_algae.

- **Julia C. Alter** earned her MFA in Poetry from the Vermont College of Fine Arts. Her poetry has been nominated for the Pushcart Prize, and has appeared in journals including *The Southern Humanities Review*, *The Raleigh Review*, *Crab Creek Review*, *Sixth Finch*, *Foundry*, *Palette Poetry*, *Gigantic Sequins*, and elsewhere. She lives in Vermont with her son.

- **Elena M. Aponte** is a writer and editor based in Michigan. Her work has appeared in *The Tahoma Literary Review*, *The Indiana Review*, *Barrelhouse*, *marrow magazine*, and elsewhere. She is a current MFA student in fiction at Vermont College of Fine Arts and editor of a charity anthology of Puerto Rican writing called *Boricua en la Luna*, the sales from which go to support organizations in Puerto Rico. Check it out on Blurb.

- **Andrea Askowitz** is a writing teacher and the author of the memoir *My Miserable, Lonely, Lesbian Pregnancy*. She's written for *The New York Times*, *Salon*, *Glamour*, *The Rumpus*, *Huffington Post*, *The Writer*, NPR, and PBS, where she was nominated for an Emmy. Andrea hosts and produces the podcast Writing Class Radio and is at work on a new memoir. You can find her at @andreaaskowitz, @wrtgclassradio, writingclasssradio.com, and andreaaskowitz.com.

- **Mariah Ayscue** *he/him/king)* is a Black, Trans, Artist, Activist, and mental health advocate from Montclair NJ. He also identifies as a Christian Witch, Disco ball Dyke, Pansexual pancake and a Demisexual dream that is expressed through his poetry. Mariah worked with the organization Girl Be Heard as a Directing Fellow and Company member under the instruction of

Ianne Fields Stuart (founder of The Okra Project*)*. This led to working with V (formerly Eve) Ensler, known for *The Vagina Monologues* and Tony Porter (founder of A Call to Men) on creating the YouthACT council. He has also worked with The Nuyorican Poets Cafe community, Ameerah Shabazz-Bilal (artistic director of When Women Speak), Rescue Poetix (poet laureate of Jersey City), Talena Lachelle Queen (poet laureate of Paterson) to create safe spaces where poetry can help us express our many intersections and learn from each other. Mariah wants to reclaim the narratives, education, and healing of the QTBIPOC community. It is the work he wants to do for the rest of his life.

- **Limi Marie Bauer** is a seeker of joy, a creatrix, and an educator. Holding a Master of Science from the University of Oxford, she provides English language services, and is part of the founding team of the app, STUCK. An expat, cult-survivor, and HSP (highly sensitive person), she enjoys creating poetry, prose, and videos about healing, travel, empowerment, and the psychology of language learning. She lives in Austria with her favorite husband, their three giant-hearted children, an orange tabby healer, Catness, and an angel disguised as a dog, Ruby.

- **Margo Berdeshevsky**, NYC born, often writes and lives in Paris. Her newest book is *Kneel Said the Night* (a hybrid book in half-notes) from Sundress Publications. Forthcoming: *It Is Still Beautiful To Hear The Heart Beat*, from Salmon Poetry. Her other books include *Before The Drought*, from Glass Lyre Press, which was a National Poetry Series finalist; *Between Soul & Stone*; *But a Passage in Wilderness* from Sheep Meadow Press, and *Beautiful Soon Enough*, FC2 recipient of the Ronald Sukenick Innovative Fiction Award. Other honors include the Robert H. Winner Award from the Poetry Society of America, and Grand Prize for the Thomas Merton Poetry of the Sacred Award. Widely published in journals in America and Europe such as *Kenyon Review, Plume, The Night Heron Barks, Verseville, Scoundrel Time, Southern Humanities Review,* and *PN Review*. Her "Letters from Paris" have appeared for many years in *Poetry International* online. For more info, kindly see her website http://margoberdeshevsky.com.

- **Danielle Bero** was born in Queens to hippie parents, given a dose of Shel Silverstein, Tupac, jazz, and classic rock. Bero is a Posse scholar, taught in Indonesia on a Fulbright, co-founded a school for students in foster care and held it down as a high school principal in Brooklyn. She holds a master's in English Education, Educational Leadership and completed her MFA at the University of San Francisco. She is a Jack Straw Fellow and Saints and Sinners Festival poetry winner. She is published in *Divine Feminist* anthology, Lavender Review, *Quiet Lightning, Juked,* etc.. She has a micro-chapbook published by Ghost City Press.

- **Keily Blair** (they/them) is an autistic, queer writer, as well as Managing Editor of the *Signal Mountain Review*. They hold a BA in English: Creative Writing from UT Chattanooga, where their nonfiction won the Creative Nonfiction Award. They are currently at work on their debut novel. You can find more details about their work at www.keilyblair.com. They live in Tennessee with their husband, dog, cat, and guinea pigs.

- **Janalynn Bliss** was not born in Los Angeles but considers it her birthplace. Descendent from a long line of makers, she believes in keeping alive the handmade arts. She works in textiles, yarn, paper, and ink.

- **Amy Bobeda** holds an MFA from the Jack Kerouac School of Disembodied Poetics where she serves as director of the Naropa Writing Center and teaches pedagogy and processed based arts. She's the founder of Wisdom Body Collective and author/illustrator of *Red Memory* (FlowerSong Press), *What Bird Are You?* (Finishing Line Press), *mi sin manitos* (Ethel Press), and a forthcoming project from Spuyten Duyvil. She writes about myth, menstruation, and language and can be found on Twitter @amybobeda.

- **Erica Bodwell** is a poet and attorney who lives in Concord, New Hampshire. Her full-length manuscript, *Crown of Wild*, won the Two Sylvias Press 2018 Wilder Prize as well as the New Hampshire Writers Project 2021 People's Choice Award for poetry. It was released in September 2020. Her chapbook, *Up Liberty Street*, was released in March 2017 by Finishing Line Press. Her poems have been nominated for several Pushcart Prizes and have appeared in *VerseDaily, Beloit, Spoon River Review* (Editor's Prize 2nd Runner Up), *North American Review* (James Hearst Poetry Prize finalist), *PANK* and other journals. Her website is ericasoferbodwell.com.

- **Jan Chronister** is the author of two poetry books and six chapbooks. She spends summers in Wisconsin gardening and winters in Georgia trying not to.

- **Ginny Lowe Connors** is the author of four full-length poetry collections, the most recent of which is *Without Goodbyes: From Puritan Deerfield to Mohawk Kahnawake* (Turning Point, 2021). Her chapbook, *Under the Porch*, won the Sunken Garden Poetry Prize and she has earned numerous awards for individual poems. She is a former Poet Laureate of West Hartford, Connecticut. As publisher of her own press, Grayson Books, Connors has also edited a number of poetry anthologies, including *Forgotten Women: A Tribute in Poetry*. She is co-editor of Connecticut River Review.

- With a Ph.D. in British and American literature and an MFA in Poetry, **Chella Courington** is a writer and teacher who's published nine chapbooks of poetry and four of fiction. Her many stories and poems appear in a range of journals and anthologies including *SmokeLong Quarterly, The Collagist,* and *New World Writing.* Her poetry has been nominated for *Best of the Net* and *Best New Poets* along with awarded individual prizes, the most recent of which is *Writing in a Woman's Voice Moon Prize* for her poem "Eurydice." Her fiction also has been nominated for *Best of the Net, Best Small Fictions,* and *Pushcart* as well as awarded individual prizes, the most recent of which is the *Shooter Magazine Flash Prize* for "Showtime." She lives in Southern California with another writer and two feline boys. You can find her on Twitter at @chellacouringto and Instagram at chellacourington.

- **Susan Darlington** is a Leeds-based poet. Her work regularly explores the female experience through nature-based symbolism and stories of transformation. It has been published in *Dreich, Dream Catcher, Anti-Heroin Chic, Hedgehog Press*, and *Ethel Zine* among others. She has three books available: *Never Wear White* (Alien Buddha Press, 2022), *Traumatropic Heart* (Selcouth Station, 2021) and *Under The Devil's Moon* (Penniless Press Publications, 2015). Follow her at @S_sanDarlington.

- **J. Lois Diamond** is a poet and playwright. Her monologues published Smith & Kraus' Best Women's Stage Monologues 2021 & 2022 and Applause Books' *She Persisted*. Her poem "On the Subway" was published in Origami Poems Project's *The Best of Kindness* 2020. Her poem "Knots" was included in the online program Healing Voices, McCarter Theatre Center, 2021. Her poem "Tea Cup," was performed by Scribe Stages, Online Reading, 2020. She has been a frequent featured poet at The Cornelia St Café. Her poems "The Bodies," "Where is Bess?," "On Thursday Afternoon," "Moon Landing" appeared in *Syndic Literary Journal*. Her poem "The Parting" appeared in *The Visual In Verse, Grounds for Sculpture*. Her poem "Hurricane Sandy" finale *NY LADIES*, Hudson Guild Theatre, 2013. She studied poetry with Harris Schiff, Alice Notley, St. Marks in the Bowery. Her play *Growl,* inspired by the life of an Iranian poet, produced Downtown Urban Arts Festival, 2019, Theatre Odyssey, 2019 (runner up for best play), Valdez Theatre Conference, 2021. jloisdiamond.com

- **Kellie Diodato** is a native New Yorker currently residing in Brooklyn. She has earned a B.A *summa cum laude* at Marymount Manhattan College and is pursuing an MFA at Columbia University School of The Arts. Kellie is a full-time Humanities educator for fourth and fifth grade students at an independent school in New York City, as she revels in working with children, as well as contributing to the guiding light of literary education. Her writing can be found in *Lifelines: The Geisel School of Medicine at Dartmouth Literary and Art Journal*, among others.

- **Ada Donnelly** is a freshman in college, studying photography, film, and writing. Born and raised in Brooklyn, she wrote the poem in this anthology when she was a sophomore in high school. Her photographs have been exhibited at the Metropolitan Museum of Art, the Bronx Documentary Center, and BRIC gallery. Her poems and photographs have both won awards from Scholastic/Alliance for Young Artists and Writers.

- **Angie Dribben** is an artist and writer creating in the Appalachian region of Virginia. She is on the Virginia Commission for the Arts Teaching Artist Roster. Her debut collection, *Everygirl*, was a finalist for the 2020 Broadkill Review Dogfish Head Prize. She has been nominated for Best of the Net and placed in a number of contests. Her most recent work can be found in *Los Angeles Review, Orion, Coffin Bell, Split Rock Review,* and others.

- **jessamyn duckwall** (they/she) is a queer, autistic poet. They are an MFA candidate in poetry at Portland State University and serve as Co-Editor in Chief at *The Portland Review*. Their current special interests include Sylvia Plath, stinging nettles, and mushrooms of the Pacific Northwest. Raised in the Pentecostal church, jessamyn is an "ex-vangelical" who writes extensively about purity culture and deconstructing their religion. Their work has appeared in *Old Pal Magazine, Josephine Quarterly, Kithe Journal, Sylvia Magazine, Pithead Chapel,* and *Radar Poetry,* among other publications. They're on Instagram as @babydeadnettle.

- **Eleanore Christine Dykes** (she/her) is a Chicago-based poet. Her poems have appeared in numerous anthologies and publications including Free Verse Revolution, Gypsophila Magazine, Querencia Press, and The Wee Sparrow Poetry Press. Her debut poetry chapbook I Don't Have the Words for This was released by Dark Thirty Poetry Publishing in March 2023. In her spare time, she enjoys reading, traveling, and sipping a good chai latte. You can find Eleanore on Instagram at @eleanorechristine.

- **Dr. Deirdre Fagan** is an associate professor at Ferris State University and the award-winning author of a collection of poetry, *Phantom Limbs* (forthcoming, 2023), a memoir, *Find a Place for Me: Embracing Love and Life in the Face of Death* (2022), a short story collection, *The Grief Eater* (2020), a chapbook of poetry, *Have Love* (2019), and a reference book, *Critical Companion to Robert Frost* (2007). A creative writer and literary scholar, Fagan's essays, poetry, fiction, and nonfiction have appeared widely in literary and scholarly journals and anthologies, as well as newspapers and magazines. She is the poetry editor at *Orange Blossom Review.*

- **Alexis Rhone Fancher** is published in *Best American Poetry, Rattle, Verse Daily, The American Journal of Poetry, Plume, Diode, Flock,* and elsewhere. She's authored nine poetry collections, most recently, *Junkie Wife (Moon Tide Press), The Dead Kid Poems (KYSO Flash Press), Stiletto Killer (Edizone Italia), EROTIC: New & Selected (NYQ Books), and DUETS (Small Harbor).* Her photographs are featured worldwide, including the covers of *Witness* and *Pedestal Magazine.* A multiple Pushcart Prize and Best of the Net nominee, Alexis is poetry editor of *Cultural Daily.* She lives with her husband on the bluffs of San Pedro, overlooking the Pacific Ocean, just a stone's throw from downtown Los Angeles. They have an extraordinary view. www.alexisrhonefancher.com

- **Anne Finger**'s most recent book-length publication is a novel, *A Woman, in Bed* (Cinco Puntos, 2018). Her short story collection, *Call Me Ahab* (Bison Books, 2009), which won the Prairie Schooner Award, takes iconic disability stories such as Moby Dick and "crips" them, rewriting them from a disabled perspective. Two memoirs, *Elegy for a Disease: A Personal and Cultural History of Polio* (St. Martin's Press, 2006) and *Past Due: A Story of Disability, Pregnancy and Birth* (Seal Press, 1990; British edition, Women's Press, 1991; German translation, Fischer Verlag, 1992) considered her personal experience of disability, placing it within a broader social context, looking at how narratives of disease are formed and of the tensions and confluences between feminism and disability rights. She is the recipient of a Creative Capital Grant, the Berlin Prize (2019), and has held residencies at MacDowell, Djerassi, Yaddo, and Hedgebrook.

- **Emily Fontenot** is a writer from south Louisiana. She is currently working on her PhD in Creative Writing at Illinois State University. An excerpt from her novel-in-progress is now available in *South 85 Journal,* where it has been nominated for the 2022 Best of the Net Anthology. Her fiction has also been published in *Children, Churches and Daddies, Quail Bell Magazine, Gone Lawn, The Southwestern Review*, and others and is forthcoming in *The Dodge*. Her poetry has appeared in *Antenna::Signals* and in *Buddy, a lit zine*, where her poem, "debris," won their first annual poetry contest. Her book *Hurricanes, Cypress Trees, and Other Synonyms for Home* was published by Press 254 in December 2022.

- **Geula Geurts** is a Dutch-born poet and essayist living in Jerusalem. A 2021 Best of the Net nominee, her work has recently appeared in *Guesthouse, Spoon River, Indianapolis Review, Pleiades, Salamander, Radar* and *EcoTheo*. Her lyric essay *The Beginnings of Fire* was published by CutBank Books (2021). Her manuscript *Tiny Bones Glowing* was selected as a finalist in the 2021 Brittingham and Felix Pollak Poetry Prizes from Wisconsin Poetry Series, was the first runner-up in the 2020 Red Hen Press Benjamin Saltman Award, and a semi-finalist in YesYes Books 2021 Pamet River Prize. Her mini chapbook *Like Any Good Daughter* was published by Platypus Press. She is a graduate of the Shaindy Rudoff Graduate Program in Creative Writing at Bar Ilan University and works as a literary agent at the Deborah Harris Agency.

- **Carol L. Gloor** has been writing poetry since she was sixteen. Her work has been published in many journals, most recently in *Trajectory*. Her poetry chapbook, *Assisted Living*, was published by Finishing Line Press in 2013, and her full-length poetry collection, *Falling Back*, was published by WordPoetry in 2018.

- **Kelly Gray** lives in Northern California on unceded Coast Miwok land. She writes about what she knows or is trying to know; parenting, eco-grief, dead things, monsters, prophetic animals, relationships to self and others, and rural life. Her work has recently appeared in *Witness Magazine, Southern Humanities Review, Trampset* and *Passages North*. Her collections and chaps are available through her website at writekgray.com.

- **Monique Hayes** received her MFA from the University of Maryland College Park. She's the recipient of a Ruth Stone House Poetry Scholarship, a Courage to Write Grant (de Groot Foundation), and an American Antiquarian Society Fellowship. Her poems have appeared in *Lucky Jefferson, SHIFT, Indiana Voice Journal*, and *The Forum*, among others. Monique is a fellow of Callaloo, VONA, and Hurston/Wright, and a Wildacres Retreat Residency.

- **Marty Head**'s work has appeared in anthologies by *Potato Soup Journal* and Gnashing Teeth Publishing. In 2019, they attended the Iceland Writers Retreat. They are expected to graduate in summer 2023 with a BA in Editing, Writing, and Media. If you would like to contact them professionally, you can do so at mheadwrites@gmail.com.

- **Raye Hendrix** is a writer from Alabama and the author of two poetry chapbooks, *Every Journal is a Plague Journal* (Bottlecap Press) and *Fire Sermons* (Ghost City Press). Raye is the winner of the 2019 Keene Prize for Literature and the 2018 Patricia Aakhus Award (*Southern Indiana Review*). Her work appears *in Poetry Daily, American Poetry Review, Cimarron Review,*

Poet Lore, 32 Poems, Poetry Northwest, Tupelo Quarterly, and elsewhere. Raye is the poetry editor at *Press Pause Press* and co-editor of DIS/CONNECT: A Disability Literature Column (*Anomalous Press*) and is currently a PhD candidate at the University of Oregon. Find more of their work at rayehendrix.com.

- **Anndee Hochman** is a writer, storyteller, and teacher. She is the author of *Anatomies: A Novella and Stories* (Picador USA) and *Everyday Acts & Small Subversions: Women Reinventing Family, Community and Home* (The Eighth Mountain Press). Her column, "The Parent Trip," appears weekly in the Philadelphia Inquirer, and her work has also been published in *Poets & Writers, WebMD, Broad Street Review*, and other venues. She's a six-time winner of Moth Story Slams and recently shared the first-place title in Philadelphia's Moth Grand Slam. Anndee lives with her partner, a housemate, two mercurial cats and an enthusiastic puppy in Philadelphia.

- **Katherine Hoerth** is the author of five poetry collections, including *Flare Stacks in Full Bloom* (Texas Review Press, 2022). She is the recipient of the 2021 Poetry of the Plains Prize from North Dakota State University Press and the 2015 Helen C. Smith Prize from the Texas Institute of Letters for the best book of poetry in Texas. Her work has been published in numerous literary magazines including *Literary Imagination* (Oxford University Press), *Valparaiso Review*, and *Southwestern American Literature*. She is an assistant professor at Lamar University and editor of Lamar University Literary Press.

- **Juleigh Howard-Hobson**'s poetry has appeared in *Valparaiso Poetry Review, Mobius, The Lyric, Able Muse, Hip Mama, Anti-Heroin Chic, Lift Every Voice* (Kissing Dynamite*), Birds Fall Silent in the Mechanical Sea* (Great Weather for Media), and other places. Nominations include Best of the Net, Pushcart and The Rhysling. Her latest book is the Elgin-nominated *Our_Otherworld* (Red Salon). Now that she is in her 50's, she has escaped the torment of PMS, but *never ever* the memory. It's a bitch.

- **Amy Hsieh** lives in Ontario, Canada. She is a Taiwanese-Canadian, bi, and neurodivergent writer recovering from post-concussion syndrome. Her poems have appeared in *IHRAF Publishes, Watershed Review, Grain Magazine, Barrie Today, Devour: Art and Lit Canada, Acta Victoriana, Hart House Review*, and *The University College Review*. She received an Honorable Mention in the 2020 Creators of Justice Awards contest held by the International Human Rights Festival of Art. She was the recipient of the 2021 Reinhilde Cammaert Memorial Writing Scholarship from Inkwell Workshops. Amy is currently working towards completing her first poetry collection with support from the Canada Council for the Arts.

- **Jessica Hudson** (she/her) received her Creative Writing MFA from Northern Michigan University. Her work has been published in several literary magazines, and her first poetry chapbook is forthcoming from Nightingale & Sparrow Press. Jessica lives in Albuquerque, NM with an experimental artist and a black cat. www.jessicarwhudson.wixsite.com/poet

- **Valerie Hunter** teaches high school English and has an MFA in writing for children and young adults from Vermont College of Fine Arts. Her stories and poems have appeared in publications including *Cicada, Storyteller, Edison Literary Review, Other Voices, Room,* and *Colp.* "Surely, This Time" is loosely based on one of her great-grandmothers, who had nine children (including two sets of twins), and who was supposedly told by her doctor on more than one occasion that she was going through menopause when she was, in fact, pregnant.

- **Vicki Iorio** is the author of the poetry collections *Poems from the Dirty Couch,* Local Gems Press (2013), *Not Sorry,* Alien Buddha Press (2020) and the chapbooks Send *Me a Letter,* dancinggirlpress (2015) and *Something Fishy,* Finishing Line Press (2018). Her poetry has appeared in numerous print and online journals. Vicki is currently living in Florida, but she is NY4EVAH.

- **Susan Ito** is the author of *The Mouse Room.* She co-edited the literary anthology *A Ghost At Heart's Edge: Stories & Poems of Adoption.* Her work has appeared in *Growing Up Asian American, Choice, Hip Mama, Literary Mama, Catapult, Hyphen, The Bellevue Literary Review,* and elsewhere. She is a MacDowell colony fellow and has also been awarded residencies at The Mesa Refuge, Hedgebrook, and the Blue Mountain Center. She has performed her solo show, *The Ice Cream Gene,* around the US. She is a member of the Writers' Grotto and teaches at Mills College and Bay Path University. Her theatrical adaptation of *Untold,* stories of reproductive stigma, was produced at Brava Theater. She lives in Oakland, California.

- **Libby Falk Jones**'s poems and creative nonfiction have appeared in more than 25 journals and anthologies, including *Ruminate, Still: the Journal, Blue Fifth Review, Literary Accents, The Heartland Review, New Growth: Recent Kentucky Writings,* and *Women Speak* (Women of Appalachia Project). She has authored or co-authored four books of poems, including, most recently, *For Your Good Health, Drink Flowers* (Bass Clef, 2023) and *Yakety Yak (Don't Talk Back)* (Workhorse Writers, 2022). Professor Emerita of English at Berea College and a member of Bluegrass Writers Studio (Eastern Kentucky University), she lives in Berea, KY, where she co-leads a writing project for Kentucky women over 60.

- **Jennifer Schomburg Kanke** lives in Florida where she edits confidential documents. Her work has recently appeared or is forthcoming in *New Ohio Review, Massachusetts Review, Shenandoah,* and *Salamander.* She is the winner of the inaugural Sheila-Na-Gig Editions Editor's Choice Award for Fiction. Her zine about her experiences undergoing chemotherapy for ovarian cancer, *Fine, Considering,* is available from Rinky Dink Press. She serves as a reader for *The Dodge.*

- **Ashly Kim** (she/her) is an over-caffeinated Philadelphian and weekend fishmonger. When not adventuring with her two kids, she enjoys eating sushi and hoarding books like a literary dragon. Find Ashly online @ashlykimchi.

- **Olivia Kingery** is a writer and farmer in Michigan's Upper Peninsula where she lives on her farm with her husband, dogs, cats, chickens, and hermit crabs. Right now, she is probably chatting with earthworms or feeding Elanor her sourdough starter or playing Mariocart. Find more of her work on our website: oliviakingery.com and follow the farm adventures on Instagram: @pileatedfarms

- **Judy Kronenfeld** has published five full-length poetry collections, including *Groaning and Singing* (FutureCycle, 2022), *Bird Flying Through the Banquet* (FutureCycle, 2017), *Shimmer* (WordTech, 2012), and *Light Lowering in Diminished Sevenths* (2nd ed. Antrim House, 2012), winner of the Litchfield Review poetry book prize for 2007. Her poems have appeared in over three dozen anthologies and in such journals as *Cider Press Review*, *MacQueen's Quinterly*, *New Ohio Review*, *Offcourse*, *One*, *Rattle*, *Sheila-Na-Gig*, *Slant*, *Valparaiso Poetry Review*, *Verdad*, and *Your Daily Poem*. Judy is also a more occasional writer of short fiction and nonfiction. Her most recent story, "The Paisley Scarf," nominated for a Pushcart, was published in *Loch Raven Review* (2020). Her most recent piece of creative nonfiction, "Operating in French," appeared in *Kaleidoscope (2022)*. She is Lecturer Emerita, Department of Creative Writing, UC Riverside.

- **Sheree La Puma** is an award-winning writer whose work has appeared in *The Penn Review*, *Redivider*, *The Maine Review*, *The Lascaux Review*, *Stand Magazine*, *Rust + Moth*, and *Catamaran Literary Reader*, among others. She earned her MFA in writing from CalArts. Her poetry has been nominated for Best of The Net and three Pushcarts. A reader for the *Orange Blossom Review*, her latest chapbook, *Broken: Do Not Use* is currently available at Main Street Rag Publishing. www.shereelapuma.com

- **Kate LaDew** is a graduate from the University of North Carolina at Greensboro with a BA in Studio Art. She resides in Graham, NC, with her cats Charlie Chaplin and Janis Joplin.

- **Kara Lewis** is a poet and editor based in Chicago and Kansas City. Her poems have appeared in *Snarl*, *Rogue Agent*, *Pithead Chapel*, and elsewhere. She has received a Best of the Net nomination, as well as been awarded the John Mark Eberhart Memorial Award for a collection of poetry. She serves as a poetry reader at *Longleaf Review* and a contributor for *Read Poetry*.

- **Nina B. Lichtenstein** is a native of Oslo, Norway who moved to the U.S. when she was 19. She holds a PhD in French literature from University of Connecticut and an MFA in creative nonfiction from University of Southern Maine. Her essays have appeared in *The Washington Post, Lilith, Full Grown People, Tablet Magazine, Dorothy Parker's Ashes,* and AARP's "The Ethel," among other places, as well as in the anthology, *Ink* by Hippocampus Books (2022). Nina's memoir *Body: My Life in Parts* is looking for a home, and she is at work on a new memoir about becoming "the Viking Jewess." She divides her time between Maine, Tel Aviv, and Oslo.

- **Sarah Lilius** is the author of the full-length poetry collection, *Dirty Words* (Indie Blu(e) Publishing, 2021) and six chapbooks. Some of her publication credits include *Fourteen Hills, Boulevard, Massachusetts Review* and *New South*. Her website is sarahlilius.com.

- **Claire Loader** is a New Zealand-born writer and photographer now living in Galway, Ireland. Her work has been published in various magazines, including *Poetry Bus, Splonk, Crannóg* and *Skylight47*. She is a Forward and Pushcart Prize nominee and was this year part of a collective poetry anthology, *Pushed Toward the Blue Hour*, published by Nine Pens Press.

- **Lorette C. Luzajic** writes, edits, publishes, and teaches small fictions and prose poetry from Toronto, Canada. Her work has been widely anthologized, and published in journals such as Axon, *Ghost Parachute, Trampset, MacQueen's Quinterly, Bending Genres, Unbroken, JMWW, Cleaver, New Flash Fiction Review, Litro, The Dillydoun Review,* and more. She has been nominated for Best American Food Writing, twice for Best Small Fictions, thrice for Best Microfiction, and four times each for the Pushcart Prize and Best of the Net. She is the founding editor of *The Ekphrastic Review,* a journal devoted to literature inspired by visual art. Lorette is also an international visual artist working with collage and mixed media to create urban, abstract, pop, and surreal works. She has collectors in thirty countries so far.

- **Eve Lyons** is a poet and fiction writer living in the Boston area. Her work has appeared in *Lilith, Literary Mama, Hip Mama, PIF, Welter, Prospectus, Poetry Quarterly, Barbaric Yawp, Word Riot,* Dead *Mule of Southern Literature,* as well as other magazines and several anthologies. Her first book of poetry, *Tikkun Olam: Repairing the World,* was published in 2020 by WordTech Communications. She works as an expressive arts therapist at an outpatient mental health clinic and teaches at Lesley University.

- **Caitlin Grace McDonnell** was a New York Times Poetry Fellow at NYU where she received her MFA. She has published poems and essays widely, including a chapbook, *Dreaming the Tree* (2003) and two books of poems, *Looking for Small Animals* (2012) and *Pandemic City* (2021) She lives with her daughter and teaches writing in NYC.

- **Freesia McKee** was the 2022-2023 Poet-in-Residence at Ripon College. She practices poetry, creative prose, book reviews, and literary criticism. Find her at FreesiaMcKee.com.

- **Kaylin Margaret** is an author and creative from Jacksonville, NC. They are co-writer on the upcoming comic book series *Compact Risk,* and have multiple mediums published in *Atlantis.* They study writing and graphic design in Wilmington, NC.

- **Nikki Marrone** is a spoken word performer, published poet, photographer, and coffee addict. She is motivated through feelings, of which she has plenty. Nikki is the winner of multiple poetry slams and has featured at various spoken word nights and festivals internationally but is based in the UK. Nikki is the author of *Psychogenic Fugue, Honey & Lemon* and *Burning Through the Bloodline.*

- **Betsy Mars** is a prize-winning poet, a photographer, publisher, and an editor at *Gyroscope Review.* Her writing has appeared widely online and in numerous print anthologies. She is a Best of the Net and Pushcart nominee. Her photos have been published in *Rattle* (as the Ekphrastic Challenge prompt), *Redheaded Stepchild*, and as a cover image for *Spank the Carp*. She works as a substitute teacher, and as a cat wrangler in her spare time. Her chapbooks and small press publications (Kingly Street Press) are available on Amazon. In addition to her chapbook collaboration with Alan Walowitz, she recently worked with artist Judith Christensen on an installation in San Diego which is part of an ongoing exploration of memory, identity, home, and family.

- Oregonian **Jodelle Marx** (@JodelleMarx), investigates gender expectations and generational trauma through poetry, fiction, and nonfiction storytelling. In 2019, Marx's poetry collection, *Rituals*, won Best Creative Writing: Poetry at the Northwest Undergraduate Conference in the Humanities. Her poem, "Oscillations," also received honorable mention in the Pacific's *Literature by Undergraduates* Magazine contest. Marx is currently working in marketing and event coordinating for Pacific University's Visiting Writers Series as well as teaching essay writing workshops to high schoolers. When Jodelle is not reading and writing, she is probably out with the horses, experimenting in the kitchen, or shooting film photography.

- **M. Boone Mattia** writes fiction, poetry, and personal essays. Her short story "No Moon Night" is listed among the special mentions in the 2020 Pushcart anthology. With an MFA from Pacific University (2015) and a background in journalism, oral history, and nonprofits, she divides her time between the Oregon Coast and Austin, Texas. She likes cemeteries, deserts, and long plane flights with a window seat.

- **Lynn Melnick** is the author of the memoir, *I've Had to Think Up a Way to Survive: On Trauma, Persistence, and Dolly Parton*. She is also the author of three poetry collections: *Refusenik, Landscape with Sex and Violence*, and *If I Should Say I Have Hope*. Her work has appeared in *APR, LA Review of Books, The New Republic, The New Yorker, The Paris Review, Poetry, A Public Space*, and the anthology *Not That Bad: Dispatches from Rape Culture*.

- **MaryAnn L. Miller** has artists' books in many special collections across the United States including the National Museum of Women in the Arts, Stanford, Yale, Bryn Mawr and Swarthmore Colleges. Miller has held residencies at Vermont Studio Center, Virginia Center for Creative Arts, Universidad Metropolitana Autonomia, Mexico City, University of Costa Rica, and the Ragdale Foundation. She was the Resident Book Artist at the Experimental Printmaking Institute, Lafayette College from 2001-2016. Miller was the featured artist in Vol. 15 Issue 1 of *Mezzo Camin*, a journal of poetry in form. Miller is also a poet with three Pushcart nominations and four books of poetry: *Locus Mentis* (PS Books 2012), *Cures for Hysteria* (Finishing Line Press 2018) and forthcoming in 2023 *Falling into the Diaspora* (Finishing Line Press) and *Time is a Snake's Tongue* (WordTech). Miller's art is represented at www.ravenfinearteditions.com and at www.maryannlmiller.com.

- **Megan Mary Moore** is a poet working in Cincinnati, Ohio, and living in a fairy princess fever dream. She is the author of two full length collections,

Dwellers (Unsolicited Press, 2019), and *To Daughter a Devil* (Unsolicited Press, 2023) and the forthcoming chapbook *And Aphrodite Laughed* (Milk & Cake, 2023). She holds an MFA in Poetry from Miami University and writes about the gorgeous and sometimes horrifying terrain of the feminine body.

- **Christina Myers** is a writer, editor, and former journalist. Her novel *The List of Last Chances* (2021) was longlisted for the 2022 Leacock Medal and shortlisted for the Fred Kerner Book Award. She was the editor of the award-winning anthology *BIG* (2020), and her work has appeared in several anthologies, as well as in magazines, journals and online. She is currently at work on an essay collection and a new novel and teaches both fiction and creative non-fiction. Christina juggles her creative work and stay-at-home-parenthood from her home on the West Coast of Canada.

- **Sarah Kai Neal** lives in Tucson AZ with Edgar Allen Poe, Asher, and Simone— her four-legged children. She graduated with her MFA from Sarah Lawrence College and has been published widely and wildly in: *North American Review, Sinister Wisdom, hoot, The Ilanot Review,* and many other journals. She uses she/they pronouns and substitute teaches when she's not driving for Lyft and Uber or watching movies. Her favorite book is Audre Lorde's *Zami,* and her teachers are the reason she's alive and writing today.

- Poet, essayist, and translator **Rachel Neve-Midbar**'s collection *Salaam of Birds* (Tebot Bach, 2020) was chosen by Dorothy Barresi for the Patricia Bibby First Book Prize. She is also the author of the chapbook *What the Light Reveals* (Tebot Bach, 2014), winner of The Clockwork Prize. Rachel's work has appeared in journals such as *Blackbird, Prairie Schooner, Grist,* and *The Georgia Review* as well as other publications and anthologies. She is a PhD candidate at the University of Southern California where her research concerns menstruation in contemporary poetry. More at www.rachelnevemidbar.com.

- **Adura Ojo** is a British-Nigerian Poet & Storyteller. Her "lost decade" story is featured here in "44 Songs to My Body." The rest is in a memoir on its way soon. Her work is also featured in *Anti-heroin Chic, Cultural Weekly, Lockdown 2020, Paris Lit Up, The Rialto, The Stockholm Review of Literature,* & a host of other publications. She is author of a full-length poetry collection: *Life is a Woman Breaking Eggs.* Her innovative chapbook, *MANIA* was published in August 2020. Mania: https://www.wrr.ng/download/mania-adura-ojo/ You can find her on Facebook at https://www.facebook.com/aduraojoauthor/

- **Anne-Marie Oomen**'s memoir, *As Long As I Know You: The Mom Book,* about her difficult and ultimately rewarding relationship with her mother, won the AWP Sue Silverman Award Nonfiction Award and a Michigan Notable Book Award. She wrote *Lake Michigan Mermaid* with Linda Nemec Foster (Michigan Notable Book, 2019), *Love, Sex and 4-H* (Next Generation Indie Award for Memoir), and others. She edited *ELEMENTAL: A Collection of Michigan Nonfiction* (Michigan Notable Book). She teaches at Solstice MFA at Lasell University (MA), Interlochen's College of Creative Arts (MI), and conferences throughout the country.

- **Abigail Ottley** is based in Penzance in Cornwall. A Pushcart nominee in 2013, her work has appeared in more than two hundred outlets including *The Lake, The Blue Nib, Atrium Poetry, The Atlanta Journal, Gnashing Teeth, The High Window,* and *Ink, Sweat & Tears.* A selection of Abigail's poems appeared in *Wave Hub: new poetry from Cornwall* (2014) ed. Dr Kent and in *Invisible Borders: New Women's Writing from Cornwall* (2020). In 2021, Abigail was shortlisted for both the Cinnamon and The Three Trees pamphlet awards and was highly commended by Penelope Shuttle in the Buzzwords poetry competition. At the close of 2022, she was shortlisted again, this time for the Nine Pens collection competition. She also contributed to both *Morvoren: the poetry of sea-swimming (2022)* and *Cornwall, Secret and Hidden, an anthology of short stories (2022).*

- **Emily Perkovich** is from the Chicago-land area. She is the Editor in Chief of Querencia Press and on the Women in Leadership Advisory Board with Valparaiso University. Her work strives to erase the stigma surrounding trauma victims and their responses. She is a Best of the Net nominee, a SAFTA scholarship recipient, and is previously published with Harness Magazine, Rogue Agent, Coffin Bell Journal, and Awakenings among others. She is the author of the poetry collections *Godshots Wanted: Apply Within* (Sunday Mornings at the River), *The Number 12 Looks Just Like You* (Finishing Line Press), & *baby, sweetheart, honey* (Alien Buddha Press) as well as the novella *Swallow.* You can find more of her work on IG @undermeyou

- **Emilia Phillips** is the author of four poetry collections from the University of Akron Press, most recently *Embouchure* (2021). They have published poems, essays, and book reviews in numerous journals. They are an Associate Professor of Creative Writing in the Department of English; MFA in Writing Program; and Women's, Gender, and Sexuality Studies Program at UNC Greensboro.

- **Raegen Pietrucha** (she/her) writes, edits, and consults creatively and professionally. Her debut full-length poetry collection, *Head of a Gorgon,* won a 2023 Human Relations Indie Book Award; her debut poetry chapbook, *An Animal I Can't Name,* won the 2015 Two of Cups Press competition; and she has a memoir in progress. She received her MFA from Bowling Green State University, where she was an assistant editor for *Mid-American Review.* Her writing has been published in *Cimarron Review, Puerto del Sol,* and other journals. Her photography has been published in *Rivanna Review, Seaside Gothic,* and other outlets. Connect with her at raegenmp.wordpress.com, on Twitter @freeradicalrp, and on Instagram @raegenmp.

- **Kristin Prevallet** is a poet, scholar, performer, and somatic practitioner who lives in Westchester County, NY and teaches at The New School in New York City. *Everywhere Here and in Brooklyn, I, Afterlife: Essay in Mourning Time,* and *Trance Poetics* are among her books. Her work casts a wide net to include archival and feminist recovery work (*A Helen Adam Reader*), performance art (*OilOilOil*), collaborative editing projects (*apex of the M, Third Mind*), and collaborations with visual artists. Prevallet is a legacy member of the Belladonna* Collaborative, a feminist poetry collective and event series, and she facilitates salons and conversations around Trance Poetics (trancepoetics.com).

- **Laurel Radzieski** is a poet and the author of *Red Mother* (NYQ Books, 2018) which won the 2020 Whirling Prize in Poetry from Etchings Press. Her poems have appeared in *New York Quarterly, Rust + Moth, Atlas and Alice, House of Zolo's Journal of Speculative Literature,* on a street sign in Wisconsin, and elsewhere. Laurel is a teaching artist and presents pop-up poetry installations in public places. She presented a talk at TEDxScranton 2020 called "Writing Poems for Strangers." Laurel earned her MFA at Goddard College. She currently lives in southeastern Pennsylvania and can be found online at www.eatmorepoems.com.

- **Catherine Ragsdale** is a Texan writer living in Baltimore. You can find her at catherineragsdalewriting.com or in your dreams, baking you a peach cobbler.

- **Lauren Rheaume** is a writer from New England. She's a graduate of GrubStreet's Essay Incubator program, and her work is published at *Breakwater Review, Boston Accent, Pidgeonholes, Complete Sentence, Thimble Literary Magazine,* and the *Neighbors* anthology from *Crack the Spine,* among others. You can find her at lauren-rheaume.com.

- **Chelsea Risley** is a writer, editor, and floral designer in Chattanooga, Tennessee. She is the editor-in-chief of the *Southern Review of Books* and has an MFA from Queens University of Charlotte. Her work has appeared in *Juked, Barrelhouse Magazine, Kissing Dynamite, Pidgeonholes,* and *Lunch Ticket.*

- **Kim Roberts** is a 2023 Poet-in-Residence at the Arts Club of Washington. She is the author of *A Literary Guide to Washington, DC* and editor of two anthologies of DC poets, most recently *By Broad Potomac's Shore,* selected by the Centers for the Book for the 2021 Route 1 Reads program. Her sixth book of poems, *Corona/Crown,* a cross-disciplinary collaboration with photographer Robert Revere, will be released in Fall 2023 by WordTech Editions. http://www.kimroberts.org

- **Dr. Verónica Rodríguez** is Lecturer in the Department of English Studies at University of Alicante (previous institutions include Royal Holloway, University of London, and University of Reading). With the research group "Contemporary British Theatre Barcelona," she participates in the research project "Gender, Affect and Care in Twenty-First Century British Theatre," funded by the Spanish Ministry of Economy and Competitiveness (http://www.ub.edu/cbtbarcelona). Publications include the monograph *David Greig's Holed Theatre: Globalization, Ethics and the Spectator* (Palgrave, 2019) and a chapter on endometriosis and spectating in the *Routledge Companion to Audiences and the Performing Arts* (2022). She is a member of the University Institute of Gender Studies Research (IUIEG) at the University of Alicante. Verónica is also a playwright, poet, and women's health coach, specializing in endometriosis, the illness she lives with. She has written the play *Bi* (Royal Court, 2019), codirected *Menstrual Care Charter* (University of

Reading, 2021), and performed and written *Performing Endometriosis* (University College London, 2022).

- **Rosemary Royston**, artist and poet, is the author of *Second Sight* (2021, Kelsay Press) and *Splitting the Soil* (Finishing Line Press, 2014). She resides in the northeast Georgia mountains with her family. Her writing has been published in journals such as *POEM, Split Rock Review, Southern Poetry Review, Poetry South, Appalachian Review,* and **82 Review.* https://theluxuryoftrees.wordpress.com/

- **Helen Ruggieri** has a new book of poetry, *The Sapphires,* from Kelsey Books and a book of short prose pieces, *Camping in the Galaxy,* from Woodthrush Books.

- **Anna Sandy Elrod** is a poet and essayist. She holds a PhD in poetry from Georgia State University and is the co-founder and editor of joint projects Birdcoat Quarterly and Ghost Peach Press. Her work can be found in Pleiades, the Threepenny Review, North American Review, Green Mountains Review, Iron Horse, Fugue, and other journals. She recently repatriated from Amsterdam, the Netherlands, and lives in rural Georgia with her husband, infant daughter, and several other small creatures.

- **Jennifer Saunders** is the author of *Self-Portrait with Housewife* (Tebot Bach, 2019), winner of the Clockwise Chapbook Competition. Her poem "Crosswalk" was selected by Kim Addonizio as the winner of the 2020 Gregory O'Donoghue International Poetry Prize and appeared in *Southword.* Jennifer is a Pushcart, Best of the Net, and Orison Anthology nominee, and her work has appeared in *The Georgia Review, Grist, Ninth Letter, San Pedro River Review,* and other publications. Jennifer holds an MFA from Pacific University and lives in German-speaking Switzerland. More at www.jennifer-saunders.com.

- **Katelyn Shinault** is an author and yoga teacher living a joyous life surrounded by her dogs, family, and nature.

- **Traci Skuce** lives, writes, and bleeds on the traditional and unceded territories of the Sahtloot, Sasitla, Ieeksun, and Puntledge. Her work has appeared in several literary journals throughout North America. In April 2020, her short story collection, *Hunger Moon,* was released by NeWest Press and was a finalist for the Rakuten Kobo Emerging Writer Prize.

- **Amy Small-McKinney** is the author of two full-length poetry books and three chapbooks. Her most recent chapbook, *One Day I Am A Field,* was written during COVID and her husband's death (Glass Lyre Press, 2022). Her second full-length book, *Walking Toward Cranes,* won The Kithara Book Prize (Glass Lyre, 2016). She has been published in numerous journals including *American Poetry Review, The Baltimore Review, Comstock Review, Thimble Literary Magazine, SWWIM, Tiferet Journal, Literary Mama, Pedestal Magazine, Persimmon Tree,* and *The Banyan Review,* among others, and has contributed to several anthologies, including *Rumors, Secrets, & Lies: Poems about Pregnancy, Abortion, & Choice* (Anhinga Press, 2022). Her poems have also been translated into Romanian and Korean. Her book reviews have appeared in journals, such as *Prairie Schooner* and *Matter*. She has a degree in Clinical Neuropsychology from Drexel and an MFA in Poetry from Drew University. Small-McKinney resides in Philadelphia.

- **Sarah Dickenson Snyder** lives in Vermont, carves in stone, & rides her bike. Travel opens her eyes. She has three poetry collections, *The Human Contract (2017)*, *Notes from a Nomad* (nominated for the Massachusetts Book Awards 2018), and *With a Polaroid Camera* (2019) with *Now These Three Remain* forthcoming in 2023. Poems have been nominated for Best of Net and Pushcart Prizes. Recent work is in *Rattle*, *Lily Poetry Review*, and *RHINO*. You can find her at sarahdickensonsnyder.com.

- **Virginia Chase Sutton**'s second book, winner of the Morse Poetry Prize, was recently reissued as a free ebook by Doubleback/Sundress. *Embellishments* is her first book and *Of a Transient Nature* is her third. *Down River* is her chapbook. Her poems have won a poetry scholarship at Bread Loaf, the Allen Ginsberg Poetry Award, and the National Poet Hunt, among many other prizes, residencies, and awards. Eight times nominated for the Pushcart Prize, Sutton's poems have appeared in *The Paris Review*, *Ploughshares*, *QU*, *Glass Poetry Journal*, *The Comstock Review*, *Mom Egg Review*, and many other literary publications, journals, and anthologies. She holds an MFA in Poetry from Vermont College of Fine Arts. She lives in Tempe, Arizona.

- **Chris Talbot-Heindl** (they/them) is a queer, trans nonbinary, mixed-race artist, writer, educomics creator, and nonprofit laborer trying to build spaces ready to celebrate when they turn up authentically. When they aren't consulting or working their day job, Chris can be found editing the quarterly compzine, *The B'K*, the biyearly themed compzine, *All My Relations*, and the Community-Centric Fundraising Content Hub; making educomics like *Chrissplains Nonbinary Advocacy to Cisgender People* and *Why Must the White Cis Nonprofit Workers Angry React to All My Posts?*; working on their serial graphic novel *The Story of Them* about what it's like to be nonbinary in a very gender-binary world; and writing essays and short stories exploring identity and belonging. Find them at @talbot_heindl on Twitter and Instagram. Links to their creative, equity, and editing work can be found at https://www.talbot-heindl.com.

- **Carey Taylor** is the author of *The Lure of Impermanence* (Cirque Press 2018). She is a Pushcart Prize nominee and winner of the 2022 Neahkahnie Mountain Poetry Prize. Her work has been published both in Ireland and the United States and is forthcoming in *The Black Spring Press Group Anthology-Before the Cameras Leave Ukraine* (London). She holds a Master of Arts degree in School Counseling and currently lives in Portland, Oregon. https://careyleetaylor.com

- **Marjorie Tesser**'s poetry and fiction have recently been published in *Drunk Monkeys*, *Cutleaf*, *Sunspot Literary Journal*, *SWWIM*, *Anmly*, and others. An MFA graduate of Sarah Lawrence College, she received the John B. Santoianni Award of the Academy of American Poets. She is the author of two poetry chapbooks, co-editor of anthologies from Bowery Books and Demeter Press, and editor in chief of *MER - Mom Egg Review*.

- **Kelly Grace Thomas** is a poet, educator, and an ocean-obsessed Aries from Jersey. Her first full-length collection, *Boat Burned*, was released with YesYes Books in 2020. She is the winner of the Jane Underwood Poetry Prize and the Neil Postman Award for Metaphor. Kelly's poems have appeared in: *Best New Poets, 32 Poems, Los Angeles Review, Muzzle, Sixth Finch,* and more. Kelly has received fellowships from the Martha's Vineyard Institute of Creative Writing and *Kenyon Review* Young Writers' Workshop. Kelly is Head of Curriculum for Get Lit- Words Ignite and the author of *Voices in Verse: Poetry, Identity and Ethnic Studies*; *Stanzas of America: Celebrating BIPOC Poetry*; and *Words Ignite: Explore, Write and Perform Classic and Spoken Word Poetry* (Literary Riot). Kelly is currently a Blackburn Fellow in the Randolph College MFA program. She lives in Benicia, California with her husband, daughter, and sister. www.kellygracethomas.com

- **Sarah Rose Thomas** lives in Northern Wisconsin. She writes poetry and fiction and teaches in a rural high school. With six sons (ages 6-15) and two giant dogs (Groot and Quill), she has been writing and submitting as often as her very busy days allow. This is mostly possible due to a very supportive husband who helps make time for writing.

- **Patricia Thrushart** writes poetry and historical nonfiction. Her fourth and latest book of poems, *Inspired By Their Voices: Poems from Underground Railroad Testimonies*, was put out by Mammoth Books. Her poems have been published in numerous journals. She is co-editor of the blog and anthology series for North/South Appalachia and co-founder of the group Poets Against Racism USA. In 2021 her work was chosen for an anthology of Ohio Appalachian voices, and for the Women of Appalachia Speaks series. Her narrative nonfiction book, *Cursed: The Life and Tragic Death of Marion Alsobrook Stahlman*, was published in December 2021 by Adelaide Books.

- **Leila Tualla** is a Filipino-American poet and author based in Houston, Tx. Leila's books include YA contemporary romance, *Love, Defined*, and *Letters to Lenora*. She has a memoir/poetry collection called *Storm of Hope: God, Preeclampsia, Depression and Me*. Leila's poetry has been featured in several mental health anthologies and she is an outspoken advocate for maternal mental health and PMDD. Her chapbook *PMDD & me* is out now. Leila is currently working on a full poetry collection on Asian American identities.

- **Cindy Veach** is the author of *Her Kind* (CavanKerry Press), a finalist for the 2022 Eric Hoffer Montaigne Medal and *Gloved Against Blood* (CavanKerry Press), a finalist for the Paterson Poetry Prize and a Massachusetts Center for the Book 'Must Read,' Her poems have appeared in the *Academy of American Poets Poem-a-Day, AGNI, Michigan Quarterly Review, Salamander, Poet Lore* and elsewhere. Cindy is the recipient of the Philip Booth Poetry Prize and the Samuel Allen Washington Prize. She is co-poetry editor of *MER (Mom Egg Review)*. cindyveach.com

- **Kelly Westhoff** writes essays and haiku. Her words weave her experiences with nature, travel, infertility, adoption, and motherhood. For her, inspiration strikes while walking. She can be spotted standing in the middle of the street watching birds in treetops or crouched near a garden photographing leaves. She has worked as an eighth-grade teacher, a freelance writer, and an independent bookstore employee. Currently, she is writing a memoir about her infertility. She lives in the Minneapolis area with her husband, their son, and two gerbils. She can be found online at KellyWesthoff.com, or on Facebook and Instagram @KellyWesthoffWrites.

- **Cynthia White**'s poems have appeared in *Adroit, Massachusetts Review, Southern Poetry Review, New Letters* and *ZYZZYVA* among others. Her work can be found in numerous anthologies, including *Grabbed: Poets & Writers on Sexual Assault, Empowerment & Heal*ing. She was a finalist for Nimrod's Pablo Neruda Prize and the winner of the Julia Darling Memorial Prize from Kallisto Gaia Press. She lives in Santa Cruz, California.

- **Allison Whittenberg** is a Philadelphia native who has a global perspective. If she wasn't an author, she'd be a private detective or a jazz singer. She loves reading about history and true crime. Her novels include *Sweet Thang, Hollywood and Maine, Life is Fine, Tutored,* and *Sane Asylum.* Her short story collection is entitled *Carnival of Reality.*

- **Toby Sturgeon Wilcher** returned to college in her 40's, majoring in Women's Studies. Today, she is a 66 year old grandmother of three lovely young women. Toby is the proud mother of an adult daughter who is a community outreach worker for AIDS testing and referral and harm reduction in New Orleans. She also has a son who is a college junior, majoring in Social Work. They make her feel like she did *something* right! Toby is involved with a statewide citizen's lobbying group that is engaged in anti-racism work and advocating for economic and environmental justice, voting rights, and other issues affecting our citizens. Writing is her favorite hobby, and she is a firm believer in the Oxford comma.

- **Erin Wilson**'s poems have recently appeared or are forthcoming in *Vallum Magazine, Prairie Fire, Dalhousie Review, CV2, Columba, The Prairie Journal,* and in *Worth More Standing, Poets and Activists Pay Homage to Trees.* Her first collection is *At Home with Disquiet.* Her latest collection, *Blue,* is about depression, grief, and the transformative power of art. She lives in a small town on Robinson-Huron Treaty territory in Northern Ontario, the traditional lands of the Anishnawbek.

- **S.L. Wisenberg** is the editor of *Another Chicago Magazine* and author of four books from university presses: *The Wandering Womb: Essays in Search of Home; The Adventures of Cancer Bitch; Holocaust Girls: History, Memory & Other Obsessions;* and *The Sweetheart Is In.* Her work has appeared in many journals and anthologies, and she's received awards and fellowships from the National Endowment for the Humanities, Illinois Arts Council, Narrative Magazine, and Fine Arts Work Center in Provincetown. She's a fourth-generation Texan living in Chicago. Find her at SLwisenberg.com.

- **Liza Wolff-Francis** is the Poet Laureate of Carrboro, North Carolina and she has an M.F.A. in Creative Writing from Goddard College. She has an ekphrastic poem published in Austin's Blanton Art Museum and was co-director for the 2014 Austin International Poetry Festival. Her writing has been widely anthologized and her work has most recently appeared in *The Phare, Silver Birch Press, SLAB,* and eMerge magazine. She has written reviews of poetry books that have been published on *Adroit, Compulsive Reader,* and *LitPub.* Her chapbook *Language of Crossing* was published by Swimming with Elephant Publications in 2015.

- **Karolina Zapal** is an itinerant poet, essayist, translator, and author of two books: *Notes for Mid-Birth* (Inside the Castle, 2019) and *Polalka* (Spuyten Duyvil, 2018). As an immigrant and activist writer, she writes frequently about her native Poland, languages, and women's rights. Her co-translations of Halina Poświatowska's poetry into English have been published in *FENCE, Cordite Poetry Review,* and *ANMLY* and won *table//FEAST* journal's inaugural translation prize. She has completed three artist residencies: Greywood Arts in Killeagh, Ireland; Braslmar Creative Project in Skopje, Macedonia; and Bridge Guard in Štúrovo, Slovakia. She works at the Massachusetts Center for the Book.

Index

Other Titles from Querencia

www.ingramcontent.com/pod-product-compliance
Lightning Source LLC
Chambersburg PA
CBHW060856210726
48293CB00006B/1829